STC:

The Sharpest Weapons

by
Jacklynn Lord

PublishAmerica
Baltimore

ISBN: 1-60563-953-2
PUBLISHED BY PUBLISHAMERICA, LLLP
www.publishamerica.com
Baltimore

Printed in the United States of America

For Mark

Acknowledgments

The following people were invaluable during the research process for STC. My deepest thanks to all of you for your time and efforts—especially my Ranger Buddy, Master Sergeant Chris Schott, his best friend Cathy, and "Ellie Mae."

Sergeant Gerald Borecky and Tau-mie Borecky, Fort Bliss, Texas. Michelle Norris and Celia Opdyke.

Master Sergeant Ed Beach; Department of Military Sciences, University of Nevada-Reno. Tech Sgt. Elaine Samborski, USAF, MEPS Station Sacramento, California.

Dr. Clinton M. Case (for his views on things nuclear), Assistant Professor, Department of Electrical Engineering and Adjunct Professor, Department of Physics, University of Nevada–Reno.

Mladen D. Kresic, Esq., President, K & R Negotiation Associates LLC, Ridgefield, Connecticut. Sgt. Michael J. Holland, Berkeley Police Department, Administrative Coordinator, Barricaded Subject Hostage Negotiation Team (BSHNT). Lt. Joey Walker, Reno Police Department.

Jim Trexler, Associate Professor of Geology at Mackay School of Mines, University of Nevada-Reno. Dr. Peter Ernest Wigand, Department of Archeology, University of Nevada-Reno.

Ferenc Szony, Sands Hotel and Casino, Reno, Nevada. Joyce Rhodes (proofreader extraordinaire), Ron Theriault (computer guru). David Holt (Airborne), Roger Weld (who lived through a shipwreck). Tim Smith and Dave Mancini.

Preston Murray, Murray Aviation. Lynn Pierson, Sikorsky Helicopters. Denis Dagoff; Silver State Arms, Reno, Nevada.

Men and women at Fort Benning, Georgia, Airborne and Rangers.

Federal Bureau of Investigation, National Press Office, Washington D. C. Office of Public Affairs, Fort Bliss Texas. Public Affairs Office, Naval Amphibious Base, Coronado

Certain factual details, information, and accounts were coordinated with officials of the United States Special Operations Command, MacDill Air Force Base, Florida.

STC:

The Sharpest Weapons

Prologue

The rubber dingy was not part of the plan, nor was the mission failing so unexpectedly.

Conversing with an unconscious man in an unfamiliar language definitely was not.

A deep sense of futility set in, and Bill began rambling.

He was weakening. And he knew it. That was the hell of it.

He wished he could fall asleep and forget the whole thing.

All the training, all the motivation, the repetition, the planning…

All of it had plummeted out of control—like the helicopter.

The wreckage had sunk or floated away and Bill was glad to see it go. Being washed into the tangled wire and blown-apart mesh seats had given him enough panic to last a lifetime.

Brushing the crusted salt from his lips, Bill grasped at dimming reality. He found himself reaching out with both hands to the foggy air, clenching his fingers. Then he forgot what he was reaching for.

"How'd it happen?"

Bill mumbled through a throat that had lost all usable moisture.

The question hung there, swirling in the heavy mist, unanswered. He reached for it again.

"This happened…how long?"

He continued in English. It was easier.

"Halfway to...Taiwan...Quemoy? Stupid."

The sound of his own voice revived him somewhat, and Bill struggled to sit up.

The man lying next to him was so frail and so important. The young woman—clasping the other body for warmth—was his responsibility. How could he face Tahoe?

Head swirling, Bill was aware enough to know they might be facing death. The thought did not worry him personally. He had come to grips with that reality some years ago. And this was real.

Although it seemed the situation couldn't get any worse, Bill's position hadn't changed.

It had been the proper thing to do. The lessons he'd learned had taught him that at the moment of highest tension, he could simply bend and move away.

At this thought, the darkness that had a moment ago overpowered him crept back waiting at the edge of his vision.

A smallish, rogue wave swept up the side of the bright orange raft. More water sloshed over his two companions. They stirred, moaning quietly. Then were still. Using his cupped hands, Bill began to bail again. He knew the ocean. It had always been his friend—until now.

Again he began to whisper hoarsely—this time in a mixture of Mandarin and English.

"That beach...the tower we sat on...*hai tzu*...Ted knows how to find us."

Bill lay back in the salt water. He quit bailing. Fingers open now, he gripped the last thought.

"Ted knows."

Chapter One
The Problems

The Master fished with a hook but not with a net.
He did not shoot his arrow at a sitting bird.
The Analects of Confucius

Reno, Nevada
15 September

Lisa caught a familiar flash of dark green in the side view mirror of her pick up.

"Damn it!" she muttered out loud. A glance into the vibrating mirror confirmed her suspicion.

"That's it! The same car again."

Lisa tightened her jaw, snarling in the back of her throat—a habit she'd developed as a young girl.

Lisa knew she was being followed—she'd known it for three days—and her guard was up. It had become obvious to Lisa that the driver was allowing her to become aware of his presence a little at a time, not unlike a wild animal that slowly adapts to human intrusion. The thought rattled her, sending goose bumps up her sun-bronzed arms; or was it the mid-September wind combined with the hot sun? This time of year the early

Nevada autumn sun and breeze mingled to create what Lisa called "hot-fudge sundae" weather. Long forgotten, discarded rock samples, and an assortment of devices—tools of her trade—rolled and thumped noisily against the metal of the grubby truck bed. Lisa had intended to clean it out today as she had for the past month, but as always, her focus was directed elsewhere.

Glancing into the mirror again, there was no mistaking the presence of the dark green TR-4.

Lisa smiled tensely, "My luck," she said out loud, "My secret admirer couldn't have driven a Mercedes."

Her intentions had been to drive out to the desert to confirm what she'd seen from the air the previous afternoon. "Ground Truthing," was what it was called. The desert could trick you, but Lisa had trained eyes and she knew what she was looking for.

She knew what she'd been looking for ten years ago, when her geological training had begun at Stanford University. Lisa was a Research Geologist—Hydrogeology was her field of passion; a passion, not surprisingly frowned upon by her well-to-do parents who would've preferred that their daughter have their grandchildren around the house, instead of rocks. In their desperation to shift her life in different directions they offered trips to Europe, Australia, anywhere. Typically, their advice was ignored, especially after the university awarded her a scholarship. Lisa saw it as a chance of a lifetime. Not in the way a less affluent student might have seen it, but as an opportunity to go for her dream without the burden of depending on daddy's money. She loved her parents, but treasured her independence, even as a little girl. Having a good head on her shoulders kept them off her back for the most part, although there'd been a few issues. But none like the one concerning her scholarship. Her father insisted that she wait a year before committing to it. Lisa made other plans.

Soon she was living in a somewhat drab apartment in East Palo Alto, months before her eighteenth birthday. This undoubtedly had created the tension between her and her parents. But, as was the norm in her family…the years began to heal the strain. By the time "Doctor" was added to her name, her father offered to buy her a house as a reward for a job well done. Lisa smiled in disgust, thinking about the proffered "endowment."

The grade steepened as Lisa shook her thoughts from her head. For now, a stalker—or God knows what—was following her in a green, mint-condition TR-4.

In spite of the circumstances, Lisa couldn't help but sneer to herself. After all, what self-respecting criminal in his right mind would have a car that might not even start when you turned the key?

But that was the problem. What criminal in his right mind? What if he wasn't in his right mind? Anxiety washed over her like a wave, causing sweat to break out and form on her upper lip and forehead. Potentially risky situations challenged Lisa. She had never admitted it to a soul but when circumstances required a higher level of thought and awareness she was at her best.

Like the time her engine failed, forcing her to land the small airplane she was piloting on a narrow dirt road cut through a forest of juniper and dense sagebrush.

Or the time when she was thirteen. A man had followed her as she walked down the beach. Lisa had grown up along the California coast. The ways of the ocean and the beach were as familiar to her as her own backyard. But there was something about the man with the big nose that set off alarms, blaring in her head. Diving quickly into the waves, she allowed the moderate rip tide to carry her out into the comforting arms of the ocean until the strange man had wandered away.

Oddly, both experiences had left a pounding in her ears and a feeling of ebullience coursing along the nerves of her arms and legs.

Then there was that brief marriage…even now Lisa winced at the memory, remembering the ache from two broken ribs.

There had been more, many more confrontations, and today was one of them.

Checking her mirror again, she made a quick decision. The desert would have to wait.

Setting the blinker she pulled off the road and into the small parking lot next to a coffeehouse. The green car followed. Spotting it from the mirror, Lisa's palms became damp and her mind habitually cleared of all thoughts except the next few steps. Her senses sharpened. Now she'd be the hunter!

Jumping out of the dusty, gray pickup, she caught a quick glimpse of her prey as he climbed from his car. He closed the door almost gingerly. Stepping back, the man paused for a moment. Lisa's eyes squinted in confusion as she watched him admire the graceful lines of the Triumph.

The man was tall and slender. His brown hair shone in the bright light. He looked innocuous enough. But something about his smooth movements kept her ready. She knew a rattlesnake could appear harmless.

Lisa's long strides carried her toward the coffee shop. Her tan work boots thumped on the wooden stairs. Taking a seat at the counter, she pulled the dark glasses from her eyes and hung them from the front of her faded red pullover. The seat next to her sighed as his weight settled on the thick, vinyl cushion.

His voice was soft and pleasant enough as he ordered a cup of coffee with cream. Lisa ordered the same. She yanked on one of the two strawberry blonde ponytails she wore hanging over her shoulders, adjusting the band holding it in place. The waiter poured the man's coffee and then hers. Lisa shifted, looking down at her jeans, noting the fact that the knees were wearing thin again—a hazard of her profession.

"You've noticed me observing you," he matter-of-factly said.

Lisa twisted to look at him.

"I know this seems a little...awkward," he continued, "But I have some questions for you."

Again, Lisa squinted her eyes. "You've got questions for me?" she shot back with an edge to her voice.

Until this point, the man hadn't turned, choosing to speak to his steaming cup of coffee instead. But now he slowly turned to look into her eyes. His manner was excruciatingly slow and deliberate, as if he feigned boredom at her show of tension.

Lisa loved it! He definitely had her attention. The man, without a doubt, was mysterious with a big "M". But then, she reminded herself, so was a serial killer.

Lisa moved carefully. The man knew exactly what he was doing. This both thrilled and frightened her.

"The only thing I want to know is, what's your problem?"

The man turned his head and his eyes back to his cup.

"Funny you should ask," he said, softly, "We do have problems. Very big problems. Professor Cummins suggested I look you up."

Lisa carefully scrutinized the man for the first time since he'd sat down next to her. He wore a green sweater with the sleeves pushed up above his forearms. The hair on his arms shone blonde in a ray of sunshine that came through the window, dancing on his skin.

"Problems? What kind of a prob…."

Lisa stopped. Suddenly, perceptively she understood what he was talking about. The mention of her mentor had jarred the memories loose. She recalled the long talks while she was at Stanford.

Politics, terrorism, prejudice, injustice, to name a few. Yes, big problems.

"Have any ideas?" he asked casually, turning his head to look out the window.

Lisa watched, eyes wide-open in wonder.

"Me? Ideas? You want to know my ideas?"

The man turned to scan her freckled face and pensive green eyes.

"Yes! Ideas. You've probably given the world's problems some thought, haven't you?" he asked, still speaking quietly.

Lisa shrugged. "Well…sure! Doesn't everyone?"

The man looked down at his coffee again.

"Everyone? No, not really. Most people talk only to hear their own voices."

Turning to her, he asked, "Do you? Do you want to help?"

Lisa's mouth suddenly went dry. She sipped her coffee.

"Do you want to know more?"

She nodded, her eyes fixed on his.

"Good!"

Abruptly he got up to leave. The spell was broken.

"Why didn't you call me, instead of following me around?"

"You have an unlisted number. Remember? And your former professor mentioned that you were here, at UNR."

Almost as an afterthought, he added, "Besides, I wanted to meet you in person."

"Who are you, and how do you know Mary Cummins?" she finally asked, trying to put it all together.

"I have a name. I even have a title. Neither is important right now."

He purposely ignored the second part of her question. She noticed.

Holding out a white business card, she saw his hands. By their looks, he hadn't spent much time outdoors.

"Here's a phone number. Use it."

"What should I say it's about?"

"Tell 'em you want to help solve some problems. They'll do the rest."

Pulling out several bills from his pocket, he placed them on the counter and left.

Lisa never saw him again in her rear-view mirror, but she knew that she hadn't seen the last of him.

Following her encounter with the man in the green car, Lisa's life was anything but normal. She couldn't shake it from her thoughts. Her days were consumed by hours spent flying alone over the Great Basin, surveying vegetation, deforestation, evapotransperation, looking at land usage and grazing patterns. Evenings she'd use data from field observations to make calculations, and download remote sensing data from the Internet. Suddenly it all seemed so pointless.

Lisa knew she wasn't getting enough exercise, promising to push herself to go swim, or ski. Anything active would have been a welcome change. She should have been more careful of that thought.

Lisa supposed the "green car" came to mind once too often. Three months later she made the call.

* * *

Monterey, California
Early October

An hour ago, Jennifer's carefully constructed professional life had fallen apart. Angrily pounding the sidewalk, she tried to pulverize it with

16

her knee-high boots. Struggling to clear her mind, the words played repeatedly in her head, driving her crazy.

"You made it, Jen…"

Jennifer resisted the next words. But they added exactly the right rhythm.

You're fired! You made it…you're fired! The perfect cadence for a perfect life.

To make things worse! A memory surfaced. Jennifer gritted her teeth, pushing it down. She failed in the attempt. It floated up again, interrupting the regularity of her steps. It was childish disappointment—disillusionment and devastating sorrow. When her nine-year old sobs had subsided, Jen swore she'd never, ever again, indulge in idealism.

Carefully building a shell of detachment, Jennifer became a pragmatist early on. Her level-headedness coupled with brains, led Jennifer to U. C. Berkeley's Hass School of Business. And with the ink barely dry on her doctorate Jennifer hooked her first job.

Many companies were eager to hire the brilliant, practical Marketing Science graduate.

For seven years, Jennifer's drive had won her consulting contracts all over the Monterey Bay. Her biggest success was landing a deal with the aquarium. Now it was over.

At first, Jennifer didn't hear the footsteps behind her. Maybe it was her distraction, or maybe it was the heavy fog muffling the sound. Bill kept pace with the blonde in front of him. Suddenly, hearing him, Jennifer turned.

"What the hell do you want? Are you following me?"

Jennifer was ready to clash with someone. Only sixty-minutes ago her previous employer had reminded her that she was too outspoken, too aggressive and forceful.

Force! That's what she needed right now. Jennifer felt ruthless, strong and, yes! Forceful. She'd never let go once she got her teeth into something. She'd step hard on anyone who tried to stop her. Jennifer's durable leather purse, swung by the strap would be an effective weapon. So would her knee. She was invincible, ready to fight.

"Hey, calm down. We've got problems, you know," the man said with a smile.

Bill saw hostile blue eyes; strong, muscular legs holding up a rather slender build. Tension puckered her brow into deep lines. Fiery, yet captivating, he hoped her anger was not directed at him. This thought took Bill by surprise. So what if she was angry with him? Did it matter? Unexpectedly Bill felt at a loss for words. He wished she'd smile.

"What'd you say?" Jennifer demanded.

She'd come to a complete stop, facing her "problem" dead on, as usual.

Bill's calm, good looks took her by surprise.

"We have problems." Bill repeated.

"Yes," Jennifer said, mockingly, "We have problems."

She tapped her boot impatiently; wishing he'd threaten her in some way.

"Business, takeovers, downsizing, hiring, firing…"

Jennifer whipped her head around angrily as she spoke. A few curls fell loose from her normally neat twist and she distractedly brushed at them. Staring out at the heaving ocean, dark with beds of kelp, she chewed her lower lip, ignoring Bill.

"Yes, that's part of the Big Problems."

He emphasized Big Problems so that all of a sudden it registered. Jennifer knew he spoke with capital letters.

Bill went on, "And Jim Joyner thought you might want to help."

"*Who?*" Jennifer almost screeched.

Vague excitement, barely recognized at first, began to replace the rage. It grew swiftly with such intensity that it nearly took her breath away. Once before she'd felt this way. It seemed silly, but the feeling was the same. She'd fallen off her horse, the jar knocking the wind out of her. It was the name. Her professor, Jim, the one who'd said, "You made it, Jen…" Jennifer's mind reeled, trying to connect Jim with this stranger. Adding to her confusion was the birthday memory, still stuck in her mind.

The stranger's brown eyes were in front of her. Jennifer didn't realize she was clinging to them like a life raft. So long ago. It was cold that afternoon too. Her parents telling her she'd never be a priest. Only men could be priests. At that precise moment Jennifer began her alliance with "the real world," putting away dreams along with her toys.

Jennifer shivered, wrapping her arms around her upper body. A lifetime of self-discipline pulled her back to business.

"What problems?" she asked, breathing hard, "and if you know Jim, why didn't you call me?"

Still smiling, Bill replied honestly, "I didn't call because I wanted to meet you in person."

From what he had learned from Jennifer's file she'd be someone to reckon with. Jennifer's stance, her elegant body starkly outlined against the mist, told him much more than what he'd read about her. There was tough pliability about Jennifer, and Bill suddenly understood it. That's what he saw in her; a powerful softness—like his own.

Jennifer studied him intently, slowing her breathing. The fog, beginning to yield to the sun, had made tight curls around her face, diminishing her generous features.

Jennifer spoke again. "Yes, Jim and I always talked about the problems. In fact, that last year at Haas, he showed me a questionnaire."

Warm recollections of Jim, UC Berkeley, the comfort of schedules, and their intense conversations flooded over her. The anger was gone, retreating with the fog. She grinned, cocking her head at him.

"Is that what this's all about? Are you CIA or something?"

She knew he wasn't.

"Nope. But I knew you'd want to help."

Bill held out a small card.

"Call this number," he said, his eyes locked with hers.

His footsteps faded. Jennifer slowly pulled a cell phone out of her shoulder bag.

* * *

San Francisco, California
20 November

The old mower was falling apart, and Don taped the handle for the last time. He'd come out to the bright November sun hoping the exertion would settle him. He'd found the mower needed attention. *He* needed

19

attention. His life was taking rapid turns in directions he didn't want to go. The DOE had called him again yesterday. They were waiting for an answer that Don couldn't give. Don's job at Berkley's lab was fine. He had no intention of getting back into a field he'd already left once.

His brush with nuclear weapons testing had left him disillusioned. There was no way anyone could convince him that there might be methods of safe disposal. Don also felt that the demand for more testing—which came from what he called a "sub-culture"—perhaps less pervasive than during the Cold War, was still dangerous.

Pushing the dull mower, sweating in the warm sun, Don didn't know that his neighbor had the answer to his dilemma.

Bill was fully aware he should've left two weeks ago. He'd already tried rationalization—that there weren't people who met the criteria. That wasn't the reason he delayed. It was easier to wait in San Francisco, where the sounds and smells, the air itself soothed him.

Moving his hands away from the keyboard didn't stop the screen from staring back at him. Bill tried to ignore the cursor blinking to the left of one name.

Standing up, stretching his arms over his head, he pushed aside the thin curtains and gazed out the second story window of the house he'd rented on the Avenues. Bill watched his next-door neighbor mowing the small patch of lawn between the driveway and the sidewalk. He dropped the curtain, staring at nothing, putting off for another moment, the inevitable.

Bill had come across the ad a few years ago. It didn't take him long to decide to take the job, the one he was avoiding today. Bill was a good man, fairly attractive, mild mannered, of higher than average intelligence. Bumming around the world, he maintained a home on Bainbridge Island. Not a lazy man, and certainly not a playboy, Bill had taught a few classes and continued his studies in conjunction with his travels. He also thought up ways to improve the condition of world. Until he'd met Tahoe, no one had listened. She'd assigned him to the Western states.

Searching Seattle, San Diego, Honolulu, Monterey, Reno, and now San Francisco, he'd recruited sixty-nine prospects, but needed one more.

Bill's other, even more time-consuming assignment, took him to El Paso where the newly established offices needed his attention.

With an effort, Bill jerked himself out of the trance and moved towards the front door. Grabbing the old sweater off the back of a chair, he pulled it over his head. He sauntered down the wide steps, pushing up the sleeves of the green pullover, jamming his hands into his pants pockets. Bill's fingers closed over the small card he'd put there.

Reaching the sidewalk on the Avenue, he nodded to his neighbor— the one whose name was upstairs next to the flashing cursor.

Bill knew Don was a physicist, working at the Advanced Light Source Lab in Berkeley. There was a more important bit of information. Those who had worked with Don did not know that Don was a patriot. But Bill's source had highlighted several lines in Don's dossier. Supplementing Don's concern for his country was his ability to convincingly present an argument to thoughtful people who had begun to listen to the impassioned physicist. Don had recently begun to lecture all over the country. He was in great demand.

Despite his height and wide shoulders, Don had that rather pale, scrawny look of someone who spent time indoors, hunched over in deep thought. His freckled arms were already turning bright pink from the afternoon sun.

"How's it goin', Don?"

Don answered slowly, taking time to enunciate each word. Strings of damp red hair, dulled by premature gray, hung over his forehead and the tops of his ears. Panting from his recent struggle with the old mower, he gave Bill a narrow smile.

"Hi, Bill. It's good to see you out and about this wonderful day! Do you have any plans?"

"Well, to tell you the truth, I've got a problem."

Don nodded, hoping Bill would keep the conversation going. Last year he'd spent three weeks at a clinic in Virginia. With an intensity and single-mindedness that earmarked everything Don did, he'd gone through an audio feedback program to relearn the basic sounds of speech. Don rarely stuttered now. He sought out casual conversations instead of dreading them.

When Bill didn't continue, Don said, "Yes, problems. I have them too. Don't we all?"

Time was running out. Bill had to get back to El Paso.

"So, do you want to help with The Problems?" Bill asked.

"Sure. Of course I try to help. Doesn't everyone?"

"Well, actually, Don, no. Not too many people want to get involved in things beyond their day to day activities."

"Bill, you don't know me well, do you? I mean, we've been neighbors for a couple of months but we haven't really talked."

Don moved his hands from the mower's sagging handle; his gestures animated as he spoke, eager to express himself. His voice took on a deeper, more powerful tone as his words flowed out. He stumbled very little.

"Bill, the problems facing this country today seem almost insurmountable. And that's what I think about day and night—what new methods can we use, what's lacking in our present system."

Bill's response was no more than a slight nod, but it encouraged Don.

"I'm a helper at heart, a big, frustrated helper. But no one wants my help. They simply want me to do the job."

Bill saw a person whose intellect demanded attention. Obviously his present surroundings didn't give Don much opportunity. Bill found himself wondering why Don has chosen physics as a profession. He didn't know that Don was more than ready to move on to something else.

Don grinned again, "The lecturing and travel is great, Bill, don't get me wrong. People are listening, but when I'm there," Don waved his hand in the general direction of the East Bay, "I'm smothered."

Don was too strong and energetic to be cooped up in a lab solving problems relating to femtosecond pulses.

Knowing he'd leave San Francisco tonight, Bill slowly drew out the card from his pocket.

"Call this number and tell them you want to help with the problems.'"

The scientist smiled at his neighbor, looking back and forth from Bill to the card that Bill had stuck in his outstretched fingers.

Bill moved leisurely toward the green car parked down the block.

"Pretty strange, Bill," Don said dryly, raising his voice to Bill's retreating back.

Bill had his hand on the car door.

"Call the number, Don, you won't be disappointed," he shouted over his shoulder.

The physicist called El Paso the next day.

* * *

El Paso, Texas
10 December

Muffling another sigh, Annie adjusted the phone on her shoulder. The call, if positive, would be her last.

"It's simple. Respond honestly and truthfully. Express yourself fully, and don't worry that you'll be boring me or taking too much time. Answer all the questions, but be sure and tell me if you're not going to answer truthfully."

"Sure, I understand," answered Lisa.

"What were the circumstances under which you received this telephone number?"

Reading from a script, Annie made very few digressions from what was typed.

"A man followed me for a few days. Finally he trailed me into a coffee shop in Reno and asked me if I wanted to help."

"Are you in good physical condition?"

"Why do you want to know that?"

"I don't want to know," Annie emphasized the pronoun, "But it's important that you either are or that you want to be. Only when you answer this question can we continue."

"Well then, I *want* to be. But my job…"

"Have you traveled to a foreign country?"

The interview continued for over an hour with questions, answers, more questions, more answers. Annie's patience wore thin. She'd interviewed what seemed to be hundreds of prospects. She was anxious to get to the next step, the interviews in person.

Her thoughts strayed. Drawing in a deep breath, thinking about what was coming in the next few days, she failed to stifle the sigh. Coughing to cover her mistake, Annie could've kicked herself. That sigh might put a huge restraint on Lisa's responses. Annie had much to learn. She was the new kid on the block.

Hired as a temporary replacement, Annie had been promoted to Interviewer. She trusted the person who'd hired her, but it was scary as hell.

Singing and dancing in New York had scared her too. She threw up backstage before her first performance. Laughing, the sympathetic stage manager had mopped her face, patted her shoulder and scooted her onstage; whispering in her ear, "See me when you come off."

Later, hidden behind the scrim, he'd explained how to manage stage fright.

"Adrenaline didn't cause you to upchuck. The chemicals that run through your body when you're scared are the same ones produced when you're excited. Think about it."

Annie hoped her present fear was only excitement. Stage fright somehow didn't fit with Annie's own description of herself. Annie lived for excitement, sought it out. The higher the carnival ride, the better she loved the fall. For her twenty-first birthday she'd wanted to jump out of an airplane, but was tied up with graduation and the resulting parties. Annie was looking forward to what was ahead. No, it wasn't fear, she decided, it was excitement.

Abruptly she brought herself back to Lisa. "One last question."

"How am I doing?" asked Lisa.

Annie said, "You're great! Holding up well to all this prying." She paused.

"What do you want to do with the rest of your life?"

This question always took a long time to answer. Back on track now, Annie waited patiently.

Multitudinous thoughts hit Lisa hard. She always had a plan, knew where she was going. Even when things got totally mixed up, she could think of ways to fix it. She remembered how she'd fixed the after effects of that ugly divorce. Flying lessons, she'd discovered, filled her mind so completely that when she landed it was easier to take a calm look at her life. Besides, it was useful in her work. Now this question was throwing her for a loop!

What did she want to do? What she was doing today? What did she want to do when she was younger?

Ancient ideas rushed back, making her clench her jaw and growl. She didn't care if the interviewer heard it.

This country, her country was in a mess, and nothing was being done to correct it. Up until now, she kept life exciting by flirting with danger. What if she decided to use her talents, and she knew they were many, and her intelligence, which was far better then average, and what if she put all that to work on solving some real problems? What would happen? Would these people laugh if she said it? So what if they did. It was time to get to the truth, once and for all.

"Look, I'm strong and smart. I'm working on some research that might explain a few water-related problems we have. It's going well, but what does it matter? There are a hundred others who can do that.

"What do I want to do? I'd like to be right in the middle of something important, something that threatens the world, not only the high desert."

Annie grinned, and her bottom bounced a dance on her chair, causing her "Captain's Chair"—that's what she called it—to roll around. What she'd heard from the research Geologist made every minute of all the hours she spent with the phone in her ear worthwhile. Annie's mentor would be pleased.

* * *

Walking to the rear of the large open room, George peered into the glass enclosed private office. He always shrugged mentally when he read the sign posted there: *Manager—Recruitment*. George wasn't really resentful of Bill, he'd tell himself, but he wondered if Bill was right for the job. Time was short and George knew that he'd be far better at the lecture sessions than quiet, easygoing Bill could ever be. His estimation of Bill couldn't be more off the mark, but George still hadn't figured that out.

Rubbing one hand over his short, dark beard, George tapped lightly. Bill looked up from the stack of cards he was reviewing.

"Hey, George. What's up?"

"Thought you'd like to know. Lisa called in."

Pushing the stack aside, Bill leaned back in his chair. It had taken her three months.

"Thanks, George. Is that the last of 'em?"

George nodded, tugging on his beard again.

"Thanks, George. Now we can get to work."

Bill put his head down and started sorting through the cards.

George turned around and walked out, closing the door carefully, quietly. *Would it work? Would this crazy idea really work?*

Chapter Two
The Plan

"In the time of GATHERING TOGETHER, we should make no arbitrary choice of the way. There are secret forces at work, leading together those who belong together. We must yield to this attraction; then we make no mistakes."
The Book of Changes

Three Years Earlier

No one knew for sure who thought of it first. People in high positions within the organization had their own ideas. They'd spent time together, exchanging thoughts, wondering out loud—as people often do. But no one really knew for sure. As with any other "good idea," their exchanges never went too far for fear that by delving too deeply, it would somehow undermine the foundation of the design. Besides, everyone agreed—it was a credible plan.

No policies and procedures in big, black binders were prepared. Business schemes and training agendas were developed and ratified by those who'd been selected first.

Obviously the initiators had the funding and qualifications necessary to launch the organization and to sell the military on the idea of allowing access by a non-martial coalition to the best training they had to offer.

* * *

Recruiters were selected from those who responded to an obscure ad placed in newspapers simultaneously all across the States—an ad that simply read:

Interested in seeing problems solved? Are you a self-starter bored with making money?

Do you want to change? Call 1-800-776-2536.

The ad ran for only one day, and three thousand and seven hundred responded before the toll free number was disconnected. From the thirty-seven hundred responses, nine recruiters were chosen.

The recruiter Bill had two interviews with someone he never saw again. He was given an address on the east coast where he would meet with an STC spokesperson. Closing his home and leaving suddenly wasn't a problem, nor was money. The person who interviewed Bill already knew that.

* * *

Cape Cod, Massachusetts

Captivated by his surroundings, Bill's slowed his deliberate steps, picking his way carefully towards a small lighthouse that had been converted into a private retreat.

Now at high tide, large breakers—encouraged by a brewing storm—washed nearly to the front gate. Driftwood tangled with other flotsam supplied stark landscaping along a brick path, which led to the back of the structure. There, Bill found a brass ship's bell hanging from a rope next to a weathered red door. Gusts of wind, scuttling through sand grasses, masked the sound of the opening door.

In front of him was a woman. A small flurry caught at her gray, silken pants and tunic. Without a word, the woman beckoned Bill inside. He followed her into a bright room overflowing with greenery. Live plants were hanging, sitting, standing everywhere. Motioning to a large chair, the woman sat next to him on a smaller chair covered with a pale rust-colored fabric.

"They clean the air, Bill," she said, noticing his eyes moving about the room.

The woman's glance followed his, fastening on the smoldering fire. Going to a wicker basket next to the wood stove, she chose two small logs and positioned them on the dying embers. The fire hissed, throwing sparks up the red enameled chimney. The woman's movements as she returned to her chair were smooth and effortless. She was dressed in gray, flowing attire trimmed in white. Bill was reminded of a graceful sea gull, and at the same time, he sensed a rudimentary strength in the woman.

Bill looked at her intently, and she returned his gaze easily. Her timeworn face was serene. Her back didn't touch the chair as she moved her tall body to face him. She folded her hands neatly in her lap

"Bill, I imagine you would like some answers."

The woman's voice gave no hint of her age or an accent to define her origins. Comfortable in the setting and with the figure in front of him, Bill sat back quietly. He was eager for details, but he waited patiently for her to begin the conversation before asking any questions.

"For reasons of anonymity, I have chosen the name Tahoe. Is that acceptable?"

Bill nodded, "Of course. Lake Tahoe is one of the most beautiful places in the world."

It was quiet for a moment as they listened to the wind and watched the fire.

Bill asked, "What's STC? The acronym, what does it stand for?"

"STC is a plan that was formulated over a three-year period," she began.

For nearly an hour, Tahoe explained. Pronouncing words deliberately, Tahoe avoided using contractions. Bill was overwhelmed by her no-nonsense delivery. Tahoe was not a typical older woman by any stretch of the imagination. She used strong words, brief and to the point, which included no apologies for what might be thought of as childish ideas—or far-fetched daydreams.

"Bill, when people are joined one by one—like tiny grains of sand—they build a structure that can make a difference."

Bill nodded, listening intently. Strikingly, Tahoe continued. The quality and clarity of her thoughts was extraordinary.

"The structure will be built by those with certain traits we have identified. These people have unique characteristics which enables them to understand and respond to specialized training."

As Tahoe's voice swept over him, Bill comprehended her complete authority and knowledge of the plan. His respect grew along with his exhilaration. He thought of an ageless sage; all knowing and untouched by opinion, single-minded in purpose.

"It may appear that we are duplicating efforts. I can assure that we are not," Tahoe explained.

"At times there is a need for powerful actions, and we would never undermine or disparage the great good done by brave individuals in existing agencies.

"There are situations, however, which may be dealt with by use of supplemental methods, and it is into those situations where STC will be called."

Tahoe stopped for a moment, clearly adding a thought geared towards giving Bill some background.

"At the beginning, we were aware that barriers caused by traditional thinking might be difficult to hurdle. But the greatest of those obstacles have now been overcome."

Bill began to see Tahoe's incredible strength. Hidden behind her calm façade, was a titan. This was something Bill recognized and understood. He was in complete accord as she continued.

"Today's peace keepers put out fires. They quell a situation. They are not solving the underlying problems. STC will be called to do both."

Giving an overview of the instruction that would be necessary to accomplish these ends, Tahoe concluded her synopsis.

"We are now ready to seek the best and the brightest from a panel of five hundred that you will select."

Looking intensely at Bill, Tahoe continued.

"We will be very lucky if one hundred stick with it. Realistically, of those hundred we begin to train, fifty percent will not make it through the rigors of the training."

Bill's assessment of his personal involvement in the plan, which had begun with a touch of skepticism, now became a powerful desire to hear more.

"Tahoe, I'm curious..." he began, standing slowly, not wanting to shatter the flow of words.

She interrupted, as if reading his thoughts.

"I know who you are, Bill, and I am quite aware of your accomplishments. More importantly I know your strengths."

Then Tahoe stood beside him, stretching her arms over her head. She was fluid and graceful. Bill didn't try to guess her age. She was ageless. Slowly shifting his weight from one foot to another, Bill was absorbed, concentrating on her straightforward language.

"Tomorrow you and I will meet with eight other Recruiters. You will be the team leader."

Moving closer to the stove, Tahoe held her hands to the warmth as the room grew dark from the scudding clouds. With the light of the fire dancing about her face she almost appeared fragile. In the next moment she was commanding. Bill could tell she was not concerned with the normal stages of life. Tahoe functioned on an entirely different level from most.

Tahoe began to speak in a compelling mode that impacted him like the blasts of winds hitting the lighthouse.

"We are on a first-name basis, Bill. It is not required, but you may pick a new name, such as I have done. As I explained, ambiguity provides protection."

Her body bent towards the wood basket as she looked up at Bill.

"I want it to be clear that your first assignment is two-fold."

Selecting another piece of firewood she added, "Go ahead and move around if you like."

"First, work with the others to establish offices in El Paso.

"Purchase whatever is necessary. All expenditures are approved. Money is not an issue at any time.

"You will determine for yourselves who to hire. I may have suggestions.

"Ultimately the staff you employ will follow your example. Some may be useful in other capacities."

Bill went to the large porthole facing the sea, staring at the storm growing in intensity. He turned looking back at Tahoe, who didn't seem to notice either his movements or the gale. Rain had begun to rattle the windows. Fixed on the fire, Tahoe's eyes focused on something far away. She began to speak again, authoritative words contradicting the tranquil expression on her face.

"In addition, you have the job as recruiter. Select only one person from each place you visit, in all only seventy people. Each recruiter will do the same.

"I will supply you with names and background. The profile on each person will provide data indispensable to your approach. They are relatively young, highly intelligent and successful. In addition, they have the necessary energy and motivation that can inspire those with whom they interact. Additional training will enhance the characteristics I mentioned. Your job is to make contact with each, and let things take their course. Do not interfere after your initial meeting."

Pausing briefly, Tahoe switched to another subject, catching Bill unawares. The tone of her voice changed, hardened as she stressed each word.

"Anything detrimental or contrary to the ideals of STC is not to be tolerated."

Gripping a brass poker, she nudged at the fire. Her movements were sure and strong. She spoke, choosing her next words with care.

"Even the most dedicated person can suffer from uncertainty. Doubt gives rise to arrogance and negativity. Those can quickly weaken an individual's commitment. Ultimately, this conduct can spread to others and will undermine STC principles."

Including Bill now in her monologue, Tahoe looked directly at him.

"Bill, you need to be aware of this phenomenon. At the first indication, you can utilize methods to encourage those involved. You will make every attempt to bring them back on track. Every person involved with STC is important. Each one is essential."

Tahoe came to the window to stand closer to him. Her eyes intense, she spoke calmly, evenly. Again, the subject had changed.

"As we discussed, experts will undertake certain instruction, but you will monitor that training and the conduct of all involved."

Bill didn't know that Tahoe's grace and astuteness, coupled with power and ability, had already combined to hold the attention of political and military leaders. It kept Bill riveted. Slowly she touched his arm, feather-light.

"Is this all clear to you?"

Tahoe's touch was soft, but it barely concealed an astonishing undercurrent of confidence. At that moment, Bill knew he could trust her completely. His response was simple.

"Yes, I understand."

One by one, Tahoe positioned sturdy fingers in her palm as she enumerated.

"Tomorrow we will meet to review field procedures for contacting selected individuals. Personal contact with each prospect is imperative. We have resources, of course, and telephone numbers are available. But they are not to be used. Your impression of the total person—not only the voice—is essential. I will assign territories, and explain the purpose of the Interview in El Paso."

Tahoe placed her hands behind her back, watching the rain.

"By the time you leave here, you will understand the specifics of your first duties. It will be intensive but enlightening."

She smiled openly for the first time.

"What I mean is…don't worry…STC grows on you; becomes part of you."

Accompanying Bill to the door, Tahoe linked her arm with his. Their footsteps were slow as she continued speaking.

"Later, you and I will come together alone to discuss STC Training."

She stopped, still holding his arm.

"Bill, you have the traits I spoke of. Your life has led you in directions that have provided the knowledge and information that you will use to develop STC expertise."

Then she spoke for the last time that day.

"What you know is invaluable to STC."

Clouds glowered in the fading light. Heavy rain pelted the brick path.

Lifting a hand in farewell, Tahoe was outlined against the red door. She slowly turned, disappearing from view. Unmoved by the storm, Bill stood a moment longer, studying the ocean.

Chapter Three
The Interview

Excellence does not remain alone; it is sure to attract neighbors.
The Analects of Confucius

El Paso, Texas
13 December, 1500 Hours

Descending into El Paso International, the airplane banked steeply over the desert. A narrow ribbon of murky yellow caught Jennifer's eye as she looked out the window.

Leaning over, she asked her seatmate, "What's that stream?"

"You're kidding me. Right?" laughed the husky geologist.

"This is my first trip to El Paso," Jennifer admitted.

"That's the Rio Grande."

Saying exactly what she thought was never a problem for Jennifer.

"You're kidding *me* now, right? That river is famous. I thought it'd be bigger."

They both laughed.

Losing altitude slowly, the runway was still far ahead of them. Turbulent air bounced the airplane and Jennifer sighed. Flying was not her favorite mode of transportation, and she gripped her hands together.

The red ponytails on the woman next to her whipped back and forth, and Jennifer thought she might be sick. She moaned.

"Hang in there. This is normal for El Paso."

Lisa drew Jennifer's attention to the sights as they continued their bumpy ride.

"Look down there. See how the city is a big V? It runs roughly north and east."

Lisa pointed out the window.

"There, see? That's Fort Bliss. That's where I'm headed. Right there, at the base of the V, see it?"

Caught off guard, Jennifer forgot her queasiness.

"You too?"

She held out her hand. "Hi, I'm Jennifer."

* * *

Fort Bliss, an Advanced Individualized Training post was headquarters for STC. Gold lettering on a sign in front of a white two-story building stated: DCD—Directorate of Combat Development. This revealed nothing about STC. The building was secure and what was inside, classified.

For the past two weeks, STC offices had been chaotic, filled with tension almost palatable to the staff. This afternoon calm had descended, accompanied by a faint humming from the air conditioning. El Paso was hot and dry—not unusual for December. At times there was snow. Other times you sweltered.

Avoiding blasts from the vents circulating the chilly air, Jeanne hurried through the nearly vacant offices, a number two pencil stuck in her wild, curly brown hair. She gripped a spare pencil between her teeth. She'd finished copying a five-page masterpiece of carefully drawn graphs needed to keep track of five hundred people. Jeanne's tight schedule had made meeting airplanes and transportation almost easy. Her organization drove many people wild.

Quick and competent, Jeanne's long-limbed body cut through the stillness.

"Mike, are you still here?" she yelled across the room. Jeanne's strident voice sometimes irritated the staff, but they never said so.

Looking up at her flushed face Mike noted that Jeanne's glasses, as usual, were off kilter and needed to be cleaned.

"I'm gettin' ready to call it a day, Jeanne."

He added, "You don't have to yell. I'm right here."

"Mike, don't yank my chain today. I'm not in the mood."

Jeanne thumped the paperwork on his desk. Her chair didn't squeal as she flopped into it. She oiled the mechanism frequently. Muscular legs encased in blue jeans whipped up to the desktop, and Jeanne's cowboy boots met the surface without a sound. There was no wasted motion. Watching Jeanne's routine, Mike grinned fondly.

The first time he'd met her, Mike's jaw had dropped and he winced at her powerful handshake. Since then he'd grown to admire the New Yorker's strength and ability.

When they'd furnished the offices, Jeanne had carried nine heavy boxes up the stairs. Neatly separating all forty-two parts contained in each box, she'd quickly assembled task chairs, rolling one to each desk. Jeanne's capabilities were legend. She often bragged that she could complete any job with one hand tied behind her back, or she'd boast of some terrifying episode, saying she'd done it single-handedly. Two summers ago she'd been battling forest fires in Wyoming.

"You gotta love this heat, Mike. Reminds me of that time in Yellowstone."

Mike grunted, his head bent over the stack of papers.

"I had to haul out this tourist."

Listening to Jeanne's colorful tales was something Mike secretly enjoyed. When she recounted her adventures, he'd tease her. They both enjoyed the banter.

"This guy must've weighed two-hundred pounds. He caught his foot in a rotten log and broke his ankle."

Glancing up, Mike commented.

"Did you have to use both hands that time?"

Joking was one thing, but Mike didn't question Jeanne's skills. He depended on their partnership. Procrastination was a life-long habit for

Mike. His slow, methodical suggestions coupled with Jeanne's efficiency had made order of duties like check-in. He and Jeanne kept in constant contact as schedules were updated, sometimes hourly.

For the last time, Mike reviewed a card with one yellow highlighted streak marking a potential change. Other than that, he was ready. He *hoped*. Tossing the stack of papers into his briefcase, he loosened his tie. Slinging his jacket over one shoulder, Mike prepared for the heat outside.

"Lock up tight, Jeanne, will you?"

Her eyes on the checklist, Jeanne slapped one hand on the pocket of her dungarees where she kept the keys. Mike understood that Jeanne's off-hand manner was an attempt to mask her deep exhilaration—an excitement they all shared.

Waving in her general direction, Mike traipsed through the office. His long legs took the stairs two at a time. Emerging into a blast furnace, Mike muttered out loud.

"This can't be nearly Christmas."

But he couldn't control a big grin of expectancy. *Tomorrow. The interview.*

Adjusting his large body to the mid-sized car, Mike continued to smile as he was flagged though the Cassidy West gate. Any plan he made was carefully thought out. Once a course was determined, Mike was resolute. This included his driving habits.

Mike had decided to exit at the Schuster off ramp. That way he could enjoy the artistic grounds adjoining the University. Their staid beauty—created with striking rock and foliage native to the area—provided a few stress-free moments. Left on Sun Bowl and another on Mesa took him to his apartment on the west side of The Hill, overlooking Mexico. This time of day traffic wasn't too bad, and he made the trip in less than fifteen minutes.

Furnishing his quarters with those things most comfortable for him, Mike was going to miss the sound of bubbling from his exotic indoor water fountain. By tonight, his earth-brown leather couch would belong to someone else. The titles and colorful bindings of his favorite books were old friends greeting him. They'd be heavy to pack up.

Unlocking the door, Mike was welcomed by his large red Chow.

"Hi, Trouble. How's your day?"

Tail wagging, the dog's nails clattered as she ran in circles, panting to tell him he had messages. The beeping and blinking red light were an invariable source of entertainment for her.

Suitcases, along with the empty book boxes were stacked here and there. They crowded Mike as he made his way to the phone. While the voices on the machine spoke, Mike began a series of stretching exercises outlined in a runner's magazine lying open on the couch.

"Hey, Mike, long time no see! What're you doin' in El Paso? I had a hell of a time finding you. Call me."

Mike groaned, more from the voice he heard than from unaccustomed muscles.

"Mike, this is Jeanne. Sorry to bother you, but I need to get an update as soon as possible. Please call. I'm home."

Giving the magazine a surly glance, Mike slipped off his leather loafers and padded to the kitchen. He grabbed an imported beer from the nearly empty refrigerator. Sitting by the still-open magazine, he dialed a number. What could he say to his former colleague? And how in the hell had he found him?

"This is Mike. Yeah. El Paso."

The voice in his ear was annoying. Gulping the cold brew in ten long swigs, Mike hurled the empty bottle towards a paper bag in the corner. Both acts barely lessened his aggravation.

"No, don't know if I'll come back. This is a great place to slow down."

While he listened, Mike bent over to rub his feet. His abdomen got in the way. Throwing the magazine on the floor, his attention was momentarily diverted from the voice. He really needed to whip himself into some sort of shape. Then he remembered. That would come soon enough.

"No, no, I know I'm too young to retire."

Mike rolled his eyes at Trouble.

"But I definitely won't go back to that war. I'm happy. I'm healthy. I make enough to feed my dog!"

Mike continued to appease his previous partner, skipping around the pointed questions.

He remembered his parents' similar grilling when he'd first left home.

Without telling them, Mike had enlisted in the Marine Corps. They were content however when following discharge, he got his law degree. During two years in private practice as a trial lawyer, the military had never been far from his thoughts. Mike stopped worrying about his ex-partner. Tonight he'd ship Trouble to his sister, and move on post. He'd disappear. Smoothly and diplomatically, Mike ended the conversation.

He groaned aloud, thinking of the evening ahead. He needed to pack the books and get the couch and fountain to the next-door apartment. First, he checked in with Jeanne.

* * *

On the east side, Jeanne prepared a quick dinner, knowing she'd probably never eat it. She'd given Mike the names of three last-minute arrivals then laughingly asked if he was packed. Like Mike, Jeanne would leave her apartment tomorrow. Unlike Mike, she'd been ready a week ago.

Alone, Jeanne didn't hide her fierce excitement as she clumped from room to room. Uninterrupted, a stream of questions kept up with her pacing. *Would the script work? Would they get the idea? Could she carry out the interviews and get STC going in her groups? Would they agree to basic training? How many would quit before they even started? Could they get the teams ready?*

Jeanne's forgotten dinner grew cold, and she answered her own questions.

It's too late to worry about it now. Get some rest, Harlem, get some rest.

She liked her new name and intended to ask everyone to use it.

* * *

Lake Tahoe, California
13 December ,1800 Hours

One person was not excited. Three years of work was about to come to fruition. Everything pointed to success. Recruits would be receptive to the interview. The interviewers were well trained and had the capacity to make the concepts clear. The military would be satisfied. Tahoe looked at the lake held like a cup in the hands of the majestic mountains. Her face was impassive. Her intense blue eyes flashed gold from the sunset mirrored in the water.

* * *

Stout Gym, Fort Bliss
14 December, 0800 Hours

Military personnel had difficulty—at first—accepting a civilian organization on a military installation. With the coming and going, the gossip ran its course, and those stationed at Fort Bliss became accustomed to the newcomers. They put STC into the same category as the German troops housed near the airport. The Germans came, enrolled their children in school, did their jobs, and then shipped out. Activity this morning did cause a few heads to turn. But in the Army, so did anything unusual.

Recruits, thanks to Jeanne's schedule, had been arriving since 0730. In preparation for the interview, she'd sent information explaining the weather, what to pack, pick-up times, and where they'd be staying. Hotels near Fort Bliss were filled to capacity.

Cleared to enter the post, a continuous stream of rental vans lined up in front of the new recreation center. They'd drop off as many as fifteen people at a time, leaving and returning with another group. Stationed at four wide entrances, STC staff kept running head counts as recruits arrived. They were asked to print only their first names on nametags.

Five hundred folding chairs, commandeered from all over the Post, began to fill as men and women from cities and towns across the country conversed quietly. Meeting for the first time, some made connections as professions were discovered and discreet inquiries into qualifications were exchanged. None of them knew they wouldn't run into someone from their own town. They found that out later.

* * *

In a small conference room off the gym, the Interviewers sat at a long table. Jeanne fumbled with her chair. Her actions, usually not awkward, brought their heads up.

"I've chosen a name," she announced loudly. "Please call me Harlem."

Clearing her throat, she immediately returned to business. She didn't feel like hearing any comments.

"Of the six hundred and thirty people recruited, four hundred and ninety-eight showed up."

Tapping the pages with her pencil, Harlem referred to her notes.

"Still, the percentage is surprisingly high."

She pushed her glasses back in place from where they had slipped down almost to the end of her nose. Mike couldn't resist.

"Harlem, darlin'. Love that name!"

Giving him a blank stare, Harlem allowed her eyes to cross slightly, easing her body into the chair.

Once the chuckles subsided, Mike held up the card he'd marked in yellow. Everyone had the same card with a list of questions. There were only ten.

"Remember the last time we met with Tahoe? She told us to air out any questions we might have?"

They nodded as Mike's searching gaze traveled around the group. He leaned forward, elbows on the table.

"Regarding question number nine," he said.

He added, "I'm serious about this. I've given it hours of thought!"

During his tenure as a trial lawyer, Mike had perfected acting skills. Over the past few months, the Interviewers had to ask several times if he was serious or performing. Besides, everything Mike did took hours of thought. Smirking, they kept their eyes on the list of questions. Mike didn't seem to notice. He ran his fingers through thinning brown hair as he read.

"Do you look forward to new situations?"

Glancing around the table once more, Mike continued.

"That question was included because we wanted know if they'd be up to doing basic training."

Mike made sure they were all following him.

"And then, doing specialized training, you know, jumping out of perfectly good airplanes…"

The others nodded, waiting for Mike to get to the point.

"Why can't we ask 'em a question and give 'em some information at the same time? Wouldn't that encourage more of a dialogue?"

Mike shrugged, holding his hands palm up. For a long moment, the others looked at their cards. When no one answered, Mike spoke again.

"So, what'd you think, Bill?"

It was Harlem who flipped a card towards Mike. Spinning around, it came to rest directly in front of him. Mike angled his head, nodded and read aloud:

"Would you be willing to experience Army Basic Training, and other essential military instruction?"

Looking at each other in silent agreement, they made the change.

* * *

Interviewers made their way to the back of the gym where a long table was draped in pale yellow. Plastic bottles of spring water were pyramided at either end. At the center of the table was a microphone attached to a heavy oak podium. There, Bill took his place, looking at the group for the first time. Interviewers assembled behind the table. Crowd noises diminished. The large-faced school clock on the left wall indicated exactly 0900 hours.

Bill's thoughts were clear. Facing a group of select individuals, he knew they'd be attentive, anticipating his words. The next days would be exhausting, eight-hour days, and he needed to set the pace right from the beginning. Bill had planned the introduction to last less than five minutes.

"Good Morning and welcome to El Paso!"

Smiles and a few voices returned his greeting.

"Thank you for being here today. It is truly an honor to be addressing you."

Raising his left arm, Bill pointed to his watch. Then he pointed to the clock on the wall.

"Take a good look. This is an extraordinary moment in time. It represents the culmination of years of planning and work, by people with the same ideals and vision held by each of you."

Even with the amplification, Bill's voice retained its pleasant pitch.

"You are here because someone asked if you wanted to help with the world's problems and you responded. Each of you have ability, vision, and most importantly—a desire to serve."

Bill grinned.

"Dynamite combination! That's not something you see every day. And we've got a roomful of it! Take a look around you!"

Practice had taught Bill to speak as if there were only two or three people in a room. Each person felt his attention—and they did as he suggested, looking at one another.

Bending his head slightly over the stand, Bill's voice became serious.

"I believe you'll find the events different from most interviews."

People settled back in their chairs. Pencils and notebooks appeared.

Picking up the small card marked *Introductory Remarks*, Bill's movements were deliberate.

"Before we explain the interview process, I want to tell you what's on this card."

Bill raised it over his head.

"Each of you is uniquely talented and capable. Let me explain:

"On this card are three letters—STC. They stand for three words or concepts. They describe how this group functions. The words, however simple, will serve as a reminder to each of us—why we came together."

Bill lowered the card, leaning forward on the podium.

"Each of you are stars, hence the letter S. You have star quality; a drive to express your talents to the utmost."

Smiling, Bill's voice changed again—became more lighthearted.

Holding his hands gripped together over his head, Bill gave a little jig like a boxer who'd just won a bout.

"Actually, you're all super stars. But somehow, SSTC didn't have quite the ring we were looking for."

The audience laughed quietly. When the amusement died down, Bill continued.

"You can consider yourselves to be members of an all-star team. Because of your focus on solving problems, you make up the team we're looking for."

Bill's expression changed again. He was composed, completely at ease. His self-possession spread to the large audience. They were attentive.

"Truth is represented by the central letter in our logo. It's the pillar, and we *cannot* stand without it. We don't believe that hostilities, problems or sufferings are inevitable. What we do believe is that by utilizing our abilities, we are able to seek a larger truth making way for resolutions to become evident and possible."

Quiet now for a moment, Bill let his words sink in.

"The third letter, C, stands for Country. We love our country, of course. But on a broader scale we love our ancestry—the larger family of humanity—with the unique heritage and culture contributed by all countries over the eons. In other words, not only do we love our country, we respect all peoples."

Holding up the card again, Bill repeated the three letters.

"STC. Become familiar with these letters and the meaning of the words. These ideas will keep STC functioning in the way it has been designed—around the pillar of truth."

At these words, the group unexpectedly began to applaud. Soon they were standing, joined by the eight behind the table. Returning their smiles, Bill encouraged them to sit down.

"I feel this is a day of destiny, in a sense. I see great friendships and accomplishments ahead of us. There is the potential for great achievement in all of you. It is because of *who* you are that you've come here today, and I again sincerely want to thank you all. This is only a beginning."

Nodding to Mike, Bill took a seat. Applause began again, and then faded as Mike stood at the podium.

"I'm here to explain the so-called *interview*. It took a while to come up with that word."

Ever the actor, Mike thoroughly enjoyed speaking to a large group. His inventiveness was something the other interviewers anticipated.

"Interviews are normally conducted one-on-one—or one-on-three or maybe two-on-four—but fifty on fifty! That's gotta be a first!"

Shaking his head and counting his fingers, Mike grinned at them.

"This morning, you'll separate yourselves into nine groups. There are four hundred and ninety-eight people here today. This means each group will consist of fifty-five people, more or less."

Gesturing with open hands, Mike pointed around the room,

"You're smart stars. You can work out what to do with the remaining three."

The group chuckled, enjoying the high-spirited fun.

"You may wonder why you need to form into groups. We *will* explain. Honest," and like a kid, he crossed his heart.

"An Interviewer, acting as team leader, will join each group."

Holding up a card, Mike feigned bewilderment.

"Wow! This could get confusing. I hope you can figure it out!"

He brought the card closer to his eyes, and then pulled it away.

"It says here that we'll work each day from 9 to 7 with a two-hour lunch break."

Looking at his watch, Mike looked up with a dejected look.

"Only three more hours. Well, after lunch—with renewed energy— you'll form groups of twenty-seven."

Speaking very quickly now, Mike rushed through rest of the schedule.

"Tomorrow, we'll interview groups of ten. That'll take all day. On Saturday and Sunday, it'll be groups of five. On Monday, there'll be two at a time."

He paused, panting, "Okay, did you get all that, or should I repeat it?"

From the back of the room a voice called out, "We got it, man, go on!"

Mike didn't miss a beat. Slurring his words together he shot back,

"I knew there must'a been at least one startmass here."

Laughter erupted, as the young man who had yelled at Mike stood and bowed deeply. Returning the bow, Mike continued.

"Okay. Make schedules, and keep track of when your group is on. That's it. The Interview will begin in half an hour. Please separate into nine groups. Thanks for your attention."

The Introduction had taken exactly five minutes. There was a brief silence as the Interviewers exited the gym. Standing slowly, Don—the physicist from San Francisco—folded his chair. His actions encouraged those around him to do the same.

The activity caught the attention of the group very quickly. Chairs were folded by their previous occupants, and carried to the large trolleys along one wall. In the process, subtle attractions, or earlier conversations formed alliances. Other, more physical actions such as bumping, stepping on toes, and the resulting apologies brought groups together.

Lisa's eyes followed Don. She was impressed with his leadership, and wondered why she hadn't thought of stacking the chairs. Glancing at him, she smiled, taken by his intense, sincere expression.

One by one, slowly, then faster and faster chairs were cleared, making space for the groups to form. Intent on the assignment, the people kept personal conversations or comments to a minimum. Everything they'd seen and heard so far had impressed most members of this specialized group. The poise and organization of the staff was acknowledged by all but a few. Tremendous thought had gone into arranging this interview. Many knew from personal experience the effort it took to put something like this together.

Once again Don took care of an awkward situation, and started the head counts by simply pointing to himself, saying "ONE. Then he pointed to the person next to him. The gym began to echo with voices counting out loud. The three extras were incorporated as Don took one, and a carpenter from Texas encouraged another. Standing alone, the third finally shoved her way into a group. No one seemed to mind. The selection was orderly and in exactly thirty minutes nine teams were formed.

Chapter Four
The Buddy System

One does not make claims and hence is given the credit. One does not compete with anyone, Hence no one in the world can compete with that person.
Lao-Tzu

Little Creek Naval Amphibious Base
Norfolk Virginia
14 December, 1100 Hours

Until recently, Balke's personal habits had not included head shaking. Such movements might be considered a weakness or—worse yet—be copied by those under his command. Nevertheless, as he forcefully pushed back his chair Commander Balke shook his head.

A veteran of two wars and far too many "encounters", Balke had considered early retirement. Now there were other matters to think about.

Striding towards the east window, he narrowed his eyes at the Eagle Haven Golf Course visible less than half a mile away. Beyond the yellow-brown fairways Balke could see the Atlantic Ocean shimmering bronze, like an ancient Roman shield.

On the third floor of an 80,000 square foot cinderblock building,

Balke's corner office had a stark, hidden away quality. Students often referred to it as the 'Eagle's Lair.' Balke's hooked nose and rugged countenance had certain similarities to that majestic bird of prey. If one squinted while sitting in the visitor's chair the image that the Lair was atop some granite outcropping became quite overpowering.

Dominating one corner was the grand piano, upon which no one was allowed to put anything. Like the piano, Commander Balke had an imposing presence. While playing Ravel's Left-Handed Concerto, he'd yell out the complicated rhythmic patterns to an ensemble of musicians. He got a great deal of pleasure explaining to his students that after WW1 a pianist—who'd lost an arm in battle—arranged a competition among the composers of the day to write a piece for left-hand only. Ravel didn't win the contest, but the concerto was one of Balke's favorites. He played rather ponderously, but there was no denying the emotion he felt.

Balke was at his most impressive however, as musical advisor to foreign heads of state. Upon hearing his suggestions regarding the power of music and its necessity to set the tone for certain functions, people found him striking.

Balke's own opinion of himself—that people found him pushy and opinionated—kept him from seeking company. He had only one close friend, an Air Force General, who he saw infrequently. Due to ship out in four days, Balke was scheduled to meet with the general at Special Operations Command in Tampa. Continuing on to Coronado the day after Christmas, he wouldn't return to Virginia for many months.

Alone in his office, Balke's thoughts made him to shake his head again. He had trouble believing he'd received orders and acknowledged them without a bit of sadness at leaving his school. Balke always thought of the Armed Forces School of Music as "his" school. He'd come up with an idea, and had finally seen the establishment of a combined school for musicians in any branch of the military. Balke was secretly proud of his brainchild. He had no idea how many people admired him and sought his advice.

Three years ago she'd come into his office. Resenting the fact that he'd been *ordered* to meet the woman, Balke was prepared to dislike her. In the course of his career, he'd met with hundreds of civilians, men *and* women, but had never been *ordered* to take a meeting. The woman was a complete surprise!

When he'd heard details of an idea even bigger than his, Balke had difficulty keeping his face in its customary scowl. During their first conversation, Balke had accepted an appointment as liaison between STC—a civilian group—and SOCOM. Further committed to the project by subsequent phone conversations with Tahoe, Balke had outlined the particulars of his duties. In addition he'd detailed records describing who and what was needed to implement the plan when the time came.

Keeping the documentation carefully locked up, Balke didn't discuss the phone meetings with anyone. He assumed that eventually his superiors would enjoin his work. Until his orders had come three days ago, it had never occurred to him that the entire combined United States Military backed the effort. How could one person have so much charisma, charm and clout all packed into such a delicate body?

Staring out the window, Balke consciously stopped himself from shaking his head.

* * *

Stout Gym
14 December, 0930 Hours

Being the youngest of the group, Jasen tried not to resent frequent jibes from the other Interviewers. They felt he was too intense—too steeped in his own personal philosophies—and they sometimes told him so. When Jasen objected, they teased him even more, telling him he was too sensitive. Knowing that before STC Jasen had been teaching philosophy at Yale University, they secretly valued his opinions on deeper matters. Bill was the easiest to talk to, and Jasen sought him out.

The Interviewers returned to the gym. Bill had thrown an arm over Jasen's shoulders. Brows drawn together made a faint crease in Jasen's otherwise smooth, round face. The cleft in his chin repeated the deep furrow on his forehead. Articulate and ambitious the young African American was, as usual, determined to make his point.

"Of course racism exists, Bill, it's the degree of commitment in each of us that can make the difference."

"Jasen, let's talk more about this later," Bill interrupted with a smile.

Clearly defined, nine groups stood elbow to elbow. Once again Bill took the podium. He came right to the point.

"Nice work. Let's get started."

For the next few minutes, Bill spoke slowly. He used short sentences interspersed with frequent pauses, but the pace was smooth with no break in the flow.

"Each of you came here with hopes of being part of a group that could assist in solving major world concerns. Many of you have already taken steps in that direction by the way you conduct yourselves in your personal and business environment. What you learn here will provide you with even greater insights."

Bill pushed his hands against the podium, leaning back and glancing at the large groups.

"Ongoing conversations within the teams you choose will be centered on three themes. Problem solving is the first. As we begin this morning's session, focus on a problem you'd like to solve."

Bill glanced at Jasen, and was relieved to see that the young man's tight expression had relaxed.

"The next subject is a series of ten questions."

Bill grinned widely.

"And there's a specific way to listen to them."

Gesturing with his hands, Bill explained.

"There are over fifty people in each group, but I can assure you that by using this method, you'll get to know everyone."

No one moved. They were intent on his words.

"As each question is read, look at one person in your group and the name."

Bill tapped his chest, pointing out the nametag.

"As the next question is read, look at another person. Continue to do this while each question is read."

Now Bill saw nodding throughout the group. People were beginning to take closer looks at one another. As usual, Tahoe was right. It worked.

"The third element to keep in mind during discussions is STC—the letters and the words."

Again, Bill saw acquiescence. They understood. He raised his hand, lifting one finger at a time.

"One. The problems. Two. The questions. Three. STC."

Bill leaned forward, again lifting his fingers.

"There are three goals. One, your exchanges on these points is a way to begin to understand how STC works. Two, team discussion is a way to study group intelligence, which you will come to rely on more completely than has been done in the past. Three, behavior changes can occur. You need to know the impact of your willingness to change. If you're not willing to acknowledge the importance of change, you're wasting your time here."

Bill removed the microphone from the podium. What he had to say next was key to the interaction today, and he began to move around and within the groups.

"Every one of you has earned degrees. Some have received acclaim, recognition."

Heads turned to follow his progress. Eyes met his, and from their movements Bill could tell they were accepting and understanding what he had to say.

"Many of you have diplomas, certificates, credentials, and have won awards. The honors you have, well...you simply did what you did. You are truly excellent, but there is no competition between you."

Bill repeated the words, "There is no competition."

Lifting his eyes to the clock, Bill turned back towards the head table, extending one hand to introduce each Interviewer.

"Please meet Annie, George, Mike and Robert."

One by one they stood and smiled.

"Jasen—with an "e"—Flavia, Harlem and Becky."

He concluded quickly, "My name is Bill. Let's get to work."

Sitting on the floor, Bill encouraged the group to move closer together. Hearing could be difficult. Although the gym was huge—the bleachers closed and basketball hoops closed to the ceiling positions—

there were only a few feet between the clusters. No matter. They'd get smaller.

Bill held the card with ten questions in his right hand, the printed side against his thigh. He looked at Jennifer first. He smiled and lifted the card.

"What changes would you make in the world today?"

Bill didn't move his gaze. He was sitting in a gym with five hundred people in El Paso, and at the same time he was in Monterey, the fog swirling, watching her walk towards him. With real effort, Bill dragged his eyes away.

"How do you describe yourself?"

They were doing it; moving their eyes to another person as Bill read the next question. Reading slowly, he allowed time for eyes to readjust to another face and name. Other Interviewers read the same questions. The murmuring was quiet harmony, echoes of Bill's voice.

"What would you like to do if you could do anything in the world?"

"Where would you want to live if you could go anywhere in the world?"

"Who are your heroes?"

"How much do you love your country?"

"Why are you here?"

"Where have you traveled?"

"Would you be willing to experience Army Basic Training, and other essential military instruction?"

At this question, many eyes jerked to Bill's face. He was calm, unmoved by the topic, and read the last question.

"When can you be available?"

"Let's stand and move around."

For a moment they were quiet, watching other groups rise to their feet. Within a relatively short time the gym resounded with voices.

Wandering through the busy groups, Bill was alerted to something needing closer attention. Strident laughter, almost raucous, came from a group at the far end of the gym. Bill recognized the laugh. From his vantage point Bill could see George, pulling his beard, a big happy smile on his face. It appeared George was balanced on the edge of becoming too familiar with the crowd, seeking out those he'd personally interviewed the past three years.

Tahoe had given Bill specific instructions. Interviewers were not to impress themselves on the teams. Over the months they'd examined the feelings of power that can sometimes emerge when in a leadership role. Learning to recognize the symptom was sometimes difficult, but even more difficult was learning how to pull on the reins and keep those emotions in check. An unbridled ego could cause problems. Some found the discipline tricky, but it was a necessary part of STC.

Even as he rejoined the mill of people on the floor, Bill kept one eye on George. It was understandable that George would be wound up. They all were. Bill hoped he wasn't overreacting. Something told him he wasn't.

For the next hour Bill spoke little, and listening to the discussions. Fifteen minutes before the lunch break, he turned on the mike. Bill disliked stopping the flow of conversation. But he did.

"May I have your attention?"

His amplified voice reached out over the other voices.

"At this time I'd like to bring up a new subject."

This sudden interruption widened Jasen's eyes, then Annie's. They knew Bill had special instructions to enhance any of the Interview sessions whenever he felt it was necessary. But they never thought it would happen on the first day. Suppressing their surprise, they looked casually at each other.

"To introduce the topic, I want like to remind you of STC. The three words are Star, Truth and Country."

Bill didn't have a script. He knew what he needed to say.

"Being a Star means you're also selfish. Understanding the power of truth means you recognize lies. Appreciating your country means you may not be concerned with others. This is perfectly normal."

Bill's face was somber, allowing his gaze to lock on George.

"It's important to remember that opposites are part of our character. The problem that faces all of us is to balance constructive and destructive, because we *need* both. The selfish, power-prone, or untruthful nature can overcome us in a very short time."

Bill's next words staggered every person in the room.

"Ask Don, over there, he's the physicist."

Bill motioned towards the scientist.

"Don, would you come up and give us a brief discussion on Uncertainty?"

Faces turned. There were a few nervous laughs as people realized they also might be called on to give a brief discussion that would be understandable to someone not in their field of expertise. Unexpectedly the atmosphere had become super-charged.

Don lifted his hands and waved and smiled as he walked towards the head table. Applause followed his progress. It rippled softly at first, and then became overpowering. Bill was taking a big chance—shifting attention to someone from the group. Like a coach who'd called the right play, Bill knew—when he saw Don come through the crowd—he'd made the right decision. Bill's thoughts were compressed into a single word. "Yes!"

Don moved through the groups, quickly formulating a brief talk. He decided to shorten the opening of a lecture he'd given many times before. Realizing this audience was discerning, he'd remind them of certain principles. Without wasting words, Don didn't talk down to or over the heads of the group.

"There's a principle of tolerance that abides in the human species. We need to ask each other 'what do *you* think, what's *your* opinion?'"

Placing his forearms on the podium, Don slowly emphasized certain words. His deep, slightly hoarse voice easily projected towards the back of the room. While in normal conversation, Don often spoke quickly, slurring many words together. When lecturing he slowed down, making sure all his words were understood. This was a skill he'd worked hard to attain.

"We need to put aside all our prejudices and stereotypes. We're connected to all points in space. We're part of the seamless whole. We need to be explicit as well as implicit."

Don paused, as Bill nodded encouragement.

"We *need* uncertainty," he stressed.

"Absolute certainty is stasis."

As these words filled the air, Don gave them a small smile.

"Gravity will always get you down."

The gym resounded with applause and laughter. Blinking his eyes,

Don looked around slowly. Physicists do not often make jokes, and he was surreptitiously pleased he'd said something the group enjoyed.

"We are all *so* trained, so extremely *sure* of ourselves, and that training can cause us to run in circles *because* everything's sure. In that kind of environment, there is no uncertainty. We walk. We talk. We respond to people, but our thinking relies *only* on what we are certain of—what we are used to. We get caught in the loop. We're trapped, caught, because we can't see beyond our own recurring personalities."

Leaning back a little, Don paused again. He swept his fingers across the strands of hair on his forehead, smoothing them.

"We get *caught* in our own personalities. We continually create our own reality."

Moving forward, Don rested put both arms over the wooden podium, hands hanging losing towards the floor.

"Quantum Mechanics came along to open an entirely new door in relation to how to think about things. This thinking is still going on."

Smiling to himself, Don remembered something he'd read.

"Einstein could never accept Quantum Mechanics. He didn't *like* uncertainty."

The crowd laughed again, Don tried to explain.

"Actually, some other physicists got together and proved that Quantum Mechanics *did* exist, by virtue of one of Einstein's own formulas."

The laughter continued. Don realized he had made another joke. He smiled broadly, completely at ease. Bill passed a card to Don. Reading to himself, Don continued grinning.

"Want me to...?" he asked.

Bill nodded.

"We need to make use of chaos in a positive way. Remember that habits form in 21 days."

Bill returned to the podium stretching out his hand, shaking Don's. He spoke under the sound of responsive applause.

"Thanks, Don. You really came through for me, buddy."

Looking in George's direction, Bill leaned into the mike.

"For the next ten minutes, discuss the constructive use of chaos. Open up that door for yourselves. Thanks."

George's attention was elsewhere.

* * *

The Inn at Fort Bliss
1930 Hours

Unlike some of the interviewers who'd maintained apartments in town, Bill checked in and out of the Inn during frequent trips to El Paso. Brand new four years ago, the Inn was well kept and comfortable.

Even with the sun down, the temperature remained in the low 80s. The swimming pool at the back of the U-shaped hotel was still open. Nodding to the night clerk on the way to his room, Bill was determined to swim before eating a late dinner in the small dining hall. Bill shed his clothes quickly and pulled on swim trunks he finally found hanging from a hook on the back of the bathroom door. In five minutes he was in the pool enjoying the evening sounds.

Bill missed the ocean. Born in New Jersey and raised on the shore, he was more at home in the water than anywhere else. At an early age, he was a licensed scuba diver determined to study marine biology. Receiving his Doctorate in Oceanography at Rutgers, he was called home two days later.

Closing up the family estate overlooking the Atlantic, Bill had traveled to the Far East. Instructing him in Eastern Philosophy and the practice of martial arts, Bill's eighty-year old Master in Taipei was his greatest friend.

Lonely at times, Bill had deep feelings about many things—but he rarely shared them. Upon first meeting him, most people got the impression that Bill was absent-minded. The few who got to know him well came to realize that this trait was a tool—used to fend off unwanted attentions.

Bill was equally comfortable reading the Chinese Classics in a small, mountain cabin, or dining at a five-star restaurant following a concert at

Carnegie Hall. Relaxed in khakis and sweater, Bill was also at ease in black tie.

Rather disorganized in his private life, Bill's rooms were clean but overthrown with books and clothing. Forever nagging him to keep his personal papers in some sort of order, Bill's accountant had finally taken over handling his affairs. Whenever Bill needed cash, which was seldom, he used an ATM. For everything else—like his tab at the hotel—he used credit cards.

Spotting the waitress, Bill softly called to her, "Hi, Juanita, could you please bring me a light beer?"

She waved an admiring 'yes.'

Toweling the water from his lithe body, Bill pulled in his stomach. His belly was beginning to tighten the waistband of his trunks. That would change soon enough. Leaning back in one of the padded chairs he pulled up to a white wrought iron table, Bill allowed himself to think about Jennifer and George.

Jennifer was a new experience for Bill. This surprised him, and uncharacteristically threw him off balance. Bill's next thought—connected to the first—was George's attitude. If George ignored the warning signs, he might be on a track that could begin to undermine the program or Bill—or both. It was a big IF at this point. But from what Bill had observed, George needed to be reminded of one of the fundamentals of STC. Bill wasn't sure if George had gotten the message.

Now, to compound the problem, Bill was contending with a swirl of thoughts concerning Jennifer. If he gave the woman any special attention, George might misinterpret Bill's motives. For a moment Bill wondered if he should enlist Annie's help, but quickly pushed the thought aside. From the first, George and Annie had been drawn together. Bill thought the relationship was stable. So, what in the hell was bothering George? There would only be one warning. If George didn't alter his actions, he'd be history. The whole situation confused Bill, and involved a complexity of sensations he'd never felt.

Bill's relationships with women had been mostly casual, friendly, and never prolonged. The intensity of his feelings after one, brief meeting with Jennifer surprised Bill again and again. Bill realized this might be clouding the issue, keeping him from thinking clearly. Putting his mind on the afternoon's sessions, Bill relaxed his body. Without focusing directly on either George or Jennifer, Bill wandered among the events surrounding the problem. This was a technique he often used. The answer usually came as a last random thought.

Accustomed to Bill drifting away, Juanita quietly brought the beer, her soft slippers noiseless. He didn't use a glass.

Reflecting on Don's talk, Bill remembered another physicist he'd met several years ago. What he'd said was significant:

"Most people don't understand each other, even though they're conversing in the same language. Physicists, on the other hand, understand what everyone's trying to say, and can get a divergent group into a working environment faster than anyone else."

Bill saw this ability in his former neighbor, Don. Bill's inherent capacity to look at things from all directions was enhanced by Don's aptitude in this area.

On the heels of this realization, another influential voice, soft and amazingly strong, burned into Bill's mind:

"Take advantage of all you hear and learn. The people who are drawn to STC will provide insights and add strength to your character."

Tahoe's thoughtful and dynamic remarks gave him energy. Bill heaved a sigh, straightening his body. Swallowing the last of his beer, he diligently kept his thoughts away from Jennifer.

Today it had become obvious that people were beginning to link up. Right from the beginning it had been decided to use a Buddy System for STC—a plan used by the United States military. The method of choosing a partner was unique to STC, but the dynamics were basically the same. Bring two people together, put them through training and they'd emerge as fighting machines, depending upon one another for strength as well as companionship. It had proven to work.

Circulating through the gym, he'd zeroed in on one couple, deep in conversation with Jasen. They were strong and full of life, well spoken and quite capable of keeping up with Jasen's rhetoric. Bill overheard the two reminding each other to keep to the questions:

"And tell the truth! No matter what," one had said.

They'd laughed, slapping hands like teenagers. The Buddies were coming together. The groups were anxious to hear the questions again, and, surprisingly, the conversations were not overly concentrated on the military aspect of question number nine. It came up, of course, but most people were keeping to the sum of the questions.

Pulling the towel around his middle, Bill took lagging steps to the shower. His eyes on the red-tiled patio, he remained deep in thought.

Bill never allowed himself the luxury of wavering. His single-mindedness was evident in every word and action. He knew exactly what was ahead. Total concentration was needed to ensure the success of STC. Facing his dilemma, Bill stopped suddenly and brought his head up. In the morning, he'd talk to George alone. This last thought brought him back to Jennifer. She matched and strengthened him. George was simply the second half of the question. Now Bill had the answer.

Chapter Five
Taking Responsibility

"If you were in charge of the army, whom among us would you take with you?"

I would not take along one who, like a raving tiger or a raging torrent, would recklessly throw away life. What is required is someone keenly conscious of responsibility, someone fond of accomplishment through orderly planning.

The Analects of Confucius

The Inn at Fort Bliss
15 December, 0530 Hours

Bill groaned and pulled the pillow over his head at the same time he slammed his hand on the alarm. The soft buzzing had awakened him with an annoying persistence. It had been nearly dawn when he'd finally dozed off, and his head felt thick. Chucking the pillow across the room, Bill clicked on the television hoping the noise would distract him from the thoughts rattling through his head, which were more unsettling than the alarm.

Every day for three years Bill had awakened with STC on his mind. Normally, early morning hours were his most productive time and he'd wake up with his thoughts together. Today was different. For the first time, Bill felt overwhelmed with the weight of responsibility.

Groaning again, Bill managed to get himself upright. Sitting on the edge of the bed with his head in his hands, he tried to focus on the blur of uncertainties that bordered on personal doubts. The newscast did nothing to organize his thoughts, and Bill vigorously rubbed his head. That didn't help either. Yawning, he gave it up.

"Let the questions run, Bill" he said aloud, "Let 'em take a run for a second or two. See where they're going."

Had he done enough? Would five days give them sufficient time? Did they have any inkling of what was ahead? Had he said enough, or too much?

At that point, Bill decided that thinking would be best in a hot shower. Plodding to the bathroom, he left the news blaring. Invigorating, the water roused Bill to full consciousness.

He knew that each phase of STC had presented sticky situations. Over time, Bill had developed a way to deal with them. He'd set his mind on some facet of STC, gearing himself up to anticipate questions and ensure he'd be on the right wavelength. It was a method similar to the one he employed for problem solving. Generally, it worked pretty well.

Four areas of performance were identified when STC first began the recruiting process. It was on these that Bill set his mind this morning. Leaning his hands flat against the tiled wall of the shower, Bill let the blast of water hit against his back and shoulders.

"First," he spoke out loud again, clarifying the points, "STC recruits have a unique talent to think, assemble, lead and follow. Secondly, those selected would form the most effective teams themselves. Third, gifted people have ideas of their own. Lastly, group intelligence would begin the process of problems solving."

Water pressure in El Paso—especially on post—was powerful. Bill was awake and thinking. Something Tahoe had said on that cold, stormy day at Cape Cod was connected to the questions he'd woken up with—something that would ease the trepidation. What was it she'd said? Bill fumbled and found the memory:

"You will be in a place where conditions are volatile, but it is not hazardous because you know you will deal with it. You are simply doing a job. You are confident. You go beyond the situation. You have a broader understanding that enables you to see all aspects of the threat. Your knowledge will have an effect that force alone could never equal."

That day Tahoe had paused, studying his face intently before she continued:

"We are not inventing anything. We are simply augmenting what has already been formulated, making it better and stronger."

The clatter in Bill's head began to settle down as Tahoe's words reminded him that the ever-increasing complexity of new technology demanded a whole new way of thinking, training, and implementation. STC had come along at exactly the right moment, and it might possibly begin to unravel the tangled maze of things now threatening the world. STC was well planned and ordered. Bill knew he needed to trust the plan.

The water swirled around Bill's feet. Catching his eye, the carioles affect gave him a sense of reassurance. The direction of the whirl followed the rules of the planet rotating on its axis—order established at the creation of the galaxy. Bill began to hum under his breath. Slowly turning off the faucets, he shook the water from his hair. This movement brought Commander Balke to mind.

Bill smiled at the memory as he stood in front of the mirror, plugging in his razor. They'd only had one conversation, and although Balke's intentions were hidden behind musical metaphors, their meaning was quite clear:

"The danger is this," Balke had said, "Increase in technology often brings about a corresponding decrease in human ability."

Waving his expressive hands in the air, Balke had quickly turned to face Bill to tell him about an old film of Toscanini conducting Beethoven's Ninth.

"Bill, the fire from his eyes and the tiniest movements of his baton were like a magician casting lightning bolts as he urged the musicians onward."

Bill's mood changed, self-doubt fading like a bad dream. Remembering Balke's description, Bill began to hum the Ode to Joy.

"Each person in the ensemble—the huge choir and the orchestra— was totally enthralled and focused on the maestro's interpretation. Not one eye could drift away from his baton. Toscanini demonstrated the perfect blend of control and power, balanced to bring out the highest capability of the musicians."

Balke had explained that in his opinion, current electronic technology—the norm in music performance today—might bring about the downfall of the original purpose to enhance performances.

"Hell," he'd thundered, "These days they even teach students correct methods of microphones and sound equipment use!"

Laughingly, Balke had admitted he was a fan of rock and roll, and certainly didn't discount true talent.

"But, Bill, at times it seems that the true nobility of music that always attempted to bring the spiritual into the physical, sometimes misses the mark in today's electronically enhanced environment. It makes for a spread of very highly polished product, sometimes seemingly at the expense of the real substance of human ability to express strength and truth. Stars on stages today are more dependent on technology, and the same is probably true in athletics—possibly every walk of life."

Still humming, Bill reflected on Balke's next comments.

"A hundred years ago, what percentage of people could build their own homes?"

Balke had turned back to the window and concluded his thoughts, "Today's recording and sound engineers might laugh at the primitive equipment used for that Toscanini film. But there's no denying the high level of technique, sometimes lacking in today's slick performances with all their high-tech equipment. Bill, we don't want to reject the possibilities of our advances. We simply want to bring out the full potential of the intent of the technology."

Finished now with the razor, Bill patted his face and grinned at the memory of Balke's mini-lecture. And how they had chuckled at the toast Bill proposed:

"To the intent of technology, and to STC!"

Wending his way to the small dining hall, Bill's mood was lighter. He chose a table reflecting the rising sun. He didn't need to order. The waiter knew he ate the same thing every morning. With a flourish, he had Bill's oatmeal, orange juice and coffee with cream on the table in two minutes.

Returning to his room, Bill made two quick phone calls and pulled out of his parking space near the front entrance five minutes later.

* * *

It was good to be driving the TR4 again. Bill had to smile at the connection the car made with the road. Perfectly designed to carry the weight equally on all four wheels, the low center of gravity gave an immediate response to his intentions. The drive lulled the faint misgivings, still lurking at the edge of his mind.

From the description he'd received, Bill immediately recognized the man standing on a wide cement berm surrounding a graveled area in front of the gym. The advisor wasn't as tall as Bill had thought. Both arms were covered in tattoos. The man's toothy grin and freckled face belied his years. In his early fifties, he looked fifteen years younger. Blue eyes, with specks of brown, moved quickly from place to place. Bill was certain the advisor missed very little. Dressed in blue jeans and a bright yellow T-shirt, the man had a baseball cap turned backwards on his head. Bill couldn't see the logo on the cap, but he imagined it would be some sports team.

The advisor had been working as a bodyguard for a high-powered executive when Tahoe had met him. Following several brief conversations, she'd recruited him. Trained as a Ranger specializing in Anti-Terrorism, the advisor had served in Viet Nam from 1969 until 1972. Thirteen years of counseling allowed him to sleep at night. The events in this man's life could have destroyed him, but he'd survived and become stronger. A highly experienced combat veteran, Steve was a patriot. When he'd heard the details of STC, he knew he'd found a better way than warfare. Recruited to work in a special capacity, the man was again on active duty. Only a few people knew what the advisor did.

Slinging a duffle bag over his shoulder, Steve held out a huge hand, "Hell, Bill, it's damn good to finally meet you."

Rough and coarse in speech, Bill knew from Tahoe's briefing that the advisor was highly intelligent.

"Really appreciate the chance to see things from the git-go."

Laughter involved Steve's whole face. Bill didn't know it was a hard-won battle for Steve to laugh again, especially at himself.

"Good to meet you, Steve."

"We have, what, 'bout five hundred recruits?" asked Steve, "All of 'em here today?"

Conversing quietly, the two men walked slowly from the parking lot towards the rec center.

"No, some have left for various reasons—mostly because of previous commitments."

Bill shrugged, "We're not too concerned with large numbers."

He pointed towards the doors of the gym ahead of them.

"Late yesterday they split into teams of ten."

Bill slowed his steps, "Let me go over this morning's activities."

Turning his head slightly, Steve grinned. Bill wondered at the smile, but began to explain.

"Yesterday—day one—we started with four hundred and ninety-eight, separating into teams of fifty-five. Last night I got a report that the number is down to three hundred and sixty."

Standing in front of the doors, they paused.

"As I said, groups of ten and a team leader will comprise the first nine groups this morning. At 1030 hours another ninety will show up. This afternoon…well, you get the picture."

Steve nodded, striding ahead of Bill as they entered the foyer. Steve peered through the wide doors of the empty gym, his back towards Bill. Bill could see the front of Steve's cap. In large gold-embroidered letters it said: STC.

* * *

Bill left Steve flirting with the aerobics trainer who came in to answer the phone and explain the gym was closed until next Wednesday. While Steve was occupied, Bill went to the small conference room.

Before leaving the Inn, Bill's cautious nature had prompted him to call Tahoe. Her response was direct:

"Bill, deal with it now. You know what to do."

Calling George had only taken a moment. George's voice was tight and clipped, but he'd agreed to an early meeting. Bill placed both hands on the table, lowering himself into a chair. The table was bare except for a note pad and a few pencils. Reaching for the paper, Bill tested the point of the lead with a finger. He began to sketch quickly. The picture that emerged was of a soldier in full battle dress complete with M16A-2.

Entering the small room, George carried two steaming cups of coffee.

"I know you use cream," he said nervously.

George looked terrible—no usual grin.

"Thanks, George. Appreciate it."

To George, the sound of Bill's sketching was as annoying as fingernails on slate.

"Jesus, Bill, what's going on?" His voice was loud, almost shouting.

Pulling out a chair, George slammed it on the floor. He tried not to pull his beard. His hands went towards his face, and then returned to the mug of coffee.

Bill dropped the pencil on the table. "Calm down, man."

George lifted his cup, eyes directly on Bill.

"That lecture before lunch yesterday...that for me?" he asked.

"That was for all of us, George, a reminder. You okay with that?"

"Oh sure, Bill, fine. But I gotta tell you, I knew you were coming down on me, and I didn't like it!"

George's grin was uncomfortable, ashamed.

"Are we on track, George, you and me? Can you tell me what's going on?"

George sighed deeply. He put both his hands on his head, leaning his big arms on the table. At that moment George reminded Bill of a tired old man. He knew George wasn't quite thirty. Lifting his head, George stared at Bill with bloodshot eyes. He looked as if he'd been awake for days.

"It wasn't only yesterday, Bill and you prob'ly know it," and he added, "I didn't sleep a wink last night."

George moved carefully, slowly as if in pain. Any anger he'd shown was now replaced by what seemed to be a great sadness.

"Men don't talk about this stuff, Bill. Not to each other. But after that thing yesterday, you know, with the physicist, well..."

George stopped, and then began again.

"I heard what he said. Did you know I was a physics major at one time?"

Shaking his head, Bill indicated that he didn't know.

"Totally gung ho on the idea. But when I realized exactly what it entailed, well…"

George sighed again, his chest heaving as he took a big gulp of air. Giving him time, Bill didn't interrupt. This was definitely an awkward situation, but Bill knew they had to see it through.

"I know I'm not making much sense, Bill, but I'm gonna try to get it clear in my head once and for all!"

Clenching and unclenching his fists, George swallowed hard.

"As I said, I went to school with one thing in mind. That didn't work out. I tried something else. That didn't work. I was going in that circle Don described yesterday. I finally got it together and started in the work you know about—engineering. I built tall buildings in a single bound!"

Forcing a weak grin, George seemed calmer now. He spoke with less strain.

"I made tons of money, and was still young enough to enjoy it. I was a whiz kid. You know the type? The guy who happens to be in the right place at the right time—get a gig, which leads to another one—and then zowie! It all comes together?"

Looking down at his hands, George spread his fingers as if seeing them for the first time. Intrigued for a couple of reasons, Bill said nothing.

"I went into physics to change the world. I couldn't do it, Bill. And then STC came along and I was gonna do something really great."

Lifting his head, George's look pleaded with Bill.

"Do you understand anything I'm saying? Am I making any sense at all, or is this too personal, too maudlin?"

Shuddering, George's voice began to tremble again.

"And, Bill, It started to go in circles again. And I've been so scared I'd lose it. STC, you, the group, everything."

George tried to still his shaking hands by forcing the fingers together, making a shield in front of himself.

"This isn't easy to say. I've needed to tell you for a long time, but I've been too embarrassed to admit it—even to myself."

Breathing hard, his words rushed out all at once.

"I've always been so damn, well, *envious* of you and your office. And whenever I even think about telling you...I'm gonna finish this if it kills me."

George rushed through the next words miserably, as if he was looking at himself with dislike.

"I've wondered if you were right for this job, if Tahoe made a mistake, and should have had *me* doing your job. And then I'd realize I *couldn't* do it, and that made me madder."

George's eyes glanced at the sketch. He shuddered again as he pointed to the picture.

"And to top it all off, I've never shot a gun in my life."

Slowly, George's breathing began to even out. Both men were very quiet. George angled the sketch of the soldier towards him, giving it a closer look.

"I could draw a better one than that!" He laughed faintly, giving Bill a chance to laugh at him.

Bill didn't laugh. He stood up, needing space to move around. Bill's thoughts had taken two paths during George's admission. He was amazed that George—a huge bear of a man, so sure of himself, outgoing and at ease with everyone—had a streak of doubt as wide as a river. Doubt, as Tahoe had explained was the beginning of arrogance. The second path was even more intriguing. George's weakness could turn out to be his greatest strength. He'd faced his limitation head-on. If he continued on a positive tack, there'd be no limits. STC would extend reminders to each other, so long as a member responded. This meeting was definitely a wake-up call for George. Bill put his hand on George's warm shoulder. He could feel the sweat coming through the fabric of George's shirt.

"Buddy, It's good we talked."

Then he told George exactly what he'd been thinking.

* * *

Somewhat surprised, Bill walked to the head table followed by the interviewers. The gym was full. Not ninety people, but all three hundred plus—it looked to Bill—were in attendance. Perhaps they'd misunderstood the instructions.

"Mornin'," he said briefly. He wanted to make opening remarks, but to a smaller group than this. Nonetheless, Bill kept to his agenda.

"I'd like to start things off with a short story."

Bill closed his eyes. Tilting his head back slightly, he quoted:

"There was a Chinese master of painting, calligraphy, medicine, poetry and Martial Arts. The master liked visiting scenic mountains with their deep gorges. Danger did not deter him. Once the master met a tiger on a narrow mountain path but was not frightened because he was internally strong and his mind was calm. The tiger passed."

Bill opened his eyes.

"Lao Tzu said that softness and suppleness could overcome hardness and strength."

There was a smattering of applause as Bill gave a little bow, glancing at George. Believing his words were not fully clear to the group, Bill had told the story for George. The rest of them would come to understand later on. This would be one of the last times Bill underestimated the capabilities of the teams.

"Well, I'm surprised you all showed up today. That's okay because we have a guest. Steve's an STC advisor observing today. You'll all get to know him better as time goes by."

Nodding to the advisor, Bill said, "Steve, let these fine people see you."

Steve waved and nodded around the room. Bill glanced again at the crowd. It was interesting to see how they'd arranged themselves. Don, Lisa and the teenagers stood with Mike. The Mustache, the Carpenter and Jennifer were together. Frequently assigning nicknames, Bill's designations often stuck.

Waving the card with the ten questions over his head, Bill got the attention of the group.

"The schedule's posted out front, but I'll review it quickly. We'll meet in groups of ten for ninety minutes…"

Bill stopped. The faces before him were smirking.

"We're ready, Bill, let's get started," called a voice from the back.

Bill shrugged and watched as all but ninety people left the room. Crowding in the foyer, they stopped and looked back into the gym. Those who remained quickly arranged chairs into nine groups of eleven. The teams sat facing Bill. With a questioning look, Bill raised his eyebrows at the other interviewers. They were as surprised as he was at the apparent organization of the recruits. Making a quick decision, Bill nodded to the interviewers. One by one they each joined a team. Bill saw Jennifer pointing to an empty chair. Still carrying the question card, he walked towards her.

Somehow, something had clicked in the group, and they were now leading the meeting. Bill's early morning reflections came back to him. *STC recruits have a unique talent to think, assemble, lead and follow.* It seemed to be exactly what they were doing.

Holding out a hand for the card Bill was carrying, the Carpenter stood. Bill craned his neck, looking around the big gym. One person from each of the other eight groups was standing with a hand out to the team leader. Shouting in Bill's head were the other three criteria:

The ones selected would form effective teams. Exceptional people have ideas of their own. Group intelligence would begin the process of problems solving.

Bill had not anticipated that the group might employ all these means on the second day. Whatever they were doing had obviously been prearranged. He handed the card to the Carpenter.

"Ok, Buddy, go for it!"

"What changes would you make in the world today?"

The man's voice was twangy, with a nasal southern drawl, but it carried easily. Rolling like a wave, question number one was loudly repeated by eight other voices. Immediately on the heels of the question, an ear-splitting cheer answered.

"STAR! TRUTH! COUNTRY!"

They'd done much more than arrange groups last night. The impact left Bill with his mouth open. The audience in the foyer shuffled for a better position to see. Jammed together, they watched for Bill's reaction. Crossing his legs, with his hands hugging one knee, Bill leaned back in the chair. He was laughing. Without reacting to Bill's laugh, the Carpenter passed the card to a small woman with jet-black hair braided over one shoulder.

For the next two minutes the huge room reverted to its original purpose. It was a gym full of screaming fans responding to each play. Each of the ten questions was dramatically read and a ninety-voice cheering section would answer.

"Star! Truth! Country!"

Whistles, shouts and stamping feet accompanied the words. The in-your-face presentation erased the last of Bill's doubts. The delivery had been both witty and sincere. Tough, intelligent and creative, they'd planned the display—not for amusement—but to let Bill know they'd heard the questions and understood the reason for asking them. They knew the purpose was only a way to get conversations started—a way to establish links between them. They were ready to get down to specifics. They'd put on the show to pick up the pace, aware that those who couldn't keep up would weed themselves out.

Bill was staggered once more when people reached under their chairs and each pulled on a cap identical to Steve's. The advisor's huge grin preceded him as he made his way to Bill and offered him a cap.

"What did you think I had in that duffle bag?"

Ending in laughter and applause—the sound echoing back from those now leaving the foyer—the opening sequence ended as Steve took off his cap. Throwing it towards the high ceiling, his voice followed its path with a huge whoop.

"Hooah!"

Bill turned towards Jennifer. "So, who planned this thing?"

Her voice was almost serious, "It was a group effort, Bill."

The rest of the session was spent in quiet conversations. Walking from team to team, Bill changed places with other interviewers who did the same. Towards the end of the session Bill overheard a woman's heated words.

"I don't have time for this...I did what you wanted, now I'm outta here!"

She tossed her cap toward the chair. There was a short silence as her footsteps echoed in the gym.

"Let 'em walk out. *We're* here," declared one of the teenagers.

His buddy added, "Look, we're on a military installation. We're using first names. We're problem solvers. We're stars, we tell the truth, and we love the good old US of A. This's intrigue, man! I love it."

Throwing high fives, they laughed.

It was obvious the teams knew they were here for something more important than simply discussing hypothetical situations and how they might possibly fit in. They were ready to hear the details of their involvement. Tomorrow Bill would tell them.

Chapter Six
Clandestine Meetings

When it is a person's fate to undertake new beginnings, everything is still unformed, dark. Hence one must hold back, because any premature move might bring disaster. Likewise, it is very important not to remain alone; in order to overcome the chaos one needs helpers. This is not to say, however, that one should look on passively at what is happening. One must lend a hand and participate with inspiration and guidance.

The Book of Changes

El Paso
Friday Night

The gym was silent and dimly lit. Bill stood with his right forearm pressed against the arm of the advisor. Both men's arms were curved into identical positions. Neither man spoke or moved. With their feet aligned closely together and knees deeply bent, they could have been performing some intricate dance step. The advisor's greater body weight looked as if it might easily push Bill over. Both men were intent on something—a test of strength or a test of will? It was neither.

After fifteen minutes, they straightened and grinned at each other. They weren't sweating or breathing hard.

Faint applause from a dark corner of the large room turned their heads. A man of about fifty years old walked towards them, slowly clapping his hands.

"Well! That's impressive, gentleman. What do you call it?"

His voice held a trace of irony.

"Jus' sittin' down relaxin'," joked Steve, flexing his knees.

Bill smiled faintly.

"Explain it to him, Bill," said Steve.

"Steve was showing me another way to relax," Bill began.

The police captain—dressed in shorts and T-shirt—looked Steve up and down. Nearly six feet tall and weighing 190 pounds, he was close to Steve in build. It was a fair match. He could take him. The captain held out his arm. "Show me."

Explaining how to place his feet, Steve gently placed his tattooed forearm against the other man's. Feeling his touch, the captain instinctively tensed, waiting for the Steve to push back. That's all it took. The burly policeman was flat on his back, staring up in disbelief at the other man. Bill gave him a hand and then held out his arm. Shaking his head, the captain refused at first.

"Naw, you must weigh 30 pounds less than I do."

Bill kept his arm out. Accepting the challenge, the Captain took the stance and made the same trip to the floor.

Looking up, Jack yelled, "Okay, you tricked me, right? It's a trick, right?"

Captain Jackson—Jack to his friends—had an advisory position in STC. When on duty in California, he served as Field Commander for the Berkeley Police Department's Barricaded Subject Hostage Negotiation Team.

Under Jack's dynamic leadership, Berkeley PD had begun looking at a new and unique way to deal with hostage situations. Tactical, negotiation and ancillary teams were incorporated into a single team. BSHNT now utilized this single team approach to address all volatile situations. Other cities, including Los Angeles, had followed suit.

Hearing of the success of the team, Tahoe had made a trip to Berkeley to convince Jack that his skills were needed. Jack had agreed to meet with

Bill in El Paso. He was still undecided whether or not to take a few months' leave in order to augment the training of STC Personnel.

As a Colonel in the Air Force Reserve, Captain Jack was familiar with the military. What he'd observed of STC had impressed him.

In excellent physical condition, Jack ran five miles a day. His pale blue eyes were in a permanent squint and he kept his mustache clipped away from his lips. Jack's closely cropped brown hair was parted on the right side. On and off over the years, his wife had attempted to get him to change the part to the left because of his receding hairline. After a while she quit nagging.

Habitual in nature, Jack was as solid as a rock. His ability to inspire those under his command was legend. Courageous under pressure, he continually perfected his skills. Until now—being knocked over first by Steve's soft touch and then by Bill's—Jack thought his only weakness was his '48 MG.

Captain Andrew Jackson returned to the darkened corner of the gym, determined to commit his talents and energy to this new group.

* * *

El Paso Airport Hilton
Friday Night

As the after-hours gathering place, Jennifer's large hotel room was overflowing. Easy-going with the group, Jennifer's persona had made a transformation from its hyperactive and sometimes overbearing ways. Maybe the southwest desert air was making its influence felt, or maybe it was her increasing interest in Bill. Whatever the reason, Jennifer was more tolerant than she'd ever been—even with herself. If anyone had asked why the change, she would have said that she felt satisfied with the way her life was going.

Most of the recruits felt the same way. Being young, they'd looked forward to the evening. They could let down and joke about the day's events. By this time they were aware of the dedication demanded by STC. They were too smart not to have figured it out. Tough, intelligent and well educated, they knew exactly what they were facing. Some dreaded it. Most were determined to give it their best shot. Others eagerly anticipated delving into the mystique surrounding military training.

Growing up in peacetime, most of them were in grade school when the Berlin Wall fell in November 1989. The Saudi war was an event that hadn't touched them personally. 9/11 had impacted them; but none of them had seen military service. Only a few had family with this background—perhaps a father here and there. Nevertheless, all of them had deep convictions about the way the world was headed and saw STC as a way to serve their country.

Tonight, sixteen people were munching peanuts they found on the bar, drinking bottled water and trying to decide where to go for dinner. In one corner, Don and Lisa's red heads were close together; absorbed in a completely incomprehensible conversation. A book was lying open and upside down on Lisa's bare legs. Catching a glimpse of the title stamped in gold, Jennifer read out loud.

"Physical principles of Flow in Unsaturated Porous Media"

"Who's Clinton M. Case?" she asked Lisa.

Briefly, Lisa looked up at her hostess. "He's the author," she said, bending her head back to the book.

As usual, Bobbie stood in a circle of women, but this time the Carpenter had joined the group. Their attire—shorts, and tank tops or T-shirts—was the deciding factor for dinner. No one wanted to change.

"How 'bout we go out to the patio around the pool?" suggested the Carpenter who grumbled something about his comfortable slacks and not wanting to put on socks.

Everyone now called him the Carpenter—shortened to 'Carp'—even though they knew his occupation was more involved than simply punching nails. Slightly bulging eyes—half-hidden behind thick lenses; and his small mouth—often pursed when in thought—gave him the look of that fish. The petulant tone he used in his speech gave the name its double meaning. The fact that Carp was tall, blonde and muscular eased the sharpness of the nickname.

Slapping Carp on the back, Bobbie spoke, "Right! They've got that great late night menu, and it's a fine evening. Let's do it!"

Jennifer interrupted the two scientists, conversing in the corner. She didn't notice the small red light blinking on her laptop.

* * *

Located two hundred yards from the Airport off Interstate Ten, the El Paso Airport Hilton was a short distance from Bliss. At capacity, the hotel could accommodate four hundred guests. The hotel had checked in over three hundred recruits on Wednesday. Others had rooms at the Holiday Inn on Gateway, also two miles from the gym.

As Jennifer's group strolled by the front desk on their way to the pool, a large group waited to check out. Nods were exchanged, but no one spoke.

Assisted by the friendly hotel staff, several tables were pulled closer to the huge swimming pool. Drinks were ordered. Jennifer spoke first.

"We've only been here two days. They didn't give it much of a chance, did they?" She nodded back towards the lobby.

Carp's twangy voice chimed in. "Those intellectual types!"

Everyone laughed; knowing they all shared that vice.

Harrison and Kurt—Bill's 'teenagers'—were seated together. Leaning his head on one hand, Harrison interrupted the laughter.

"All kidding aside, most of us are certainly connected—not only by our 'fancy degrees' as Mike might say—but we're also on the same wavelength concerning the problems facing the world in general."

Pointing his chin in the general direction of the hotel lobby, his silver earring caught the light.

"I believe those people are too. And if that's the case, what's their problem?"

Kurt turned to his friend and answered in a few short words. The others listened; intrigued that Kurt had somehow picked up the information.

"Well, for example, take that chemist. She's got some test tubes cookin' and cannot *wait* to get back to them. And that astronomer has some glitch in his readings. The surgeon told me he has two major operations scheduled next month."

Bobbie had his two cents to add, "That group of lovely women I was with last night? They all decided to leave because they're scared of doing the military gig."

Looking around the group, Bobbie asked, "Can anyone here give me a good reason why we have to do it?"

Bobbie's question was delivered quietly, but with his usual intensity. His silky voice had an east coast inflection—a little New York and not quite New Jersey—added to some Middle East heritage. It was an arresting combination. His worldwide clients felt Bobbie's voice was one of his greatest assets. So did Bobbie. It would be unproductive not to be aware of one's talents. But talented or not, Bobbie had his concerns.

Before joining the group in Jennifer's room, Bobbie had plugged in his laptop. The information he'd reviewed at the Army web page terrified him. He couldn't even begin to think what firing an M-16 would be like.

Two years ago, he'd arranged a meeting between two high-powered corporations determined to fight it out over a conference table. Bobbie's company had mediated. During the heated discussions, a CEO had jumped up and pulled out a Beretta 9 mm semi-automatic pistol—Bobbie was told the make and caliber of the weapon when it was all over—and waved it around the boardroom. Yelling and screaming, the man made violent threats before he put the gun in his briefcase. It scared the shit out of Bobbie. He hated violence of any kind.

Now, he was facing a decision he couldn't make until he'd heard the ending.

"Bobbie, you still don't get it? Bobbie!"

Lisa's voice pulled Bobbie out of his reverie.

"You really don't understand why we need this bad-ass training?" Lisa was laughing at him. Something else Bobbie couldn't tolerate.

"No, I do *not*. Can *you* explain it?" Bobbie's voice had a dangerous edge to it.

"Sure I can. Look, Bobbie, I didn't mean to insult you in any way. Honest. Here's the thing. We may be on the same wavelength concerning world problems, but what do we know about team discipline outside our own fields? Do we understand coordination in dangerous situations?

We've all admitted we're high-tech intellectuals—free spirits who've all done our own thing. We're a diverse group, you know?"

Bobbie was in a mood, pushing his hands over his eyes. In his line of business, it could be disastrous to forget the basics of bargaining skills or good manners, but remembering the gun had evoked unwanted emotions. He nodded, elbows on the table and his head covered. Bobbie didn't look at Lisa as she continued.

"OK. So, here we are, separate individuals, all on our own. What we need to do is come together as teams. Oh sure, we can talk all day, getting ideas out. But ideas can only go so far. What happens when we need to take action? Do we know how to follow orders? Maybe in our own fields, we do. But how about in a situation we've never faced? And are you strong enough physically? And can you face certain in-born fears—like falling, or having someone shoot at you, or chase you—and know exactly how to react without coming unglued?"

Lisa's questions were point blank and delivered with passion. She'd obviously questioned herself in these areas.

"And what moves would you make when some emergency comes up? Are your reactions so well-developed that you don't need more training in those areas?"

Lisa's grin softened the sharpness of her questions.

"Hey, man!" Kurt's voice broke up Lisa's discourse.

He waved to a man standing on the far side of the pool. The man waved back and motioned to two women behind him. Pulling up another table, the three newcomers joined the group. If the man noticed any tension, he chose to ignore it. The others were ready to change the subject, and welcomed the interruption.

"I was thinkin' about checkin' out this here hotel. They tell me there's rooms now, and I saw ya'll sittin' out here."

"Great day, huh?" he added.

They knew he wasn't talking about the weather.

Some found James uncomfortable to be with because he was always on the verge of rudeness. He'd growled at several groups, "Don' *never* call me 'Jim'!"

James used insolence, along with his drawl, as a tool. He'd make off-the-wall comments—complete with poor grammar—and wait for a response. James had discovered early in life that he could learn a great deal about people if they assumed he was a bumpkin with no manners. Sophistication was not a goal James sought. He liked people, but had little time to socialize.

Fully educated and highly trained at an early age, James was a much sought-after historical archeologist. He'd returned from China—on a dig with the University of Hartford—only a few days before Flavia caught up with him and had given him the phone number for STC.

"So, where's all the heroes at?" asked James.

The others smiled. They'd begun to see through James' uncomfortable speech patterns. Tonight, James caught them off guard.

"I've been thinkin' about that hero business, and wanted to tell ya'll one of my favorite hero-stories. Do ya'll mind?"

The waiters had taken orders for dinner, and came back for the newcomers.

"Wha'ever they're havin'," James said, waving his hand around the tables.

"Okay, James, tell us your very favorite bed-time story," said Bobbie.

James flipped him off, and everyone laughed.

"What happened was, there was this quar'back, can't 'member his name—some state I think. Anyways it's a long time ago. Played for San Francisco; the Super Bowl, maybe, and there was less than a minute to play."

James paused to gulp the beer in front of him, his prominent Adams apple bobbling as he swallowed. Tall and painfully thin, James' large hand nearly hid the bottle he gripped.

"Well, anyways, here's this quar'back. They gotta score to win. They've got the ball but it was hopeless. So anyways they're in the huddle, in this des'pert situation. Everyone is scared and full of doubts."

One by one they began to listen as James' voice took on an entirely different quality. Dropping the garbled speech, he told his story with depth and feeling. There were no interruptions.

"The team was pumped up for their last shot, waiting for the quarterback to call the play, maybe say a word or two. But what happens?"

James looked around at the faces, but no one said a word.

"The quarterback looks up, and then downfield over a hundred yards towards the end zone. He spots a movie star in the bleachers. And he says, 'Hey look who's here!'"

James paused again. By this time, the entire group was listening, wondering where this was headed. James' normally offensive tone was completely gone. Remembering something important to him, he wanted to contribute to the group.

"So? What happened?" asked Don.

Living in San Francisco, Don was a 49'ers fan, but he'd never heard this story.

"Well, this quarterback, not only does he break the ice for his team, but his casual remark makes time stand still for a moment. His teammates begin to sense what's about to happen, slightly before the crowd senses it, before the other team does, and before coaches on both sides do. Before the game is over, everyone knows how it's going to end. Do you know how it ended?"

Don asked, "Did they win?"

James grinned, "Sure, they won—but not by a big miracle play or by some terrible mistake by the defense. Both of those can leave everyone walking away thinking it wasn't somehow fair—even if your team wins."

Nods from the group encouraged him to continue.

"What happened was a series of precision plays perfectly executed. There must have been eight or ten plays, each one taking only a few seconds off the clock. You felt like they couldn't miss. But then you wonder if there's time. The distance is so great. Then they score…with three seconds left. That's the rarest of performances that leaves everyone involved—the other team and the fans for both sides—thinking, 'Wow!'"

"Yeah," said Bobbie, "I can relate."

"Yeah," said James, in perfect imitation of Bobbie. "You think to yourself, 'It doesn't get better than this. It was meant to be.' No matter how many years go by, you get this big, satisfied feeling whenever you think about it."

James drank the last of his beer and added another few comments.

"A few years ago I heard the Chicago Symphony play, and went backstage afterwards. I told them how much I enjoyed the performance. Some of the brass players have been together for over forty years. They told me they played good that night, but went on to tell me about one gig they'll always remember. It was a performance of Strauss' *Don Quixote* in 1996 where everything worked and they could almost feel flawlessness."

James stretched his arms over his head and flagged the waitress.

"That ball game and *Don Quixote*—that's teamwork, perhaps our only chance to taste perfection in this life."

Silence greeted his story. The group was bowled over. Bobbie scraped back his chair, stood up and slowly began to applaud.

* * *

Fort Bliss
STC Offices
Friday Night

"About your beard, George, you'll need to do something about it." Annie's voice murmured in the stillness.

A half-empty bottle of wine sat on a notepad on top of Bill's otherwise empty desk. Realizing George and Annie needed time alone; Bill had offered the office for after-hours privacy. Along with most of the other interviewers, George and Annie had temporary quarters on post—but they weren't housed in the same building.

"I've been out on the net getting some information about Airborne School."

She showed him a stack of colorful pages she'd printed, which included a shot of a 250-foot tower used in training. George ignored them.

"What about my beard?"

Pulling out one sheet, Annie laid it in front of him. She moved her head to read it, pointing her finger to the passage.

"*FACE. Male students will be clean-shaven unless a valid medical shaving profile has been issued.*"

George ran a hand over his chin. "Well, it makes sense. Gotta be aerodynamically correct."

Annie drew back, feigning alarm, "George, you're not going down face first, are you?"

Then, reading further, she poked George's arm. "It says here that students can't wear make-up or jewelry in the training area."

Laughingly, Annie commented, "I guess Harrison and Kurt will have to go elsewhere to wear their earrings and eye shadow."

"Cut it out, Annie. You can't joke like that. They are really bright, you know. Flavia showed me their profiles before they got here."

She changed the subject.

"George, do you think I can do 19 sit-ups and 36 push-ups?"

"You know you can do anything you set your mind to."

Resting his forehead in one hand, George was silent. All day he'd looked forward to talking with Annie. Straightening his back, he told her what was on his mind.

"Remember the short lecture Don gave?"

Annie remembered it very well.

"That was a new beginning for me, Annie. Bill came to my rescue and got me back on track."

George told her everything. It was easier this time.

Annie loved the talented engineer and often wished she could share her secrets with George as readily as he did with her. Her appointment as recruiter had been planned. She was the only one who hadn't answered the ad. Having accepted from the beginning that her musical career would be short-term, Annie hoped her talent would be useful to STC.

The close relationship with George had added a new dimension to her work, but there were certain things she couldn't tell him. She had to prove herself first.

Eyes clear for the first time in days, George went on.

"This morning I heard an interview with a famous Irish music group. The leader said, 'First you do what you *want*, perfect your skills, then you can do what you *like*.' So, Annie, I was thinking all day, one should *want* success; get out of the living room, so to speak."

Annie listened patiently. She knew George would make his point.

"I remember this 16-year old jazz musician, so humble about his talent. Someone commented, 'He doesn't need to hear he's a genius. He needs to go New York and get his butt kicked.'"

Annie knew George listened to radio interviews—was almost addicted to them—on many subjects. He was a sports enthusiast, and Annie could predict his next thought would be in that arena.

"Annie, most people involved in sports at a high level will admit they want fans, and they want competition. They may be real polite outwardly, but inside they're all egomaniacs. The light comes on, and they're stars. See what I mean?"

Annie nodded, leaning closer.

"You gotta do what you want—master it *first*—then you can do it. That's what I've been pondering all day. You can't jump ahead. You must keep going and growing."

Annie got up and cuddled herself into George's lap, pulling his head down to her shoulder. With Annie, George knew he could do anything— even jump out of an airplane.

* * *

The Inn at Fort Bliss
Late Friday Night

Always looking for the best in people, Bill was an idealist first, and a realist second.

Levelheaded enough to recognize people's weaknesses, he nevertheless sought the finest. When he met Jennifer he was taken with her strength and candor. Her physical appeal was obvious—it was the inner person that Bill was most drawn to.

He'd learned that Jennifer had a great love for her fellow human beings, but was always disappointed—she'd told him—by her inability to deal with the realities of life. Alone in his room, Bill was reflecting on Jennifer's words during a short, private talk they'd had in the vacant foyer of the gym between sessions:

"I had this drive for success in the business world. I learned what it took to make it to the top. Being a woman was an advantage, to be sure. I was promoted pretty fast. Of course the degrees helped too."

But frankness had been Jennifer's downfall

"I couldn't get into the game. I'd conveniently ignore the means to a problem, see the solution quickly and bull headedly demand a quick resolution."

Most of her colleagues wanted endless meetings. They'd draw their huge salaries, delaying a conclusion for as long as possible.

"It irritated me no end. I'm not a patient person—something I've thought about correcting."

Suddenly released by the company, she'd been told they were downsizing.

"Looking back on it, I believe I was a threat to a way of life my contemporaries treasured. They complained, and the CEO in New York listened."

Jennifer had concluded the brief summary on a positive note.

"It was over—and then I met you."

Hearing her voice in his mind, Bill looked at the phone, willing it to ring.

"Bill, It's Jen. Sorry it's so late. Were you still awake?"

Bill reassured her. "Yes, it's fine. I'll come pick you up?"

Twenty minutes later they were in a place Bill knew they'd be alone.

"I missed the light on my laptop. Sorry. I knew you'd be tied up until late, but I should've called earlier."

"No problem. Good dinner?" Bill asked.

"The best! Not so much the food, but the conversations. They were great."

Jennifer laughed, throwing her hair back and moving closer to Bill. They were sitting at a small table upstairs at Bombardier's on Mesa—an out-of-the-way tavern on the west side of El Paso. The bar downstairs was L-shaped, and Bill had stopped to order two beers on tap. The table, dimly lit by a small lantern candle, was near the balcony that overlooked a sunken area where two pool tables sat vacant. Bill knew they wouldn't run into anyone from STC. You had to know where the place was in order to find it.

"So?" Bill asked.

Jennifer told him about Lisa's questions for Bobbie. She laughed again at James' clever story, and Bobbie's reaction. She related Kurt's rapid-fire accounting of who had left and why. Bill sipped his beer.

"Get your groups all set up for tomorrow?"

Jennifer grinned at him, "Indeed, but you'll have to wait to see."

Jennifer was circumspect, if nothing else. It was one of many things Bill admired about her.

"You remember Steve, the advisor?" he asked.

"Oh sure, the hat man! What about him?"

"We worked out at the gym before you called. He's a great guy, you know; a real asset to the team."

Jennifer led the conversation easily, knowing Bill would only make general comments about anything to do with STC. He gave her no details when they were alone. Bill talked to the group, not individuals. Jennifer already knew this.

"Bill, what country haven't you visited?"

It was a variation on a game Jennifer had played as a child—daydreaming of far-away places. Bill leaned his elbows on the table.

Jennifer had met and worked with many men. But Bill was entirely different from anyone she'd met. After their first encounter, she described him in her journal: "*He is careful.*" They'd seen each other twice—if you counted the street meeting in Monterey—but the calm that surrounded him made the foundation of their friendship secure. Bill might be the leader in their relationship—but the role was amplified by Jennifer's outspoken honesty and high-spirits. It was obvious to both of them that they balanced each other.

"I haven't been to Israel, have you?"

"Oh, God, yes! Greatest food in the world, next to Monterey."

Jennifer sighed at the memory.

"I ate chocolate cake and drank the darkest, sweetest coffee *al fresco*—near Caesarea, on the Mediterranean."

Reaching out, she touched the back of his hand with one finger.

"Is this okay, Bill, I mean being together like this? Does it break any rules?"

He put her at ease. "Don't worry, it's right."

Taking her hands and leaning towards her, Bill spoke quietly.

"Jen, on Monday we have to select one other person. Remember, groups of two?"

She nodded, "I know."

"We're going to do this stint in the Army. It's been part of the plan from the very beginning—to make sure each of us has someone we've chosen ourselves."

Bill turned one of her hands palm up.

"I have something that belongs to you."

Placing a small silver and turquoise ring in the center of her hand, he closed her fingers around it.

"I chose you that day in Monterey. It's right."

Chapter Seven
The Right Assistants

It is important to seek out the right assistants, but you can only find them by avoiding arrogance and associate with those found in a spirit of humility. Only then will you attract those with whose help you can combat the difficulties.

The Book of Changes

El Paso
16 December, 0800 Hours

Intent on the task at hand, interviewers had strewn papers across the conference table. Scrawled notes for today's opening remarks were in Bill's shirt pocket. Now and then he'd pull them out and shuffle the cards before shoving them back into his pocket. Making few comments, Bill didn't participate with his usual energy. The others wondered at this, but kept to the job of tagging certain files and jotting quick notes on the pads in front of them. They'd been at work for over an hour.

Harlem had given her report. One hundred and ninety people remained. Comparing notes, the interviewers could predict with fair accuracy that at least a hundred more would leave by Monday. With assurances that they'd be "on call" should the need arise at some later date, most of those who'd left had given their reasons to Bill personally. Their departure did not threaten the plan. Details remained undisclosed until each person's commitment was certain.

For now, interviewers continued to step around pointed questions. If discussions intensified and began to approach the intricacies of their part in military or political involvement in civilian crisis, group leaders would carefully lead the conversation in a different direction. The finer points on the subject of how STC would interact with other agencies were something that did not need to be known by anyone returning to his or her previous life style. Until then, the recruits might guess, but that's all it would be—speculation.

Interviewers weren't concerned about how many would stay. Nor were they involved with the formation of the teams. The decision to remain and the selection of team members were both personal decisions. Nonetheless, interviewers considered it necessary to know as much as possible about each individual on the list of names growing in front of them. Each had special capabilities.

Things were heating up. The relatively relaxed atmosphere of the proceedings would change over the weekend. It would be grueling work for the nine interviewers who'd cautiously outline some of the more interesting aspects of STC.

Annie shoved a folder towards Mike. "About this man, Bobbie. Here, read this."

Bill raised his head, scowling.

"Who is this guy, anyway? Who found him?"

Flavia waved a lazy hand without looking up, her eyes intent on something she was reading. The table grew silent for a moment. Bill was not himself this morning. He looked down again, beginning to sketch.

This time he drew a couple dancing under the stars. Quickly forming the night sky Bill outlined a woman and finally a man with a huge villainous mustache. The figures were quick cartoon-like characters, but it was clear that the man had swept the woman into his arms, obviously hissing...

Bill was thinking about a conversation he'd heard. Circling the room late yesterday, he'd been stopped by a fast-paced interchange of words.

"So, Bobbie, what makes you think you're a star?"

"Well for one thing, they tell me I dance like an angel; since ninth grade, girls yelling, 'Dance with me, Bobbie.'"

What in the hell was this guy was talking about?

Bobbie's name badge was pinned in the middle of his silk shirt below the fourth button. The other three were open, exposing curly black hair on his chest. His bushy mustache barely moved as he spoke. His voice was as soft and dark as his hair. Slim and wiry, he gave off an air of overconfidence. As he'd spoken, Bobbie leaned towards the group—arms on his thighs, hands dangling between his knees.

"You asked, and I'm telling you the truth. That's what they said."

The sound of voices—conversations more wide-ranging than before—swirled around the gym like the noise of moths batting their wings in a vain attempt to get to a light.

"Another futile conversation," Bill thought. But he stayed to listen.

"Look, that's sort of a silly example, I know."

The others nodded as he continued.

"What makes me a star? I'm president of a business back east. I never ask more from anyone than I can give myself. The characteristics we look for in our employees are the ones I already have."

Something in his manner—although it seemed supercilious—kept Bill listening. Supple as a snake, Bobbie was undeniably sure of himself He went on to tell how he'd started the business along with his partner and best friend after getting his law degree. Bragging that he'd skimmed through undergrad studies in history and philosophy of law, Bobbie admitted to the group that he'd succumbed to pressure from his father to make something of himself. Apparently, from what Bill had overheard, his business was a booming success. Bill walked away, wondering how this attention-grabbing individual could make a success of anything. It wasn't the first time Bill had made a mistake in judgment. Bobbie's expertise and sensitivity was going to be useful in a way that Bill never dreamed.

Looking at the sketch, Bill crumpled it and threw it hard in the general direction of a large industrial wastebasket on the far side of the room.

Eyes followed its trajectory and looked away quickly as the ball hit the wall. It fell to the carpeting and slowly rolled into a corner.

George spoke out. "So, Bill, got somethin' against the *bigote?*"

George chose the Spanish word for *mustache*.

Bill told them what he'd overheard. Mike looked up from the folder and shoved it across the table towards Bill who reached out at the last second and stopped it from scattering on the floor.

"Take a look, Bill. You may not like him, but the guy's a negotiator for crissake! Besides, he's got star quality, man!"

Everyone chuckled and Bill had to smile at himself.

* * *

El Paso International Airport
0830 Hours

It was a weekend and the long passageways were crowded with travelers. Geckos woven into the carpet stared up impassively at hurrying feet. Teal-tinted windows gave off an unusual but comfortable glow. Located near the security terminal, the smoking lounge exuded white billows every time the door was opened. The odorous haze mixed with the aroma of gourmet coffee wafting up from downstairs.

Standing impatiently at the gate, the advisor watched the arrivals and wished he'd been less self-conscious about stopping for a super-latte. Dressed in BDU's, the star with oak leaves nestled between the three-up three-down stripes showed his rank—Command Sergeant Major. A ranger tab sat comfortably on his shoulder. His uniform didn't draw attention, as the airport was jammed with military.

Steve was to pick up three men flying in from Fort Leonard Wood. They'd never met and Steve carried a small placard—Harlem's idea, part of her organization. The card said 'WELCOME.' Steve held it offhandedly at his side, tapping it against his thigh. He knew he'd recognize them.

* * *

Stout Gym
0900 Hours

Things were different today. Interviewers had greeted the recruits and encouraged them to remain standing. Fifty-five people noted the changes in the gym, empty except for nine sets of six chairs arranged in tight circles grouped close to the walls. Quiet anticipation radiated from the people in the center of the room who, from habit, faced the direction of the absent head table. Making his way to the back of the gym, Bill turned towards the group. His voice was serious this morning. Any banter was gone.

"Come in closer, please."

Pushing his hands into his pockets—elbows out, Bill slowly walked towards them as they moved to join him. Bill's body was relaxed and casual, in contrast to the seriousness of his words. The timber of his voice was intimate and low pitched.

"Today we'll respond to the questions you've had. Keep in mind that there is only so much we can discuss at this time. Until you've made the decision to stay, we can only answer in generalities."

The faces before him were serious as his own.

"If any of you feel inclined to leave, that's okay."

No one smiled as they waited.

"STC, the problems you've identified and the ten questions have been the topics these past two days. The results of your discussions have decided the groups you've chosen today."

Slowly, Bill stressed his next words.

"You all know the importance of seeking the right associates. You also know that overconfidence or arrogance can hinder any endeavor. In the type of work you'll be undertaking in STC, it is vital that any such tendencies be replaced by something much more valuable and stronger than any personal confidence. We will explain what that is, and how to develop it."

Speaking softly, Bill's next words had a greater impact.

"When you're in confrontational situations, you need assistance. No one can do it alone."

Not one person moved. Not one eye wandered to the large clock. Time froze.

"We asked the question about military training. How many of you are willing to seriously consider this?"

Eyes searched among the groups of five. They pulled closer together, as if making sure this was real. Was this the time for decision?

Bill moved on quickly to his next comment. "We don't ask this lightly. You'll need to make changes in your lives; changes that are a necessary part of your commitment. So before you answer the question, think it over carefully."

Hands, almost of their own accord, reached out to touch the person nearest them. Bill kept his in his pockets, slowly moving side to side. Then he stood still, upright.

"You've talked—spent time together here, and on your own—asking questions. Why are we on a military installation? Why are we using only first names? Why is military training necessary?"

Pausing briefly, Bill smiled slowly.

"And you want to know more details about the problems. Right?"

There were many nods. The team members stayed close together.

"Let me say that STC is quite aware of escalating tensions. We'd all like to soften the glare—so to speak—so that our world can progress towards greater alliance. This won't happen by itself. You've all indicated that this in an area of personal concern to you. I can only say that STC will introduce specially trained people into situations to assist in resolving problems."

As if thinking aloud, Bill spoke even more softly. The group strained to hear his next words.

"Problems sometimes take turns that make them impossible to solve and the end result can be loss of life and destruction."

Bill clenched his hands behind his back. He leaned forward a little, involving them all in his words. Interviewers, one by one, moved among the groups. Heads turned at the motion and the interviewers returned the looks, smiling calmly.

"I'm not talking about problems handled by public agencies, normal business or political negotiations, or through military intervention. Those are dealt with by procedures already in place. We do not interfere."

Arms were thrown over shoulders, leaning against a special buddy. Everyone looked at Bill, encouraging him, as well as themselves.

"Those of you who decide to stay will learn special skills. These include sharpening your minds and opening them to some different ways of thinking. You'll need to strengthen your body and learn to face new challenges not normally met by any of you."

People drew even closer, waiting for Bill's next words.

"I think you'll agree that this is an exciting time in our history. Life, though the ages, has always been a great gift and a great mystery. Those of you who are involved in the scientific world understand that everything is somehow accelerated. Advances in technology seem to be rocketing forward to greater understanding—or greater confusion and destructiveness."

Nodding to one or two people in the front of the gathering, Bill cleared his throat quietly.

"I assure you that your expertise and experience will be used by STC. Think of them as tools for problem solving. As far as training, we'll engage the best experts in the world, but our discipline will rely on you— members of STC. Group intelligence and inspiration will come from your interaction. We'll study this, and rely on it more completely than has been done in the past."

Bill concluded his opening remarks.

"Military training is only the beginning."

It took a moment for these words to impact them. They resounded off the wooden floor and brick walls of the half-empty room like the sound of gunshots ricocheting off granite cliffs. Motioning to the chairs along the walls, Bill ignored the inquiring looks. He knew the statement would lead to more questions. It was planned to do exactly that.

"Discussions will be among six of us in each group. The chairs are in a circle, like a six-pointed star. Take advantage of the intersecting lines. Feel free to ask any question, without intimidation. You've gone way beyond that point."

Moving closer to Carp, Bill put his hand on the man's shoulder.

"Anyone who wishes to leave, please do so now."

Ten people standing in the back looked at each other and left without a word. Carp watched them go. The fun was over. This was serious.

* * *

McGregor Range
1000 Hours

"We're gonna train a bunch of civilian hot-snots here, at Ma Gregor?" the Drill Sergeant asked. "Why not bring 'em down to Leonard Wood, or Knox? And where the hell is my equipment?"

Steve grinned. "Well, for one thing there's women in the group, and Knox is *not* co-ed."

"Shee-it!" Stanley snarled. "You mean there're scientists AND females?"

"Stan-Lee," said Steve, "You were briefed. Remember? Don't go pitching stones at people you haven't even met."

"I'll reserve my judgment, but don't call me Stan-Lee," barked the huge Drill Sergeant.

Steve answered Stanley's other question.

"And you know damn well we dropped the other two at Bliss. You'll get what you requisitioned."

Steve enjoyed the Sergeant's fake bad humor. He knew it was part of the act.

"They'll get it together; building materials, and all the equipment."

Steve changed the subject.

"Balke's headed for SOCOM, you know, to get Benning ready to accept your highly-trained soldiers."

Steve laughed and pointed to the barren grounds.

"They'll march out on that field in their Class A's and give you all the credit."

"That old man, Commander? Navy? Doesn't he run a music school or some such shit?" asked Stanley.

"Yeah, but you should know something. That old man was one of the first to complete SEALS when the program began. Did some incredible top secret stuff too."

Stanley didn't have anything more to say.

Thirty miles northeast of El Paso, McGregor Range is completely desolate. Withdrawn from public domain, McGregor is used by U.S. and Allied personnel to train in the use of air defense weapon systems, including missiles and conventional weapons. In addition the Range is utilized for gunnery, bombing, and tactical training for helicopters and fixed-wing aircraft. The southeast corner is set aside for tank and other vehicle ground maneuvers.

Knowing that training needs were changing, what with new technologies and policies, the Army felt McGregor was essential to near and long term preparedness. In October 1999 the Defense Authorization Bill was signed. This meant that Fort Bliss could continue to train at McGregor through 2026. Fort Bliss controls access to the range, but the Bureau of Land Management is responsible for the withdrawn lands. BLM's state director and the Fort Bliss chief of staff signed an agreement setting out policies, procedures, and responsibilities for both agencies. The agreement included an annual report, tracking activities on the range. STC was not included in the report.

Kicking at the sand burrs with one spit-shined toe of his Cochrans, Steve watched a few scorpions scuttle in front of him. He shrugged at the dust, and lifted his head, nodding towards the buildings. "Let's take a look."

Five sagging barracks, newly painted a tan color, resembled heaps of unbaked chocolate chip cookie dough. Window frames and doors, highlighted with a flat brown, enhanced the image. There were no lawns, no greenery and no sidewalks. Nothing broke the desert expanse except a barely discernable road, outlined with roughly hewn rocks, leading from the so-called Fort Bliss gate to the WWII style barracks. A flagpole recently erected in front of the largest of the buildings was empty, waiting for the stars and strips to be hoisted.

Striding towards the renovated buildings, Steve continued talking.

"You realize, Stan, that one of those females used to spend her summers climbin' and fightin' fires in Wyoming. I heard she carried more weight than the men. I shook her hand. She nearly threw me down!"

Stanley grunted.

"Another one, a psychologist, backpacks seventy pounds up and down 12,000 feet. Bet she'll outrun you, training like she does at altitude! Says she does it for fun."

Stanley looked at Steve and grinned.

"Fun. Ha! I'll make sure she carries that much and more."

Squinting at his companion, Steve didn't mention a third woman he'd met the day before. There was something special about the tough, spunky Mexican-American biologist, and Steve wasn't one to make casual comments that might reveal personal feelings. Instead he spoke sharply.

"Okay, great. But remember it's up to y'all to get 'em ready for Airborne and Rangers."

The Drill Sergeant pushed his face towards Steve, raising his voice.

"Fat chance! Those babies'll never even make it through what I've got for 'em."

At loose ends when he graduated from high school, Stanley John Lee had taken a job at a gym in Atlanta. In a short time the likable young man was in demand as a personal trainer. During those years, Stan kept his black skin hairless, glinting with oil to enhance his physique. He'd had his tongue pierced. His female clients loved to watch Stan roll the ball bearing around in his mouth. Barely escaping an angry husband's threats, Stan removed his tongue ring and joined the Army.

Soldiering became an affair of his heart, but Stan knew he needed more than was offered by carrying a weapon and practicing "just in case" scenarios in the Infantry with 11 Bravo. After four years, his CO had suggested Drill Instructor School. Stan jumped at the chance. He'd discovered his forte: teaching recruits. Whipping them into shape, Stanley secretly cheered their successes.

Shoving hard to break up the dried paint that had dripped between the frame and the door, Stanley pushed open the entrance to the main building. His doubts increased as he walked through the dusty bay. First thing, he'd have everything scoured, top to bottom, by those cherry recruits.

* * *

Stout Gym
1500 Hours

Thirty minutes into the session, eight groups of five were deep in conversations—knee-to-knee, as planned. Bill floated from group to group. Harrison and Kurt sat with Mike and three others. Suddenly a chair was pushed back so hard it fell to the floor. Turning on her heel, a woman left the gym, her rubber-soled shoes squeaking loud as her voice.

"You people are nuts! You'll never do it. I'm gone."

The teenagers waved to her back.

"Bye, bye, Sally, nice to've met you," Kurt said in a sarcastic undertone.

His face was steely hard as he turned to his cohort. They didn't smile.

"So, what about basic?" asked Bobbie, looking around his group.

Jasen answered. "Here. Fort Bliss. Well, not on the post, out in the desert a few miles."

Bobbie shook his head, "No, no, I mean I still don't get why all this emphasis on military training. What does it matter?"

Toning down his first impulse to lean closer to Bobbie and involve him in a forceful interplay of words, Jasen tried to answer reasonably.

"Bobbie, you know how people respect a uniform?"

There was no response. Jasen tried again.

"If you see someone—police, fire, military—in uniform, don't you feel some sort of awe for what they do?"

Bobbie attempted to hide a sarcastic smile, not quite succeeding. Raised in one of the less affluent neighborhoods of Hoboken, Bobbie had grown up with little respect for anyone in uniform. They represented violent situations.

Jasen kept his temper with difficulty. He tightened his jaw.

"Try to look at it from a different perspective, Bobbie. People see you all loaded down with heavy equipment, carrying a weapon, fighting…"

Bobbie's expression changed as he peered intently at Jasen. Constantly

99

demanding clarification, Bobbie had the unique ability to adjust his viewpoint when necessary.

Others in the group, more astute perhaps, were benefiting from both sides of this conversation. They wanted to jump in with their own ideas, but held back, wanting Jasen and Bobbie to get through it.

"Jase, man, I think I'm getting the picture. What you mean is, if I wear some heavy-duty uniform, I command respect, whether or not I feel it myself…"

Bobbie's white teeth flashed in a huge grin.

"And not only do other people respect me, because I'm good at what I do…"

Then, his smile faded along with his voice. Something new had occurred to him; some vague idea was tickling around in his agile brain. He talked it out.

"So, it's sort of like me in my suit and tie when I sit in a conference room with a big client. My clients can tell by looking at me I know my part—I've got what it takes to get the job done: *attitude*."

Bobbie drew a deep breath, looking around the group.

"From their point of view, I'm the best. Their point of view affects me, and now I know I'm the best. We can solve their problem. Everyone benefits. It's a teamwork thing."

And he flashed another smile, this time directly at Jasen.

"I knew that."

"OK, so I'll learn to shoot one of those weapons, you know, M-something? I've only ever shot my snake pistol," Lisa spoke. "It's my baby; a Rueger, .22 long barrel. An associate calls it my assassin's pistol. He wanted to get me a silencer for it, but I told him I'd never use it for that!"

The group laughed.

"I'm a pretty good shot too. I've still got all my targets from the range. One has the whole damn bull's eye shot out."

"What about STC Training? What's that all about? And why did you say…?"

Hearing the question, Bill walked towards Bobbie.

Bobbie stood as he raised his voice. He stuck his hands in his pockets, rocking from side to side, parodying Bill's stance.

"How did you put it?" he asked, looking directly at Bill, "military training is only the beginning?"

Everyone in the gym heard Bobbie's question. They all looked at Bill.

Bill had read a line in Bobbie's profile: *Adaptable, the man challenges everything, learns quickly and retains it all.*

He slapped his hand on Bobbie's back, smiling.

"Monday," he said.

Chapter Eight
The Hidden Dragons

The person who has the character of a dragon remains concealed. The person does not change to suit the outside world. The person withdraws from the world, yet is not sad about it. The person receives no recognition, yet is not sad about it. If lucky, the person carries out principles; if unlucky, withdraws with them. The person cannot be uprooted; the person is a hidden dragon.

The Book of Changes

El Paso
18 December, 0900 Hours

Ninety chairs waited as recruits marched up the wide steps and into the gym. Footsteps seemed somehow stronger, heavier, taking on a distinct resonance familiar to anyone who heard it and took the time to listen. Motivated by common principles, the group's confidence was audible and the environment reacted—similar to the concentric circles created by a stone thrown into still waters that can be seen and felt.

Responding to their surroundings—an atmosphere that demanded a certain code of behavior—the recruits were transforming themselves into a cohesive whole. At first some may have been hesitant. Picking up friends and joining in varied conversations had assured them that they'd made the right decision. Now they could put their minds to what needed to be done.

Nothing about their outward appearance had changed. They were still a fun-loving bunch, dressed casually, interested in each other, excited about trying something new. Only a perceptive person would notice any difference. The changes were internal.

Standing in a sunlit graveled area filled with huge aloe, small Joshua trees and assorted cacti, Bill watched. He hadn't planned to be there when they arrived. Stepping out for some air before the group meeting, he was going over the remarks he'd make at the close of the session. He'd be the last to speak today.

Painted desert-red, the huge letters *Mitchell W. Stout Physical Fitness Center* loomed over the heads of the recruits as they pounded up the cement stairs. Recognizing the sound they made, Bill was glad he'd been there to hear it.

Mike glanced at Harlem. He stood alone in the front of the group. Nodding to Mike, Harlem took her place in the front row. The chair next to her was stacked high with papers, stapled into neat packets. Recruits were seated, two by two; their chairs arranged in nine neat rows. Harlem's report this morning had indicated that eighty-one recruits remained in El Paso. It made no difference to Bill, who hadn't looked at the list. Names listed on a piece of paper meant little to him at this point.

Taking his place next to Jennifer, Bill didn't stop to observe who was with whom. *They* knew; that was the important thing. They were the selected ones.

* * *

Soquel, California
9:00 AM

Absorbed in the news broadcast, the youngster perched on the edge of his bed his thin legs tucked under him at an impossible angle. At seventeen, he was still young enough to be anticipating Christmas. Even so, there was a dark cloud over the holidays, affecting his mood. His father was in a mess at work. Enforced retirement, his dad had called it. Seeing it coming, the man had talked openly with the family about his feelings of resentment. Later, the man would regret those discussions.

The boy's brown hair was disheveled. He'd been running jittery fingers through it all morning, trying to sort through his emotions. On top of it all, the unrelenting drone from the vacuum cleaner was driving him crazy. He couldn't even hear the news.

The boy stood up and walked quickly out of his bedroom on the second floor of the large, comfortable family home built on the side of a hill above the San Lorenzo River. Leaning on the decorative railing along the balcony, he looked down at the huge living room his mother had carefully designed and furnished.

The maid sang along with the vacuum. Equipped with tiny earphones, the personal CD player was hooked to the strap of her denim overalls. The headset kept the household from hearing the music, but not her whining voice.

Annoyance grew and the boy stomped back to his room, slamming the door loudly. With the remote in his hand, he turned up the sound. The man was in the middle of a sentence.

"...and so for all the inconvenience we have caused, we apologize. We'll be reducing the number of scheduled flights to solve the problem..."

The boy clicked off the news, muttering under his breath. Clumping downstairs to his private place in the basement, he shoved aside papers and flipped on the computer. The boy searched the Internet, surfing for ways to make a bomb.

* * *

El Paso
Stout Gym, 0915 Hours

"Background for what's coming next month!" Mike shouted, getting their attention immediately.

Conversations stopped in mid-sentence, trailing off into silence. Mike grinned at them.

"Personally, I'm dreading it, but then, I already know what to expect."

There was no head table, no podium, and no amplification. Mike stood on the same level with the group, moving at times to make sure they could all see him. His trained voice carried well.

"Great! You're here, and I assume that means you've all answered a resounding 'YES' to question number nine?"

Smiles and nods acknowledged him.

"If there are any of you that can't commit for whatever reason, you're excused."

Mike waited a moment. No one moved.

"Basic Training in the Army. Where, when and what to do—all the "W" words—I'm here this morning to tell you."

He pulled up his belt and pointed to his stomach.

"This is history!"

Running his hands over the top of his head, Mike smirked. The short haircut camouflaged his premature baldness.

"One of the things you may want to experience after Christmas."

Mike's hair had been buzzed at the Post's barbershop late last night. Barbers took turns opening the facility on Sunday nights for soldiers who needed to report early Monday morning and had failed to take care of this detail before family weekend activities.

Jonesy pulled on her braid, pointedly displaying the black length.

"Don't worry about it, Jonsey. I doubt you'll have to cut it, although you may be asked to wear a hair net on occasion."

The group began to relax. Mike was very good in front of an audience. Court appearances had taught him to take advantage of reactions from spectators to bend a group in his direction.

"Okay. First step is MEPS."

Looking at his notes, Mike raised his head and saw questioning looks.

"Oops, sorry, Military Entrance Processing Station."

Mike continued, knowing that military acronyms would soon become second nature.

"At MEPS, which is here—today and tomorrow—you'll need to qualify physically for your own safety."

Mike beamed at them.

"Seeing as how you've all qualified mentally due to the incredible number of degrees conferred on you, we can skip the aptitude tests."

He paused for some laughter.

"But you do need to take a physical."

Loud groans and a few comments vibrated throughout the room. Mike ignored them.

"It's pretty simple. They'll check your ears, and eyes for color blindness and depth perception. Then they'll take some blood and urine."

Mike shoved the notes into his shirt pocket.

"Anyone who can wait until tomorrow for the physical please let Harlem know. There are ninety of us to process, and the docs will need two days."

He let them think about that for a moment, and then continued.

"We'll skip the job counseling part, because your MOS has already been determined."

Only a few were familiar with the acronym, but they waited patiently. As Mike had already determined, they knew they'd eventually pick it up.

"The good news is that I understand you'll hop and skip right through AIT due to the fact that you're all heavily armed with those framed documents in your offices back home."

He nodded to Harlem who picked up the pile from the chair and began to count out stacks of ten. She handed each stack to those sitting at the end of each row.

"Pass these along. This tells you what to pack and how to spend the next month getting into shape."

Again, Mike patted his stomach and then flexed his arms. He was ignored. They were reading the information.

Mike spoke up over the rustle, "You can read those later. Let's continue."

"OSUT is basic infantry training and AIT all in one; One Station Unit Training—OSUT. Advanced Individual Training—AIT."

Mike knew exactly what was ahead for all of them and he shook his head.

"Anyway, I'm gonna read your schedule for the next few months. In a nutshell."

He pulled out the cards again and shuffled to the one he wanted.

"Write this down."

Waiting while they pulled out notebooks, Mike couldn't control a sigh of resignation. He'd already done it once—the long days of training and even longer nights with interrupted sleep. He was not looking forward to it.

"17 January OSUT. 24 March BAC…oh hell, let's forget the acronyms for now.

Your Basic Airborne Course begins on March 24 and lasts three weeks. Ranger School's next and is completed in about 2 months. That takes you into mid-June next year."

Mike moved his finger down the card.

"So, you'll report back here on January 17. For the next couple of days, you'll be housed—squeezed is more like it—into barracks here at Fort Bliss."

Mike looked up, continuing, "They tell me the waiting time for housing at Bliss is two years. Someone pulled some strings for ya'll."

His expression serious now, Mike paused again, jamming the cards into his pocket.

"Now, listen up! This is important. During the two or three days you're here at Bliss, keep to yourselves. Do *not* discuss anything you do with anyone outside your group. We'll tell you more about that later."

Mike had a good reason for knowing he could trust them. He nodded to Harlem. She stood next to him. Holding up a card, Harlem read in a drone.

"Most of what you'll do at Bliss is necessary to keep an obverse pretense that you're all regular Army. You'll be civilians, but don't discuss it."

Watching them, Harlem could guess what they were thinking as they looked at one another, starting to whisper.

"Bill will brief you and answer any questions you have, but for now, I'll continue with this list."

The whispers stopped. Harlem continued reading in the same repetitious voice.

"Those first days are called in processing. There will be some work detail cleaning host barracks and some KP. There'll be minimal training in military courtesies, some drill and ceremony—D and C—so you won't be totally lost. You'll get haircuts if necessary and get your blood typed. Initial clothing will be issued and measurements for alterations."

Adjusting her stance somewhat, Harlem unconsciously straightened her back.

"You won't get dog tags or Military ID cards. You're civilians. But you will have your weight and height checked, a free dental check and vision check. Shots if deemed necessary."

Adjusting her glasses, Harlem looked up.

"Oh, that reminds me. If you've got shot records, bring them when you return next month."

Harlem resumed her impersonal tone.

"Pick up altered clothing and visit the PX."

The next two sentences were more personal.

"We'll bypass the normal selection of which school you'll attend, as Mike already mentioned. You're classified STC."

She droned on, "Corrective glasses issued if necessary. You'll meet your Drill Sergeants and ship to McGregor. Don't expect to sleep much."

Harlem grinned, "Finally. I'll get some glasses that fit."

Amidst the laughter, she and Mike sat down. What Mike knew but didn't tell them was they'd been screened for top-secret clearance.

* * *

United States Special Operations Command
Mac Dill Air Force Base, Florida, 1215 Hours

With only fifteen minutes to spare, Steve arrived at SOCOM on Mac Dill Air Force Base. A van from the General's office had been waiting for him at Tampa Airport.

Mac Dill was only 30 miles or so from the airport, but the ride had taken nearly an hour. They'd crossed and re-crossed Tampa Bay via two bridges—one going southeast, one northeast. Mc Dill is located near the southern tip of a peninsula that hangs into Tampa Bay like a child's Christmas stocking. From the air, The Bay Palms Golf Course painted a green toe on the sock.

Balke, who'd arrived the night before, was waiting on the lawn in front of a long white-stone sign that read: *Special Operations Command.* The two-story building behind him was surrounded with palm trees, nearly twenty of them. It was sweltering for December, and Balke wished the trees provided more shade. He was looking forward to seeing the General. The last time they'd met in person was nearly eight years ago.

During one of Balke's early conversations with Tahoe, she'd indicated the need to have SOF accept STC Personnel, male *and* female, into their training programs. She'd come up against a huge block. Tahoe's Army contacts had informed her they were anticipating another five to ten years before females could participate in Ranger School. SEALS wouldn't even discuss the matter. Tahoe was adamant that all STC Personnel would receive exactly the same training.

When Balke had mentioned the General James Jamison was soon to be assigned CINC at SOCOM, she saw it as a great opportunity to pull a few strings.

Jamison and Balke had graduated from high school in the same class. Balke had enlisted in the Navy, Jamison in the Air Force. Jamison's career had been a blazing comet, while Balke's was low-key, and in his early years, top-secret. Leaving SEALS, Balke had worked towards seeing the Armed Forces School of Music become a reality. Promotions didn't follow this move.

A four-star General, Jamison had been at McDill since September and played two major roles. Providing fully trained Special Operations Forces was only one. As a supported Commander in Charge, he was also prepared to exercise command of special operations missions when directed. It was a weighty job for anyone, and STC was an irritation, an intrusion into Jamison's already heavy responsibilities.

It was Tahoe who had arranged today's meeting and had managed to negotiate a fair compromise. Jamison had agreed to admit a small group of civilians, including thirty females, for Ranger School. He wouldn't budge on SEALS. But he did offer to lend one of their top-notch SEAL instructors to STC.

Getting out of the van, Steve saluted Balke. They shook hands warmly; Balke's face creased in a big smile. Balke and Steve both hoped the CINC had orders already on their way to Benning and Coronado, but Balke doubted it. Balke's back-up hope was that the CINC would have them ready for Balke to hand-carry.

Promptly at 1230 hours they tapped on the door. The CINC's desk, neat as a pin, had only one folder placed exactly in the center. Heavy legs, carved into what Steve thought looked surprisingly like dolphins, supported the highly polished maple desktop. Decorations on the CINC's uniform were mirrored in the shiny surface as he stood near the desk. Balke and Steve saluted.

The General acknowledged, indicating two high-backed straight chairs with seats upholstered in black leather. The General made himself comfortable in the huge, black leather chair behind his desk. Steve carefully kept his face straight and serious. Wanting this meeting to go smoothly there was no way he'd let on that he was amused at the sight of this powerful man seated at desk trimmed with dolphins!

As he struggled inwardly to hide his smile, Steve silently cursed himself. When nervous, Steve—like many people—fought laughter.

"Right! You two want orders from me directing Rangers to accept a group of ninety civilians—including thirty females—and orders for SEALS to lend you a man. Right?"

"Yessir," they responded in unison.

"How long do you need the SEAL?"

Balke answered, "Hopefully they can send him TDY to McGregor for at least six weeks, Sir."

"Right!"

Jamison tapped the file with an index finger. The CINC still felt out of sorts whenever he looked at the damned thing. He'd drafted the orders following Tahoe's visit. It was an outrageous plan, but it might work. Besides, how could it hurt? However, Jamison had stipulated that he'd expect a personal visit from Balke and at least one other person. He wanted a face-to-face briefing; wanted to look Balke straight in the eye, and hear Balke say, "Yes, it's worth it." This meeting was only a formality.

"So, tell me about STC."

The General continued to look at the unopened file

"I'm not sure of the pro-cess here. Can you fill me in?"

The General enunciated 'pro' so that it rhymed with doe.

"Sir, we can, Sir," said Steve, receiving a small nod from Balke,

"Sir, I'll answer the first part of your question, and then Commander Balke will discuss the operation, if that's agreeable, Sir."

The CINC waved a hand for him to continue.

Staring out the window to his left, the General rolled his chair exactly two feet away from the front of his desk. His left elbow on the armrest of his chair, he massaged his chin between two fingers of his left hand.

"Sir, STC, as you know, involves a special hand-picked group of civilians."

Steve paused and waited to see if it would be necessary to continue.

The CINC turned the chair backwards, directly away from Steve and Balke, and stared out the window behind his desk. Facing south, the window had been letting in bright sunlight, which had nearly blinded Steve and Balke. The large back of his chair blocked the rays. It was a welcome relief. Jamison waved his hand again.

"Yes, go on. Go on, Sergeant!"

"Yes Sir. Sir, they'll be back at Bliss on 17 January and then out to McGregor for basic."

The general grunted, whirling his chair around, "That place was due to be closed; some BLM stuff going on."

"Sir, yes Sir, but in October, a year ago, the bill was passed…."

The General interrupted, "Right! OK. I remember."

Steve doubted he did remember, but he went on. Steve was in awe of the four-stars; his second encounter with a high-ranking officer. His nervousness prevented him from instantly realizing the CINC, in his position, would know and remember almost everything.

"Sir, while at McGregor, they'll continue STC instruction concurrently with Basic Combat Training. They'll do six weeks AIT at

McGregor, Sir, before reporting to Benning for BAC on 24 March. Their MOS is STC."

The CINC pulled himself forward, hitting his desk and nearly scattering the neat file.

"Concurrently? They'll have *time* to do something besides *run* and *shoot?*"

Pounding his fist in tempo with the words 'time' and 'run,' the General slammed his open hand at the word 'shoot.' Even Balke hid a smile.

Steve continued, "They're civilians, Sir."

"Thanks, Sergeant, that'll be all."

Steve stood, saluted and left the office.

Alone with Balke, the CINC looked at his old friend.

"Good man?" he asked, nodding towards the door Steve had exited.

"The best, Jamie" said Balke, "I've known him for many years."

Balke was one of only three people allowed to call him Jamie. The CINC nodded, got up and sat next to his friend.

"Still doin' the music gig, Jimmy?"

The CINC was the only one who ever called Balke by his childhood name; Jimmy and Jamie—their choice of names for one another. Rowdy boys in high school, their friendship did not include visits to each other's homes. They kept their friendship personal, never sharing family relationships—until Jamison had married. Upon the birth of his daughter, he had asked Balke to be Godfather.

"Yes, at least until now. I'll be attached to STC for a few more weeks, then back to Virginia. How's Helen and the kid?"

"Doin' fine, Jimmy. Got myself four grandkids, you know. Three girls and a boy. Their Daddy is Army, by the way."

General Jaminson laughed and slapped his knee.

"Can you believe it? Jamie married a GI!"

The General had given his daughter his name; the same one carried by many women in the Jamison family. Balke was not aware of the tradition.

"My goddaughter. Maybe when I'm back in Virginia?"

"It's a date, Jimmy. It's a date."

Walking to the window, the CINC put his capable, deeply tanned hands directly on the glass. Between his outspread palms, his forehead leaned hard against the pane. Looking at his slender, wiry frame, Balke found it hard to believe that his friend had accomplished so much and continued to carry even more complex assignments on his skinny shoulders.

"Tell me, Jimmy, this STC, it is OK?"

And he turned to face Balke.

"Tell me it's OK. That's what I asked you here to tell me."

"It's definitely OK, Jamie. I'm very impressed. The kids are born diplomats. They're professionals, and have great potential. They're strong and tough. It's not only OK, Jamie, it's exciting. These people are constantly thinking around all sides of problems. They're incredibly smart and eager."

Balke's voice was reassuring, but intense. He had an excitement about him that transferred itself to the CINC. General Jamison was glad his friend was part of the plan; he trusted Balke. Encouraging Balke to continue, the CINC nodded now and again.

"You've heard the plan from Tahoe, right? I feel it's thorough, well-thought out. The folks, these kids who responded are determined to use all the resources they came with. In addition, they're motivated to get through military training."

Pausing briefly, Balke leaned closer to his friend, placing one open hand on the General's upper arm.

"They'll learn, Jamie. They'll be ready to do what's necessary when the time comes, within the guidelines of STC."

Reaching out his own hand, the General placed it over Balke's familiar gesture of comradeship. Slapping Balk's hand once, he stood up, straightening his jacket. Moving towards his desk, the CINC picked up the file and handed it to Balke.

"Orders. For civilians and females in Rangers and one Navy SEAL."

Sitting in the back of the vehicle assigned to drive them to the Airport, Balke and Steve looked at each other. Steve made a vain attempt to stop the question.

"Did you know about those fish on his desk?"

Both men collapsed in laughter. They looked at one another, wiped off the smiles, and started snickering all over again. Finally, Balke became serious.

"Steve, there's something you should know."

Balke's face was intent now; it was important.

"My friend back there has the Military's highest award for bravery thrown in a drawer at home."

Peering over his shoulder at the building they'd left, Steve no longer felt like laughing.

* * *

El Paso
Stout Gym, 1430 Hours

The intelligence and knowledge in the room was greater than any individual agency had ever enjoyed. One or two may have recognized the effect and even utilized group intelligence on occasion. But no college or university taught the process by which a nebulous field of intelligence can occur. It was only hinted at in theoretical discussions. STC counted on that intelligence, and knew it was heightened by each person's background and way of thinking.

George had finished his comments, explaining that by joining STC they were not signing on for rank, salary or recognition. For the most part, they'd already figured that out. Those who'd come to STC had freed themselves from worldly responsibilities. They knew they were stars, destined for greatness, but didn't seek the rewards most people sought. While in Texas they weren't tied to their day-to-day jobs. They had time to concentrate on concepts they hadn't had time to consider in recent years.

Among the eighty-one people gathered together, most were financially comfortable and had already given up their jobs. But all of them, without exception, had no fear of being successful in the world. They knew that within six months, if necessary, they could start all over again. These were rare individuals not enslaved by career or external appearances.

This afternoon they'd heard George explain that STC was not a new military, not a new FBI, that it was something different. They'd agreed when he told them that military and law enforcement agencies need exceptional individuals. They also knew what they had already suspected. Only certain people got this training. They were tough, and ready to take on whatever was thrown at them.

Bill took his place in front of the group. Using no notes. Bill spoke from what he knew, clearly and precisely. Picking up the theme begun by George, Bill explained fully for the first time the need for military training, the use of first names and the reasons for secrecy.

"STC will provide specially trained people to be introduced into volatile situations to resolve problems where political, military or existing intelligence organizations are ineffective. We will work with all of these entities, and will be trained in all the same areas. We're on a military base for a reason, you know."

Although the theme was heavy, frightening perhaps to the untrained, Bill spoke clearly and without emotion. He applied the same method used by Tahoe three years ago, when she first explained the plan. Bill's voice was calm and strong, clear and precise. He used very few contractions.

"Additional training will be provided in all the areas George mentioned—military, intelligence, diplomacy, negotiation—but our goal will not be to replace any of the professionals in these sectors. We must be familiar with the idioms and methods because we'll work with them behind the scenes if need be—or be ready to go where they can't.

"We will not train to become soldiers or mercenaries, but we will understand the professional soldier. We will have the tools of a diplomat or politician without seeking a career in these areas. We may be called on to assist in difficult negotiations but will not be known as negotiators. We will have mutual respect with all these professionals, and will bring the tools needed to the problem at hand, and then move on.

"Among other requirements, STC must be familiar with the language, culture, history, politics, religion and philosophy of many countries. We need to know what causes conflicts. Is it human suffering or injustice? We need to know what people want.

"We've already explained that we do not interfere. We must wait for an invitation. Let me explain. STC is the first of its kind—an undisclosed civilian group of highly trained individuals that can be called upon to defuse situations ranging from low to high intensity in many arenas. Before the U. S. Military intervenes in civilian situations, whether circumstances are high intensity or low, there must be an invitation. Even then, should developments explode into a political crisis, deniability needs to follow. STC will supply this. We are a civilian group.

"STC personnel must work to gain the respect of all. STC could be last-ditch negotiators coordinating with the military before force is used. Military on both sides of the conflict as well as all factions—the civilian population, politicians, rebels or terrorists—must respect our capabilities.

"We will become familiar with Military Rules of Engagement, which will apply to STC."

Bill stood with his head down, his mind on Tahoe's words. They stayed with him night and day, a litany to hold to. Bill knew he'd repeat what he was about to say many times, answering the same questions, discussing the same themes over and over. Eventually they'd get it.

"The ever-increasing complexity of new technology demands a whole new way of thinking, training, and implementation."

He looked around.

"Those are not my words, but they are words to keep in mind as I take you through the basics of STC."

Bill spoke exactly fifteen minutes. At the conclusion, Harrison stood, pulling Kurt up beside him.

"We're committed, man, bring on that doctor!"

Chapter Nine
The Time for Waiting

Waiting is not mere empty hoping. It has the inner certainty of reaching the goal. Such certainty alone gives that light which leads to success.

The person who goes to meet fate resolutely is equipped to deal with it adequately.

Then that person will be able to cross the great water—that is to say, the person will be capable of making the necessary decision and of surmounting the danger.

The Book of Changes

Connecticut
December 24, Christmas Eve

Pleased with the nickname Bill had given him, the tall builder felt the shortened version "Carp" was part of his destiny. Because of the tag, he was beginning to take a closer look at himself. Carp was twenty-nine, and personal insight would have come many years later if he hadn't come across STC—rather, if STC hadn't run across him! Carp sometimes felt that he'd found STC, and had to remember that he'd never be that lucky.

Returning to his home in Houston, Carp had met with his twin brother. It was easier than he thought. Both boys had learned the general construction trade working for their father—who'd retired when they graduated. Growing even more successful in their capable hands, the business was their life. Specializing in heavy commercial and industrial building and renovation, Carp's twin had grumbled a little when he'd been left alone to complete a large high school project while Carp was in El Paso. But things have a way of working out.

When he'd finally taken the time to look back at the chain of events—college, the contracting company, STC—Carp began to realize he'd been on a well-designed path from the moment he'd left high school. More importantly, he was becoming aware of his own part in the design. Their brief conversation had taken place the day after he'd returned from El Paso.

"Bro' I've gotta leave it in your hands."

It was simple as that. Carp realized it was what his brother had secretly hoped for. His twin had always wanted total control. Be in charge. That was his brother. Carp was relieved that he hadn't asked too many questions. Carp wouldn't have known how to answer. The next day, early Christmas Eve morning, he'd packed his gear into a long sports bag and resolutely caught a plane to Hartford. It was that easy.

Meeting him at the airport, Bobbie drove faster than Carp was comfortable with. Bobbie's mellow voice kept pace with the speeding car.

"Man, so good to see you. I've been on pins and needles wondering if you'd make it. Got the gym lined up for us, and a trainer too. There are several places we can run, even this time of year."

Nestled into an unlikely housing development, the route to Bobbie's house proved to be a maze of turns. They wove deeper and deeper into a heavily wooded area; different from the wide-open spaces Carp was used to. It was drizzling and late afternoon. Carp lost all sense of direction. Huge, platter-sized splats of moisture dripped from the cedars, hitting the windshield. Disoriented from the narrow, weaving roads, Carp felt claustrophobic. Bobbie's constant chatter added to Carp's discomfiture.

"I've leased the house, and turned the business over to my partner.

Told him I'd be gone indefinitely. He'll make sure money gets deposited into my account. Guess I'm all set, Carp. How' bout you?"

What a strange combination these two formed. Their differences had drawn them together, as often happens. From the first, this disparity had opened a flow of active and diverse conversation. As they learned more about each other, their respective personalities were modified. Tall and blonde, Carp was pensive, grouchy, and bigoted at times. Myopic in vision as well as thinking he was at one end of the character gauge. Bobbie, talkative, charming, small and dark with keen eyesight, was at the other.

Carp looked at a problem exactly as he'd been taught. He'd look over a blueprint splayed in messy array across a drafting table in some construction shack while people paced outside waiting for answers. Carp could peer through his incredibly thick lenses and immediately see any errors. He never had to think about it. The solutions were instantly there, and always right. On the other hand, Bobbie's problem solving methods were long, tedious, time-consuming processes. Both methods would be invaluable to STC.

Pulling into the driveway, Bobbie's voice asked again, "I said, what about you?"

Carp's inner convictions pulled him away from the disorientation he'd been feeling. The days he'd spend waiting in Hartford would be the time to reinforce his decision. Taking a deep breath and pumping his arms back and forth, Carp grinned at his new best friend.

"I'm set, Bobbie. When do we start with that weight training?"

* * *

Trancas, California
The Same Day

"Rugby players don't look like anything. And how about those Apache warriors who could run for days, chewing on dried venison and juniper berries? They didn't look like anything either. So what if we don't look like anything, Kurt, it don't mean nothin'."

119

"Yes, I know. And you used a double negative again, Harrison. Watch out or someone might think you're dumb as well as overdeveloped."

Picking up the colorful towels thrown on the sand, Harrison couldn't resist.

"Kurt, is that a Ghostbusters towel you've got there?"

Harrison's thigh stung from the whip of the damp, sandy towel that Kurt rolled up snapped at him.

Harrison and Kurt. For some reason they'd stumbled across each other the first day in El Paso, and now they knew why. Their names sounded good together. Of course that was not the only reason, but it was a good sign.

Kurt had been sitting in the back of the gym when Harrison walked in. The large group was talking and laughing and Harrison doubted anyone would hear him as he took a big chance and whispered in Kurt's ear. It turned out to be the best pick-up line Kurt had ever heard.

"Can I play with those blonde curls?"

Kurt Kenneth Walters, D.O. was grateful his father's family name didn't begin with the letter K. Initialing orders would have made room for more teasing and possible ridicule. Times were changing too slowly, and Kurt was impatient; waiting for the day when people wouldn't question one's personal life. This was one of the reasons he'd decided to see it through with STC. Not one person had bothered to say anything.

This had not been the case in high school, college or even Medical School. Soft spoken, of medium height and build, Kurt had determined for himself at age ten that he would be a doctor, but in an area where he could utilize methods different from those traditionally used by the medical doctors he knew.

When he was sixteen, a friend of the family had introduced him to an Osteopathic Physician, and after a few encouraging conversations, Kurt knew where he would head. Throughout his courses of study, Kurt battled his fear of entrapment and the resulting sting of rejection. Over the years, his smile had developed a perpetual ironic twist. Attempts to keep his secret hidden made him feel haunted. Kurt knew he could only explain or share with someone who'd been there.

His mother knew that Kurt was a spiritual warrior. She'd wept many tears for her son who might never overcome his dread of being trapped or pinned down.

Graduating at age twenty-eight, he'd been grateful he hadn't had to fulfill any military obligation. Kurt hated regimentation, even though he insisted on it and counted on it in his profession. He'd told Harrison that it was probably the fact that shouting would most likely be part the military. He abhorred loud, angry, challenging voices.

The fear that his slight body might not allow him to participate physically in the military training ahead of them filled a large part of his conversations with Harrison—that and his fear of a potentially loud and violent life-style.

Harrison had a hundred exemplars for him during their self-imposed training sessions. The Apache was only one of many he'd thrown at Kurt over the past few days. Military training was something Harrison looked forward to. He wouldn't have to pay to jump out of airplanes.

Thrill seeking was a way of life for Harrison, even though, during the day, his profession kept him pinned down in front of computers in small cubicles. At least three times a week, he'd tuck his surfboard under one arm, throw it in his car and race twenty-two miles west along the Pacific Coast Highway from Santa Monica to Zeros Beach near Trancas.

Harrison looked like a surfer. He kept his brown hair cropped closely to his well-shaped head. He used disposable contact lenses at all times. Wearing low-slung brightly colored surfer shorts, Harrison drew every woman's eye. But Harrison was not interested.

When he wasn't surfing, he jumped out of airplanes or flew sailplanes. He rode every roller coaster he could find—the more bloodcurdling the better.

As the youngest-ever head of the Information Technologies department at Santa Monica, Harrison had plenty of free time to pursue his hobbies. Until STC, Harrison felt he'd had the perfect job.

Waiting to report for Basic Training, Harrison and Kurt ran from Zeros to the cliffs at Leo Carillo and back—a round trip of three miles. They'd increased the speed and distance daily, and today they'd celebrated Christmas Eve by doing the run in a little under half an hour.

"Great!" panted Harrison, letting his tongue hang out more than necessary by way of encouraging Kurt who was nearly falling down.

"You know, Airborne doesn't require nine minute miles until the second week. You're way ahead of the game, Kurt."

"Harrison," gasped Kurt, "I'm gonna shave my legs and cut off these curls you're so fond of. Maybe I'll be able to run faster."

"Don't bet on it, sweetheart, remember what happened to Sampson?"

Catching their breath, they lay on the warm sand. Harrison was somber.

"Kurt, I've been thinking about the people we've met—such a diverse group of engineers, scientists and professionals. They're so highly motivated."

Harrison paused for a moment.

"Go on," said Kurt, "What're you thinking?"

"Well, they're not afraid to climb those towers, run obstacle courses, fire weapons, because they know that's not the important thing. There's a lot more involved than physical prowess."

Harrison sighed, moving his body restlessly, digging his feet and legs into the comfort of the sand. Kurt whisked his fingers over Harrison's face, making sure the grains didn't get into his eyes. Kurt wore his glasses held with a band to keep them in place as they ran. He knew Harrison would have a problem wearing regulation glasses.

"I mean, you know you can succeed, you can resolve problems. But here's the thing. I'm not on any one side. There are no short-term fixes. We want to get to the bottom of the situation."

He paused again, and this time Kurt picked up the theme.

"Hey, you mean like about the Rugby players. STC people might not look like anything. They may be unprepared and apprehensive at this point, but at the same time they're like fifteen-year-old kids at baseball Dream Camp, or maybe Space Camp. They're eager as hell to find out what they can do. They believe in themselves."

Harrison grunted, "Yep. Self-doubt's probably not a normal part of their natures."

Kurt sat up brushing off his chest, looking askance at his friend.

"I think, Harrison, that they're like us. Concerned with humanitarianism."

They stood up, ready now to return to Harrison's apartment.

"Here's a scenario, Kurt," said Harrison.

They didn't touch each other as they trudged across the sand. Both were very circumspect.

"We're in this tenuous position. Say we've been sent to a country that's been defeated. Maybe we're like those weapons inspectors, making sure they're not hiding anything."

Kurt stopped still on the dirt steps cut into the cliff, leading from the beach to the road.

"Oh God, Harrison, something like that? We'll have to do something like that?"

Harrison shrugged, balancing himself carefully on the narrow path.

"I don't know. I'm only brainstorming here. Maybe we'd have to go into the oil arena. Remember the UN still has a ban on flights to Baghdad, uh..."

"Yeah, Iraq," Kurt responded, "What about it?"

He didn't move as Harrison continued.

"Well, I remember hearing about a plane full of artists and scientists, going in as a cultural thing, when in reality they were smuggling business people in to do oil deals."

Kurt's voice rose angrily in his urgency to make himself clear.

"We're not spies, Harrison, Bill told us that. And we're not mercenaries, and never will be. We're after the truth!"

Harrison grabbed Kurt's sunburned shoulder, knowing his friend's aversion to anger. Kurt's face had already changed as he shrugged away Harrison's hand. It took on the same determined expression he'd worn when the woman had upset her chair when she'd left their group. Now the culmination of personal trials— spanning a lifetime of fear and denial—hardened his resolve. Turning his head towards the infinite sea, Kurt gritted his teeth. His expression was resolute. Hanging on the side of the cliff, Kurt repeated his last words.

"We're after the truth."

* * *

Watsonville, California
Christmas Day

Alicia Gomez Jones sat with her family around the brightly lit tree; its scent mingling with the incredibly salubrious air coming in from the open front door. Pine and sea added to the mélange of chili and chocolate cooking aromas.

The sprawling house sat at the end of Beach Street next to an unused lettuce field. The Pajaro River was due south and 500 feet behind the huge brick patio. Due west and three miles from the redwood deck built overlooking the dunes, was the Pacific Ocean.

When she was born, Alicia was given her mother's maiden name as her official middle name. She signed it firmly—*Alicia G. Jones*—on all documents, including her personal checks. The family simply called her Jonesy.

Her father's name was William Jones, and he'd married Alicia's mother forty years ago in Tijuana after a whirlwind courtship. Both families said it would never work. They were wrong. Her mom and dad still sat close together in the living room late at night, lights turned down low, discussing private matters.

Owning many thousands of acres in the fertile Pajaro River valley, Bill Jones was a successful grower. His main crop was lettuce. But occasionally, when nagged by his wife, he set aside a few acres for strawberries. Further south, towards Castroville, he grew field upon field of artichokes.

Bill's four tall sons were as blonde as he was. But Jonsey looked more like her mother. She also had her mother's volcanic temper. When she was younger, Bill would shout at her.

"Jonsey, your lava has overflowed on me for the last time! Something's got to be done about this temper of yours!"

He'd pull her into his large arms, comforting her immediate tears. Hating to disappoint her father, she'd sob.

"I'm sorry, *Papacito, me puede mucho haberte herido.*"

"I'm sorry I hurt you, Daddy."

The diminutive, *papacito*, was an endearment, not a description of his size.

On her eleventh birthday, Jonesy stood in front of her parents. Her small bare feet, substantial and firm as rock, were pushed into the carpet.

"I'm going to UCLA and I'm going to be a biologist and learn how to make giant strawberries that are always sweet."

That's exactly what she did until three months ago.

Bill had followed her to St. Patrick's church on Main Street—was it really only three months? Her life had taken a turn she'd never anticipated. The church—condemned after the 1987 earthquake had destroyed parts of the brick structure as well as much of downtown Watsonville—had been rebuilt. It was Jonesy's place for comfort and self-examination. In the quiet, incense-filled sanctuary, she would kneel and beg God to give her patience with herself "…and with others," she'd add as an afterthought.

Jonsey kept her body and mind as clean as she could. She'd read somewhere that Latin women were fanatical about personal cleanliness. She'd shrugged, thinking it was absolutely correct, at least so far as she was concerned. Sometimes Jonesy showered twice a day. She kept her clothing—even the shabby jeans and T-shirts she preferred—clean and smelling of soap and fresh air. Her hip-length, black hair was washed every day.

Jonesy would spend hours in beauty supply houses, sniffing each bottle until she found the best scents for both shampoo and conditioner. She hounded the shops at the Capitola Mall in Santa Cruz, searching for exactly the right smells. Concocting various fragrances in her lab, she sprayed the air in her room and rotated the bottles from day to day.

Her mother thought Jonesy was adorable and was pleased that her youngest still lived at home. All that had changed.

Sitting with her parents, telling them as little as possible, Jonsey prepared them for her absence. They were impassive; hiding their sorrow, knowing the day had finally come when their twenty-nine year old daughter would leave home. Their stoicism was totally unexpected and almost changed Jonesy's mind, but there was another reason—and she'd prayed about it constantly—that she wanted to go back to El Paso.

Discussing the fact that she'd not yet chosen a cohort, Bill had encouraged Jonesy to think about it during the month. Despite her eccentricities, Jonesy was excruciatingly honest. Waiting at home, she admitted to herself, and to God, that there was more than STC with its appeal to her higher nature and her desire to see justice and truth in the world. There was also Steve. The powerful advisor had only been in the gym once. When Jonsey saw him, she knew he belonged to her.

* * *

Fort Bliss
Stout Gym
17 January, 0500 Hours

Winter had arrived while they were gone. Two inches of snow covered the ground. It would melt by mid-afternoon, but it was hazardous going in the early morning hours. Heavy flurries swirled in the wind, making the streets nearly invisible. Driving with extra caution, STC Interviewers arrived at Stout Gym more or less simultaneously.

Army terms were becoming part of Bill's vocabulary, and he chuckled to himself when the words *High Mobility Multipurpose Wheeled Vehicle*, Hum-Vees, came immediately to mind. The vehicles had made several trips to the airport and were lined up preparing to make their last run to pick up recruits. Interviewers' breaths mingled with the exhaust from the vehicles. Individual white clouds followed each person across the parking lot and into the entrance of the rec center, were they dissipated in the relative warmth.

Joining the others who were carefully picking their way up the steps at what must seem to most of them an ungodly hour, Bill had fleeting doubts.

During the holidays he and Jennifer had worked hard to build unaccustomed muscles. Spending long hours pounding the hard sand along the beaches of the Monterey Bay coastline, they forced themselves to keep control of the passion growing between them. This last had taken an emotional toll on Bill. The worst part was that he knew the others were suffering many of the same reservations that he was. He could see it on their faces. It was up to him to bring it all back together after being away from the initial excitement. They'd had time to reflect on the challenges and wonder if they'd made any mistakes.

Getting up the first step with anything new is always the most difficult. The Army had allowed access to McGregor Range. The wheels were in motion, and Bill wanted them to slow down. He needed more time.

Talking with Tahoe, hearing her calm voice explain again the importance of his role, Bill thought he should have spent more time with her. Duty should have come before his personal desires. Bill was growing up and feeling the burden of leadership.

Stamping their feet in an attempt to shake off the clinging snow, Bill and the Interviewers laughed at the adventure of a blizzard in El Paso. Finally they slipped off their boots rather than leave trails of wetness on the immaculate wooden floor of the gym.

Quietly taking their accustomed chairs in the small conference room, no one said much. They busied themselves with pouring coffee and arranging notes; intent on making sure their thoughts were in order. It was like culture shock, having been away from each other while waiting out the time with various duties. They looked towards Bill, anticipating that he'd set the tone with his first words.

Most of them knew Bill practiced a kind of martial art, although they'd never seen him do so. They suspected that because of these disciplines, Bill had the ability to exemplify certain principles in his everyday actions and speech. When standing, he was at ease, unbiased, straight. When speaking to the group, or an individual, his ideas were organized, clearly expressed, interesting—but never forcefully delivered. People rarely interrupted when Bill spoke, but if they did he didn't look surprised or offended. He was always respectful, and never gave the impression that he would lose balance in thoughts or actions.

He made mistakes but he learned quickly, and was always the first to admit any error. Today Bill was right about one thing. The other interviewers as well as the recruits were going through varying degrees of uncertainty.

The mind-set of the group was in its infancy, growing and formulating as ideas were exchanged. They had no intentions of slitting anybody's throat, even though they might learn how to do this. They were not spies, not secret service. They knew they'd begin to learn the basics of military strategy, and certainly understood the benefits of discipline, but they didn't consider themselves killers. They understood the value of diplomacy, but they were not civil servants or attachés. There was no supervised rank. They were unique. Group intelligence was their biggest weapon.

For the past four weeks they had mulled over potential scenarios, and wondered: how do we fit in? Helping with *what* was the big question. No one, not even Bill at this point, knew exactly what might be in store. They could only guess. With some variations, the questions were a theme; a melody stuck in memory that wouldn't stop until it played itself out. The trouble was they didn't know the ending.

This morning, when Bill had plodded up those cold cement steps into the same gym they'd left a month ago, he knew their reticence was exactly like carefully placing one foot in front of the other on some dark, unknown, icy path in the dead of winter. What if I slip?

Once again Bill stood in front of the recruits. If they were who he believed they were, they'd jump into training, strengthening their determination. Bill knew he'd need to do the same.

"Ladies and Gentlemen, once again, welcome to Fort Bliss."

Keeping his face still, Bill maintained a tight hold on his emotions. He suddenly realized he was glad to see them, and because of them he was actually looking forward to the next nine weeks. The awareness hit him hard and fast and he looked over at Steve standing arms akimbo, leaning casually against the far wall at back of the group. They exchanged a deep, comfortable look. Bill was, for the first time this morning, ready. The grin, that had been only a microsecond away, burst out as he spoke.

"Damn, that was cold. And I'm not talkin' about the weather. What I wanted to say is much better."

Bill raised his voice, shouting at them for the first time.

"Are you ready?"

Their voices called back to him, warming him as they warmed themselves.

"READY!"

They shouted in unison, laughter barely hidden underneath the word. They responded as if they'd studied some military manual or had watched old war movies over the holidays. Harlem's list of exercises had been utilized. They looked fit, and tough.

"Time's short this morning, but we're gonna create a few minutes here to do what we need to do first."

Following Tahoe's final instruction, Bill moved towards the front of the still-standing group. Along with the other Interviewers, Bill connected with each recruit. Clapping backs of some, hugging others, Bill encouraged the recruits to do the same. It was a gathering before the storm, a reunion of apprehension. Most of all it was a meeting filled with renewed conviction. They were on equal footing now, beginning something new. All were at the same level.

The resonance from heavy boots broke into the greetings, squashing them flat as if from a steamroller. An earsplitting voice yelled sharply.

"Recruits, my name is Sergeant Lee, and I'm gonna be your worst nightmare for the next nine weeks. Ten-shun!"

Sergeant Stanley Lee marched his recruits into the U. S. Army.

Chapter Ten
The Range

That which would be shrunken must first be purposely stretched.
That which would be weakened must first be purposely strengthened.
That which would be overthrown must first be purposely set up.
The one who would take must first purposely give.
Lao-Tzu

McGregor Range
23 January, 0530 Hours

It was a thing of beauty. Sergeant Lee couldn't stop staring. He found it hard to believe they'd knocked the whole thing together in less than five days. George had looked over the sketches. Carp had painstakingly printed up a lumber list and the two of them had selected a five-person crew from the recruits still at Bliss. Everything was there and Lee couldn't wait to use it.

The rappel tower stood sixty feet in the air, its training ramp skinnying down to the desert at a sixty-degree angle. The soaring giant dwarfed the remainder of the confidence course. Hanging from thirty-foot telephone poles, a cargo net waited patiently next to the platform fifteen feet below the peak. The five-level team-building exercise, built from lengths of glue-lam and four by fours, begged for action.

Over his shoulder, nearly half a mile away, Lee squinted in the early morning light at the obstacle course. He couldn't see the details, but he'd been there—nearly salivating in his eagerness to have it completed—when they'd pounded in the stakes and built up the belly buster, the reverse climb and hip-hop. They'd even put up an inverted rope descent that crossed a small gully and was tied down to two scrub pines on the other side. In all, there were eighteen obstacles and Lee couldn't wait to try them all.

Behind him doors crashed open. Ninety recruits emerged from two buses and stood huddled together in the damp morning air. They hadn't had time to learn a damn thing. They were dressed in Army PT's. The black and gray warm-up suits matched overcast skies. Duffle bags were thrown out at random by the bus drivers. Clouds of dust began to mingle with the light drizzle. Rain meant nothing to Lee.

"Ladies and Gentlemen, as you know my name is Master Sergeant Lee. I'm the senior drill sergeant. These are my assistant drill sergeants. I know you are all motivated, intelligent people and I do not expect any trouble from you."

Lee paced back and forth in front of the recruits who were standing at random. Most had dozed off during the bus ride from Bliss and were in the process of waking up as the cold air and Lee's strident voice hit them.

"I know you are not typical privates who come to us after having spent eighteen years in front of a TV watching Scoobie Doo."

Pausing momentarily, Lee glared at them.

"Nevertheless, I am here to tell you that we are God. I am God. This is my world. You are in my world now. Life, as you've known it, has ended."

The drizzle became a downpour. Lee was unruffled.

"There ain't no use in lookin' down. Ain't no discharge on the ground. Here you are, and here you'll do it!"

Standing at one side, the two assistant drills stood with hands behind their backs, water beginning to stream down closely shaved faces. Not making eye contact with a single person, they stared straight ahead at nothing. The whole thing was nightmarish, a crazy art form—harsh and unreal—the voice of the sergeant providing discordant background music.

"The caliber of you, uh—subjects don't make one bit of difference to me. This tells me I've got one factor in my favor. Only one. I don't have a bunch of immaturity to deal with."

The rain beat on the new clothing, slowly seeping through to the skin. The troops shivered. Summoning the assistant drills to his side, Lee increased the volume of his voice. Not once did he wipe his face or otherwise indicate they were all soaked.

"I know you've got nine team leaders in this group. Where are they? Let me see you!"

Slowly moving towards the front of the group, Bill led the way. George, Flavia, Jasen Annie and the other interviewers lined up in front of the group, instinctively pulling their shoulders back.

"You!" Sergeant Lee pointed to the tall carpenter, "They call you Carp, right? Come up here. I need ten team leaders and I want nine other people in each team."

Lee pointed his finger at random.

"You, you, you! Take one step forward."

Annie, Bill and Mike looked around. What now?

"You three will task-organize three thirty-person platoons."

What did that mean?

"I understand you all have paired together. You're on the buddy system. This gives you some stability, somebody to lean on. Let's start leanin' and learnin'!"

Soggy and miserable, the platoons prayed for clearing skies.

"You haven't learned anything yet. But once I show you, once you learn it, you *will* be expected to retain it!"

Slowly, the rain increased. Rivulets of water coursed between small rocks and humps of straggly undergrowth.

"Watch us! Everything you do from now on will be explained first! Every position we teach will be demonstrated fully. Listen up!"

Lee held out his left arm. One assistant moved and stood with his shoulder against Lee's outstretched hand. He, in turn, held out his arm and the second drill stood next to that hand. Streams of moisture ran from their outstretched fingers.

"Do it!" Lee screamed.

Mud streaked everywhere as ninety newcomers attempted to comply. Lines were straggly. Hair dripped under caps. Lee and his drills ignored the discomfort.

"This is pathetic! Straighten those lines. YOU! Bill? Get at the end of your line. Assume the normal interval! Get those hands out!"

Annie was intrigued with the power of Sergeant Lee's voice. Appreciating the seeming ease with which he was able to make himself heard, Annie determined to learn his secret. Lee's yells rang true and clear through the downpour. How did he do it?

"Oh, my God! Every ligament and bone in my body is exhausted."

Permeating the air, industrial-strength cleaner and the smell of sweat annoyed the more fastidious in the group. Some headed for the showers, others stepped out into the desert night.

Lying flat on his back in the center of the waxed floor, staring at a bulb swinging in a breeze from the open windows, Bobbie pointed his finger at the garish light. The nightmare continued.

"I'm gonna get that carbine Lee told us about, and I'm gonna kill that glare! I gotta get some sleep!"

Bobbie rolled over into a fetal position, ignoring the smooth bunks positioned side by side in the immaculate barracks. The others laughed, busy settling into their new quarters. The rain had finally stopped, the mud disappearing as quickly as it had emerged. The sun had heated up the bays until one by one most of the teams had discarded outer shirts and had changed into shorts.

Pulling himself up slowly, Bobbie wandered to his bunk, searching for an electrical outlet.

"Carp, help! Did you put in the plugs for me?"

"Yeah, over here, Bobbie." Carp tossed an orange ground cord towards his friend, plugging in the other end.

Pulling out his laptop, Bobbie attached his cell phone and logged on.

Bobbie's inquisitiveness into all aspects of the business world was not dimmed by his present situation. Tired as he was, he wanted to look into a subject that had been on his mind all week. Returning to El Paso, his flight had been cancelled. He and Carp had scrambled to find a carrier that could get them back in time to report for duty. He'd made several phone calls during the five-hour wait.

One of those calls was to his neighbor, a pilot for a major airline. The significance of their conversation was something Bobbie couldn't ignore:

"Hey, this is Bobbie. What can you tell me about this pilot slowdown nonsense?"

"Not nonsense, Bobbie. It's a very real problem. What do you want to know? Got a new client?"

Bobbie's smooth voice had answered truthfully.

"No, no. It's personal curiosity, pal, what do you know?"

"I know everything! It's hittin' all of us."

For the next twenty minutes, Bobbie's friend had given him considerable information. Bobbie's scrawl had filled several pages in his notebook.

"Can I quote you on this, man?" Bobbie asked.

"Rather you didn't, but it's all true. I swear to you. You can't use it, but at least you know."

Working quickly under the still-swaying light bulb, Bobbie began to verify the pilot's account, step by step. What emerged was an incredible but perfectly believable story.

Lee stretched his long frame on the comfortable bunk. The hefty drill sergeant couldn't believe his good fortune. Not only had they built the courses and the laid out the firing ranges—complete with perfectly square target frames—but they'd also put up this house for him. There was no other word for it. It was a house. For a joke they'd climbed up on the roof and installed a fake chimney, using leftover mortar and smooth stones they'd gathered from the desert. Sharing the hootch with the other two drills was not a problem. They each had separate rooms.

Carp's team had taken one end of the largest barracks and installed a complete kitchen with a dining facility. Dividing walls, framed in what seemed to be a matter of minutes, separated the DFAC from the open bay sleeping quarters. All three barracks had undergone transformations in an incredibly short time. Bathrooms were updated, prefab showers installed;

even a laundry room with four washers and dryers were now available to the troops.

Phone lines had been run to each of the barracks, and Lee reached for the cordless phone he'd purchased only yesterday in El Paso. It was late, but he needed to know what the hell had happened to his M4's.

24 January, 0530 Hours

Someone had raised the flag in front of the main barracks. The rising sun and breakfast was an hour away. Lee's voice screamed—crisp and clear as the dawn.

"The next movement I'll name, explain and have demonstrated is the position of *attention*. The command for this is *fall in* or *attention*. You'll hear a two-part command. *Squad* or *Platoon* is the preparatory command. It sounds like this," and unbelievably, the volume of Lee's voice increased. It shattered their ears.

"Platoon, attention!"

Annie's jaw dropped. She had to know his secret. There were four or five tenors in New York who'd kill to have this ability. How could Lee project his voice with no visible signs of effort? The sides of his neck were smooth, no veins popped out on his forehead.

Facing the group from the center position, Lee's assistants stood at either end demonstrating each movement.

"To assume the position of attention, put your heels together. Point your toes so they're at a 45-degree angle. Flex at the knees slightly without locking them. Shoulders are to be squared. Hands *will* be along the seam of your trouser leg. Close your fingers so the fingertips are touching the palms of your hands. Head *will* be erect and straight. Eyes *will* be forward. You will not move or speak unless spoken to."

At last the voice stopped. The momentary silence was welcome.

"You need to square your shoulders up. There you go! Just like that." Lee walked up and down the ranks.

"You *will* rest the weight of your body evenly on the balls of your feet. You want to keep your knees flexed. Do *not* lock your knees. If I told you to lock your knees, and I kept you there for ten minutes and then told you to fall out, you'd drop over."

Lee paced, and looked them over.

"This is the base position for all other movements."

Satisfied, he continued.

"On the command of at ease, you *will* move your left foot approximately shoulder-width apart, simultaneously bring your hands behind your back. While at ease you may turn your head and look around. When you're in formation, you *will* direct your attention to the person in charge of the formation. While at ease, you will *not* move your right foot."

The emphasis on *will* and *not* gave a certain rhythm to Lee's instructions.

"Now, we'll cover parade rest. The command for this movement is *Parade Rest. Parade* is the preparatory command, *rest* means command execution. Go back to attention! When I say *Parade* that tells you to get ready to move. On the command of *rest*, you *will* move your left foot approximately 10 inches so that your feet are shoulder width apart. You'll simultaneously move your hands to belt level at your back. You *will* place your right hand over your left hand with interlocking thumbs. Like so. See that?"

Their eyes were directed to the assistant drills—backs towards them.

"That's the position of parade rest. You'll keep your head to the front as in the position of attention."

It went on and on for an hour. The voice. The commands and shouted corrections. Most took it in stride. Only a few felt uncomfortable. It wasn't so bad.

0830 Hours

"It's half a mile to that course. We'll run."

Running, it seemed, was the only way to get anywhere. Annie thought they'd be marching, like in the movies. She wanted to lead the singing. She'd already composed a jody call, but Lee didn't want to hear it. He yelled, he didn't sing. They ran.

"I've got such a treat for you out here in the boondocks. You won't believe your eyes. I've got eighteen different ways to play on our own personal playground, ladies and gentlemen. Fun and run!"

True competitors, no one could keep up with the man, but they were trying.

31 January, 0900 Hours

In the past, privates who were under Lee's tutelage had averaged ten and a half years of schooling. Working with people who had more degrees than Lee could even imagine, was a new experience for him. Most times Lee and his drills explained, demonstrated, and the teams executed with precision and understanding—with one notable exception.

Deciding to change the pace, Lee had separated the group into thirty-person platoons and taught them to march. All went as expected—except for George. Lee allowed him to make the same mistake only three times. The man could not tell his right from his left.

When Lee yelled "Left Flank!" George would invariable turn right.

At first Lee considered marking a large X on the man's boot tip with whiteout, but then he had a better idea. Walking to the rock pile, Lee selected a baseball-size stone and slammed it into George's left hand.

"This is your *left* hand. When I say left, *that's* the way you turn."

George got that hang of it, and one day he threw his ball into the desert.

7 February, 0530 Hours

If it wasn't one thing it was another, and this morning at roll call it was her braid. It had slipped out of her cap again, and hung down her shoulder, *totally against reg-gew-lay-shuns*, Lee had reminded her several times.

"Jones-see, front and cent*er*!"

Lee was uncomfortable calling, what he considered to be privates, by their first names. His orders were clear, even though he'd hoped somebody had screwed up. They hadn't, and he'd scrambled at the last minute to begin to memorize 90 names.

She double-timed, using the most expedient route to stand one step in front of him, coming to parade rest. He carried it too far. Jonesy lost her temper, and this time there were no comforting arms to hold her as the hot tears began. There was only the Drill Sergeant's persistent voice.

"I've told you a hundred times, Jones-see, that braid's gotta go. It's a hazard, a gosh darned, 100 percent totally humongous hazard. If I see that braid again, I'm gonna cut it off with my bayonet!"

That's when she lost it.

"Drill Sergeant, You cut my braid, you lose your balls to my teeth, Drill Sergeant, Sir!"

The thing was, hardly anyone understood what she said because she yelled it in Spanish. All they heard was the *Drill Sergeant* part. That was fortunate, because someone might have snickered, enraging Lee even more. English or Spanish, it made no difference. Insubordination needed immediate correction, and if it didn't stop, Lee was well within his rights to remove her from the Army—if she'd been in the Army.

"Jones-see, how many pushups can you give me?

"Drill Ser*geant*, I can give you…" Jonesy thought fast. If she said a high number he'd double it and if she gave him a reasonable number he'd triple it, but if she gave him a low number he'd probably ask for a thousand. She was caught no matter what she said. She decided on a reasonable number. Maybe she could do one hundred.

"Drill Sergeant, I can give you fifty, Drill Sergeant!"

"Drop, Jones-see, and give me two hundred."

It was unreasonable, and he knew it. She pissed him off, the smart little biologist, making genetically engineered strawberries, when she should have been home making strawberry shortcake. She was strong and capable, making incredible progress. Lee grudgingly acknowledged these facts, and pushed her even harder.

"Jones-see, don't forget to count!"

Louder, he added, "In English!"

"Drill Ser*geant*! Yes, Drill Ser*geant*!" and she dropped.

Before she began, Jonesy slowly lifted one hand off the ground, balancing herself with only one hand down. Pulling the jet-black braid into her mouth, she gripped it in her teeth as if it were the threatened bayonet. Lee didn't push his luck. She might kill him. He left her there alone, the rain pelting down on her already-slimming body

"One, two, three…"

By the time they were half-way to the obstacle course, they heard her screaming.

"…'wenny-four, 'wenny-five…."

Her voice was slightly muffled by the rain and her hair.

12 February, 0830 Hours

All the equipment had arrived in a timely manner—except for the rifles. Knowing his trainees were a high-speed, top-secret unit, Lee had insisted on the M4Carbine. They had not appeared. Boxes of 5.56 mm NATO ammunition stood ready—but no weapons. Following procedure, the drill sergeant had used the Army system of getting the things he needed. Lee couldn't pick up the phone and say, "Hey, I want ninety M4s here tomorrow." He'd done the paperwork in a timely fashion and followed up with calls to the supply people. Finally, almost desperate, he'd called Steve.

The advisor had showed up two days ago with the rifles. He didn't give details about how he got them.

This morning, Lee divided his people into one more than the usual nine-person rifle squads. In the Infantry, the smallest unit is a Fire Team—consisting of a team leader, a grenadier, an automatic rifleman and a rifleman. A squad consists of two teams plus a squad leader. A Light Infantry Platoon consists of three squads. The Army uses what they call a Span of Control, allowing team leaders to control four people; squad leaders to control two team leaders; a platoon leader to control three squad leaders.

Sounding more complex than in reality, the method allowed Lee to oversee the ninety people with help from his drils and leaders down the line. He'd had to juggle the numbers somewhat, but the system worked well, and the people were now able to assume their correct positions in formations.

For the past two days, Lee and his drills had taken the three platoons through the first part of rifle marksmanship in addition to the other daily activities. The kids were incredible. They made it look easy. They'd learned to assemble and disassemble the Carbines so quickly; Lee wondered if they'd done it before. He didn't know that some of them had.

They approached the firing range for the first time. Lee held up a heavy buff-colored sheet of paper, his heavy voice droning.

"This is a standard twenty-five meter zero target. If you notice, the target is on a grid and it tells which way to move the sights to achieve your zero."

Standing with his back to the target frames, Lee explained further.

"We'll staple the targets to these E-type silhouettes made from hard cardboard. Then we'll slide them into these frames behind me."

Assistant drills passed targets through the groups as Lee continued.

"I want you to group your shots. I don't care where you hit the target, so long as you aim center mass, here. Your rounds may go here, or here. I don't care so long as when you shoot three rounds, they are in a four-centimeter group. Like so."

And Lee pulled a black marker from his pocket, drawing what looked like very tiny circles all over the target.

"Once you achieve that grouping, then we can go ahead and move your sights left or right to make slight adjustments to achieve the zero."

Pointing to the bulls eye, Lee yelled.

"Right here!"

Lying in the foxhole-supported position, Lisa placed her Carbine on the sandbag. The foxhole was concrete, but the desert had drifted everywhere. She could feel it rough and gritty through the sleeves of her BDUs. Aiming, Lisa fired off three rounds. Echoing shots came from up and down the line.

Waiting, as instructed, she wondered how far off her sights were. The group walked to the frames. Checking her target, the three rounds were clearly and precisely dead center. Lisa shrugged. It was not much different from target shooting with the .22 long barrel. Upon qualifying, Lisa would hit forty of forty—a perfect score.

1900 Hours

The main barracks was full. All ninety had gathered, along with the advisor. Hoots of laughter echoed from the crowd as James—acknowledged to be the best storyteller in the group—related the tale of Jonesy's two hundred pushups.

"Yeah! She did fifty and fell over in the mud. By the time she double-timed to Russet, the rain had washed her clean. But her braid was under her cap!"

Steve casually leaned against the wall, arms across his chest. Looking over at Jonesy from his position, he gave her a slow smile. Seated Indian-style on the floor she returned his glance. She stood easily and walked towards him. She'd lost over ten pounds and was proud of her accomplishments. They quietly walked out into the darkness.

The troops were building up. Teamwork of a kind they'd never experienced was giving them exactly what the Army had intended. Stretching to their limits, they toughened mentally and physically. Each day was an adventure.

"Let's go play on the playground!" became a standard command, and they'd double-time to the course.

Coming up with unusual colors to name the three sections of the course was the brainchild of Don and Lisa. The two of them, more than any of the others, were having the time of their lives. Faster and faster, they'd race each other, hitting each obstacle in Russet Group. Vaulting a log, climbing up and down an inclined ladder, weaving their bodies through some bars, hip-hopping over others, running over four logs positioned across steep gullies they'd end the run by jumping to nine stumps, tip-toeing in their rush. Each day they increased the speed.

Loud shouts, including many laughs, accompanied the exercise as eighty-eight others followed them across and headed for the next six obstacles. It was a race to see if another two would beat Don and Lisa to the next section. George and Annie were their best competitors—particularly on Vanilla Group's inverted rope descent. The two would climb the tower slower than most, but the trip down more than made up the time. George always went first, whooping like a kid the whole way. Wrapping his long legs around the rope, he had an uncanny ability to distribute the weight of his body for maximum speed. Braking with his feet and legs, he'd slide down the rope, the trees on the other side of the deep gully shaking madly.

When he was halfway down, Annie would grab the other rope and she'd be on her way. First George, then Annie let go of the rope at precisely the right moment. It was instinctive. No one could touch them.

Concerned about rope burns, Lee had advised they slow down, but they seemed impervious to the friction. They were even faster when it rained.

Lisa had named the confidence course Midnight. Sixty feet of sheer terror the first time George tried the rappel tower. Now, it was too easy.

23 February, 2300 Hours

Robert had left this morning. One of the original nine interviewers, he'd been unable to meet the heavy physical demands. He'd hitched a ride with Steve back to El Paso.

Thinking about Robert, knowing he would be available if needed for consultation, Jennifer nonetheless was having a difficult time sleeping. She'd begun to dread each day—the monotonous routine. Still awake, she sat on her cot. Tightness in her throat threatened tears. Bill rolled over in the cot next to her, raising his head and leaning it on one hand. He could see the strong muscles in her upper arms as she calmly braided her hair in readiness for the next day. Jennifer kept her outward appearance composed, but Bill knew she had something on her mind.

"Jen, you all right?"

Huge blue eyes stared at him, seeking comfort and reassurance.

"Sure. Thinkin' about Robert."

Bill threw his legs over the edge and sat up facing her directly.

"You're tired and probably a little bored, I think."

Suddenly she grinned, self-pity fading.

"Tomorrow we go camping, Jen. You'll like that."

They laughed together quietly. Camping, indeed. Jennifer had packed her CT 50 with load bearing equipment, kevelar helmet, poncho, and sleeping bag, shelter half and so forth. She knew the field operation would not be a family outing, but at least it would be something different. Restlessness and boredom was something Jennifer had fought all her life. Along with many others, she had the perfect temperament for what was ahead.

8 March, 1830 Hours

Grenade simulators exploded on two sides and behind the pit. The night sky was like the Fourth of July. Tracing overhead, the M-60—using live ammo—kept up a continuous barrage of noise. One hundred meters of desert awaited them across the infiltration course. By comparison, the field training exercise seemed like a walk in the park. Practicing and tossing first dummy grenades, then real ones had been exhilarating. Those training exercises had been held in full daylight.

They'd all done well, according to Lee who handed out compliments grudgingly. Harlem had laughed about the drill sergeant's tightfisted nods of approval.

"It's like he's got this huge box of candy, picking out the best pieces— never offering us any while he chews away."

They knew they were probably the best he'd ever had.

They could low crawl, high crawl—probably even stand and run the course. The tracers were high over their heads. Chewing her fingers, Harlem looked at her buddy, Mike.

"Don't sweat it, babe, I'm right behind you. Just like when we did the live fire exercise last week. Think about the weekend! Go!"

Harlem crawled out into the night—head buried in her helmet— weapon thrust across her arm, the muzzle of the M4 pointed dead ahead.

* * *

El Paso
10 March, 2200 Hours

Ted joined the others at Bombardier's. General Jamison had asked Coronado to send the best, and the SEAL had arrived at the airport an hour ago. Steve had planned to take Ted to the Range to observe the teams first-hand—but the flight had been delayed. Escorted by Steve, Ted edged his way into the crowded tavern.

Somewhat unwillingly, Bill had suggested the location for their first sortie into El Paso. Nearly everyone had jammed into rented cars or vans, more than ready for a night out.

"Would you look at that!"

Ted's voice was uncharacteristically jovial. His eyes were fastened on an old upright piano nearly hidden in one corner. His husky voice spoke to Steve only once more that evening.

"Be with you in a few."

The man could play. Streaked blonde by the sun, his head bent over the keyboard. His stringy build seemed to melt into the piano. Hearing the sounds, Annie was drawn to Ted's side. Softly at first, then building volume, the two began a series of show tunes. Their music would prove to be very useful to STC.

* * *

The Range
12 March, 1200 Hours

Marching with no audience, no band and no high-ranking officers in attendance, the STC unit graduated. Annie's voice floated alone, soaring over their heads.

"...and the rockets' red glare, the bombs bursting in air, gave proof through the night that our flag was still here. Oh say, does that Star Spangled Banner yet wave, o'er the land of the free, and the home of the brave."

Turning smartly, Lee faced his three platoons.

"Attention!"

They'd miss that loud voice. For the rest of their lives, they'd see his stern face and hear that voice in their sleep.

"I don't have candy, but I do have something for ya'll."

Lee winked at Harlem. She blushed, knowing he must have overheard her teasing.

"Platoons. At ease! Annie, front and center!"

None of the others heard the private message he gave her. Following her smart salute and about face, they could see the huge grin with her back to him.

"Awards time!"

Lee's assistants presented him with two large, flat boxes. Carefully removing the tops, Lee handed several plastic bags to the assistant drills. They began to walk among the graduates.

"You can sew these on your sleeves. If anyone asks, tell 'em you're a special National Guard Unit. If they don't ask, don't tell 'em."

Master Sergeant Stanley John Lee struggled with his emotions for the first time in years.

"The paperwork involved in getting these made up was about as high as that tower you built, Carp, but we pushed it through. This unit's mission is so hush-hush, I couldn't even type up a proposed motto. But TIOH completed the manufacturing and we got an authorization letter."

Holding out a paper, Lee yelled again.

"Bill, front and center!"

Before handing the authorization to Bill, the drill sergeant lowered his voice one decibel.

"This letter is in accordance with AR 672-8, which probably don't mean a damn thing to you, but I can tell you it's almost worth its weight in gold. I've never seen anything like it. But ya'll deserve it. Frame it and hang it in that secret office of yours."

Dismissing Bill, Lee went on with his closing remarks.

"I've never seen higher PT marks. Each of you should get through what's next, thanks to me. I'm proud of every one of you." And Lee saluted the unit.

The Distinctive Unit Insignia they held was quite unique. In burning shades of gold and blue, a peaceful lake was surrounded by jagged, snow-covered mountain peaks. Under the chevron patch were the words *Wei Ming*. Embroidered in deep blue across the top were the letters *STC*.

"Bill, tell 'em what it means!"

Bill swallowed hard, looking at the patch. He raised his eyes.

"The words...the literal translation is 'wonderfully minute and obscure, yet brilliant.' What it means is that the sharpest weapons of the state cannot be displayed."

Chapter Eleven
The Next Three Weeks

The path must not be left for an instant. If it could be left, it would not be the path. On this account, the superior person does not wait until things are seen to be cautious, nor until things are heard to be apprehensive.

The Doctrine of the Mean

Lake Tahoe, California
23 March, 1600 Hours

Dry pine needles blanketed the faint trail. Brilliant blue sky, half obscured by the towering trees, flitted in and out of her peripheral vision.

Tahoe looked down at her feet—pacing rhythmically—crunching the ground. Her mind was not on the surroundings. Normally, Tahoe did not waste time thinking or worrying about what might happen. Once a course had been determined, she followed the plan precisely; rarely interfering in what had been set. Her commitment was never overshadowed by stray feelings of uneasiness. Innovation was always a temptation, but Tahoe was well aware of the dangers inherent in changing things based on personal whims.

Raising her head, Tahoe watched the giant trees swaying overhead.

The wind was rising, increasing along with her apprehension. The smell of the pine trees was rich, almost overpowering. Tahoe made the connection.

The fragrance was the link. Tomorrow they'd be heading for Fort Benning where the heady scent of pine was everywhere.

She'd walked for over an hour. It was time to return. Retracing her steps, widening her stride, Tahoe glanced at her watch. Only two people knew that her dedication to STC covered a thirty-year-old obligation. One of them was Balke. He'd still be in the office.

* * *

STC Offices, Fort Bliss

Permanent location for STC had been decided. Once training was completed, STC Personnel would be at Bliss—at least temporarily.

Spending time between Virginia and El Paso, Balke had been assigned quarters at nearby Biggs Army Field. From there he'd be able to catch hops back and forth from the east coast.

"They'll arrive tomorrow morning, Major."

Talking to Benning's Basic Airborne School Operations Officer, Balke had one more item of business.

"They've completed basic, however, they'll need to fulfill the NBC confidence chamber exercise. You'll have eighty-nine to begin training."

"No problem, Commander, I'll set it up with our guys and put 'em through first thing tomorrow."

The major chuckled.

"Should give 'em an introduction that'll soften ground week."

Five minutes later, Balke was on the phone again. The voice he heard was somewhat of a surprise. Balke had received many calls from Tahoe in the past, but not since the recruits had arrived in El Paso.

"Commander, I hope I'm not interrupting anything."

"Not at all, Ma'am. How can I help you?"

"Brief me, please, on what's been happening."

The request was unusual, but Balke complied.

"They've completed Basic Training and are headed for Georgia in the morning. All but Robert made it through quite well. Lee has doubts about a few others, but for the most part, the drill sergeants were impressed and feel the people will have no problem with the next three weeks."

Eyes focused on the shimmering lake, Tahoe sat back in her chair

"Tell me about the people, please."

Again, Balke was somewhat taken aback. She'd never asked about individuals.

"Bill has been conducting the specialized training the past ten days— along with Captain Jack and Steve. Ted's been involved too, giving them some insights to prepare them for Rangers."

Tahoe nodded to herself. That had been the plan.

"Did the Jones girl find a buddy?"

One by one, Tahoe asked about each person. Balke answered, astonished at her concern.

"Ma'am, is everything all right?" Balke dared to question.

"Yes, of course, Commander."

There was a moment of silence. Then her voice came across the miles, strong and calm as usual.

"As you know, there have been times when we have questioned our inspiration. We have wondered if STC is the answer to some problems. Certain agencies have agreed to keep us in mind, so to speak, once training is completed. Everything is going as planned. But it never hurts to check on progress, to be attuned to potential mistakes or gaps in our thinking."

At her words, Commander Balke searched his mind for an appropriate response.

Tahoe continued, "We must never ignore any questions that may arise. Being prepared for eventualities is paramount, and this includes any feelings of apprehension. Please rest assured that I am monitoring all aspects of this endeavor, and will continue to ask you to do the same."

Straightening in his chair, Balke spoke slowly.

"Ma'am, all seems to be going well. Can you pin point any area in particular that you'd like to discuss?"

Sighing deeply, Tahoe did not attempt to mask her uneasiness.

"Commander, keep up with any potential situations. Use your sources. Talk with the people, especially Bill and Steve. Encourage them to question everyone involved. The people in training will continue to have ideas. Don't forget that. We must anticipate, Commander. Anticipate. Do you understand?"

"Yes, Ma'am."

"Now, Commander, tell me about Annie. Is she still with the engineer?"

* * *

Taipei Taiwan, ROC
24 March, 7:30 PM Local Time

She was very young and very pretty. Her soft voice pleaded with him.

"Please, Minister, you must understand the precariousness of your situation."

The sudden explosion knocked her off her feet. The girl wouldn't die, but it would be many months before she could speak again—and she'd never be quite as pretty as she'd been.

Cheng stood—disbelief locking his arms and legs as tightly as if he'd been trapped in quicksand. Hands still leaning on his desk, the ambassador's body remained in the same position as when she'd been pleading with him from across the room. His young, normally gentle face was frozen into a mask of horror. He'd never be able to explain exactly how he missed seeing two dark figures come through the window—now open from the blast—on the second floor of the Yuan offices.

Rough arms grabbed Cheng from behind. Hands threw bands of black cloth over his eyes and mouth. His slender wrists and ankles were bound. He fainted.

* * *

Fort Benning, Georgia
24 March, 0500 Hours

Dampness hung everywhere. The smell of it stuck to them. It had been raining—they'd been told—for two weeks.

When the C 141 touched down at three in the morning, thunderheads were building, glowing faintly from the almost new moon. Already irritable from lack of sleep, the trainees had been bussed to the 1st Battalion's processing center—affectionately called "Patches" because of the twelve or so window-sized insignia hanging on the outside of the low, white structure. Now this!

Even two months later, Harrison and Kurt would grumble again and again about the Army's nuclear, biological and chemical training requirement.

"Kurt," Harrison would complain, "I'd rather do one of Lee's five-mile marches than *ever* go back into the gas chamber."

Amidst teasing from the others, Kurt and Harrison would pretend to wipe their eyes again—coughing and choking.

1900 Hours

"What I'm trying to explain is that soldiers take care of soldiering. General Patton didn't trust the Russians. He wanted to push them all the way back. He didn't accomplish this, and we got the Berlin Wall. This is what can happen when politicians get involved."

Sitting closely together, they strained to hear Ted's gravelly voice. His projection was not quite on a par with Lee's. The SEAL was giving the last of what he called his "Campfire Talks." The lectures had begun the last week they were at McGregor, and Ted was preparing to return to Coronado the next day.

"Rangers and SEALS must have the killer mentality in order to survive. STC is not Rangers, SEALS—or governmental diplomats. You have the good fortune to be immune to those pressures. STC is an evolution, a higher way of thinking. The intelligence you have, and the intelligence that will be provided to you, can give all sides to what's causing a hostile situation. STC's objective will be to resolve situations in a fair and truthful way."

Eighty-nine STC personnel had grown to appreciate Ted's matter-of-fact way of talking about higher ideals in combat situations. It was an entirely unique approach. General Jamison had chosen the right person.

"If there is enough knowledge and truth no one can trick you. You'll be in a position to show the enemy a better way. We all realize that the world and society suffers from injustices, but there will be a positive way to work out of the crisis at hand. In addition, your training will show you how to face the bigger set of circumstances that caused the crisis in the first place."

Leaning back on his heels, Ted clenched his hands behind his back. His expression became thoughtful. Then he grinned.

"Lest you think I'm soft, let me tell you that I'm not alone in this philosophy."

The trainees chuckled. They'd all had the chance to test Ted's toughness during the grappling sessions. His slender frame—relatively short at five feet, ten inches—was sinewy and supple. No one but Bill could stand up to him.

Moving closer to the group, Ted continued.

"I have a friend—former Navy SEAL—who is teaching at one of the Police Corps' academies. This guy is tough; trust me. But he's also thoughtful. Not only does he teach cadets unarmed combat, he makes them read essays on Aristotle. He wants 'em to understand the philosophy behind the use of force—the justifiable use of force."

Staring above their heads, the SEAL seemed to reflect on what he'd told them.

"But here's the thing. You've got to be ready, mentally and physically for all eventualities. Sure, your objective is to settle peacefully whenever possible, but there will come a time when you'll have to rely upon decisive action."

Looking around at the group, packed into the larger of the two housing units that had been assigned to them, Ted stretched his arms over his head before continuing.

"You must understand things in such a way that there's no limitation in your thinking. Training is largely mental. Sure, it's technical, but it's also a mindset. You'll combine the killer mentality with more knowledge than we've had before. The edge you carry is strength of character balanced with your military training."

Motioning around the room, including them all in his words, Ted ended his remarks.

"It's a fine line you walk, folks. It's easier to walk barefoot on naked blades than to keep this attitude—knowing you can kill, and restraining yourself to think about it first."

Ted raised his hand in farewell, and reached down for his duffel.

"It's been great, folks. I have a feeling we'll be seeing each other again."

The groups of people were quite different from the ones who had gathered in Stout Gym only three months ago. For one thing, they were all dressed alike—in standard battle dress uniform. Most faces had tanned and taken on a harder, more determined expression. Both Bill and Mike had already forgotten their former worry over tight waistbands. All of them had begun to transform themselves into a hard, fighting unit.

They'd been through additional weapons training with Captain Jack who'd also briefed them, in the short time they'd had, in certain techniques used by his Berkeley unit. They'd been apt students and Jack had returned home with the same feelings Ted had expressed—they'd see each other again.

The most obvious difference was not visible. They were no longer strangers to each other.

26 March, 0900 Hours

The small mock-up looked like kid's toys lined up on a play table. Carp and George admired the miniatures, crowding closer to the long display.

"Everything you see here shows what will be accomplished during Airborne School."

Sergeant Airborne, wearing a black baseball cap with the U. S. Army insignia, was painfully thin. Weathered, tan, and wrinkled from the sun, he was graying—grizzled. He could have been anywhere from his mid thirties to early forties. He looked sixty. His uniform was loaded with ribbons.

Noticing the stares from the group, he growled and pointed to the front of his shirt.

"Pick 'em, I've got 'em!"

For thirty minutes, Sergeant Airborne explained the PT requirements, ground week, tower week and jump week, using a long white pointer to indicate the various elements so carefully crafted in small detail.

"I'm guessing we're gonna lose at least five of you this afternoon and five more tomorrow. If you don't pass PT or keep up on runs, you're his-to-ry! And one or two of you will probably break a leg during tower or jump week."

His grin gave them little comfort. He repeatedly slapped the wooden pointer into the palm of his left hand. Among the eighty-nine, two in particular were scared. George and Bobbie dreaded what was coming. As it turned out, they needn't have worried.

Sergeant Airborne was quite correct. The PT test was too demanding for exactly five. Fifty-two sit-ups and sixty-two pushups in thirty minutes smoked the first two. Immediately on the heels of these exertions, three others had dropped out on the two-mile run.

"Nine minute-miles—plus or minus ten seconds!" had been the shouted instruction.

Divided into eight, ten-person squads and one nine-person group, they'd chased each other for the first mile without incident. With less than five hundred yards to go, a man fell.

Lisa jumped over him, followed by Bill and Harlem. The rest of the squad, leaping like deer over the inert body, looked back. Around a bend thundered the next squad, who failed to see the bulk on the narrow dirt road. All ten fell like dominos. Struggling, two others never made it up and all three lay gasping in the mud. Five people left Benning that afternoon. Now they were eighty-four.

27 March, 0530 Hours

"Stretch and grow! Stretch and grow!" Sergeant Airborne shouted in the early morning light, pacing back and forth as they began the second day of Ground Week.

"Every day begins with forty-five minutes Physical Training, Airborne, fifteen different exercises every day. I'm the headwaiter and I've got the menu right here in my head! There're thirty different ways to exercise, Airborne, and you'll try 'em all! I don't care if you don't like what I serve up."

No confidential information about Sergeant Airborne ever came to light. No personality emerged from the façade he'd carefully built over the years. He was an aggravating voice, anxious for their safety and ability to fulfill each training phase. His teaching philosophy was geared towards strengthening cohesion and discipline. Obliged to provide the best possible training, his supervision never became personal. His presence was simply and always there. Hovering like a ubiquitous mother hen, he seemed to be everywhere at once, prodding and poking them without feeling.

"Today we'll begin with squat thrusts, followed by jumping jacks and sit-ups, and for dessert we'll do a ton of push-ups."

Watching them now, the sun beginning to drift in and out of the heavy overcast, he readjusted his black cap, pulling the bill close down over his eyes.

"Grass Drills! And I wanna see choppy steps, folks. Just like football workout. Do it,

Airborne. Down on your tummies, Airborne! Jump up! Don't roll up! Jump! Jump! Down on your backs, Airborne! Jump up! Energy, Airborne! Let's see some energy!"

Sergeant Airborne was wrong about one thing. They didn't lose five people that morning. They lost seven. It was the three-mile run.

0900 Hours

"I wanna see *good* PLFs. Good means you fall correctly. Dissipate that weight! Start on the balls of your feet, Airborne! Then hit your calves, thighs, buttocks and lats! Those are your push-up muscles, Airborne! Hit all five points or you go again. I'm counting, Airborne! One thousand, five hundred PLFs this week, Airborne! Do it!"

Standing at one side of the pit filled with old rubber tires ground up to approximate the size of number two gravel, the voice continually harangued them as they practiced the required parachute landing falls. Seventy-eight made it through ground week.

2 April, 1000 Hours

PT and a five-mile run had filled half the morning. Next, they looked at their first tower—the Swing Landing Trainer. Only twelve feet high with a platform on top, each was expected to climb the ladder and hook on to a thick rope attached to a pulley. One by one they stepped off the platform. Sergeant Airborne, swinging the rope with a gleeful expression, released the hook, laughing as they fell. Twenty successful falls completed the phase.

4 April, 1100 Hours

Squinting up at the four-tiered structure, George asked, "Does that have a name?"

"Yeah. We call it the thirty-four foot tower."

Dry humor was something George appreciated, and he laughed.

"Pretend it's an airplane. See the door? See that cable?"

Sergeant Airborne talked them through the drill.

"It's like a carnival ride, Airborne! Slide down that cable. Make five satisfactory exits and we'll call it good!"

6 April, 1300 Hours

Unfortunately, the weather had cleared. Sunshine was blinding as they walked across the plowed ground. Yesterday Sergeant Airborne told them in no uncertain terms that the tower would be off limits if lightning were expected. He'd told them to listen for his voice over the bullhorn.

"If it's bad weather I will announce 'Everybody out of the pool!'"

No such luck awaited them. The weather was beautiful. Ruts of freshly overturned dirt spread out for a hundred-yard radius around the bottom of the tower. Looming like a red and white four-armed construction crane, "Mongosso" soared over their heads. This two hundred fifty foot tower had a name.

Run on a winch system, cables ran to the ground and were attached to big steel hoops. Fully deployed parachutes, secured to the hoop, awaited each jumper. Sergeant Airborne, bullhorn close to his mouth, reviewed instructions as each jumper's harness was attached.

"I will ask you if you are OK. IF you are OK, open your legs like scissors and signal me. I will tell you which way to steer. Hang onto those toggles and follow my instructions. Piece of cake, Airborne!"

George tugged at his harness. Palms wet, he wiped his hands on his pants.

"Get your hands on those risers, Airborne!"

Hanging on, George felt his body leave the ground as the crew began to crank up the cables. The voice boomed from the bullhorn.

"Are you OK?"

Signaling with his legs, George squeezed his eyes closed. He didn't open them until later. He dropped.

"Steer right!"

George fumbled for the toggles, which were like wooden handles attached to the cord used to start an old-fashioned lawn mower. He found the right one and pulled.

"Release! Release!"

George didn't release the toggle. He couldn't. Coming around 180 degrees, he hit the tower at the fourth section. Of their own accord, his hands found the metal of the tower, and he held on. The red and white parachute blew into the tower and stuck like glue to the girders. It took climbers on ropes nearly an hour to get him down.

The thing was—when it was all over—George went back and demanded to try it again.

This time, it was picture perfect.

8 April, 2000 Hours

"Okay, here's a little-known piece of trivia for you. You'll do your first jump tomorrow morning and I wanted to give you one of the finer points of my many years of experience. As a going away gift."

Balke sat with the trainees as they traded stories from the past two weeks. The big news was that Flavia had broken her ankle on Mongoasso. One of the original interviewers, Flavia had landed, catching her foot in a rut. Running to her side, Kurt took one look and motioned to Sergeant Airborne.

"Well, I'm pretty sure it's broken. Better get this looked at. Sorry, Flavia."

She was comfortably propped up in a hospital bed, and would go home in a few days. Like all those who had left, Flavia would be on call to assist in other capacities.

"Let's hear it, Commander," said Bobbie, "I'm ready for a present."

Comfortable with the group, Balke grinned at them. He didn't often smile, and his face changed when he did. It became amiable, rather than morose. It was a definite improvement.

"On static line, you've got about three seconds until your parachute opens. Right?"

"Yessir!" A chorus answered.

"Three seconds can seem to last forever, so they tell you to count them, right?"

They nodded.

"In musical terms, if you count each second as a beat, the tempo is called *andante*—walking tempo. If you count one, one-thousand; two, one-thousand; three, one-thousand, you'll be pretty close to andante."

Balke began to snap his fingers.

"Now, here's what we say in music school."

Balke snapped and spoke rhythmically.

"One chimpanzee, two chimpanzee, three chimpanzee."

The seriousness of his delivery kept them all from laughing, and one by one, the group began to snap or clap along with Balke.

He explained further, "For some reason, that word takes exactly the right amount of time to say, no matter who says it. I'll leave it up to you to decide if you yell 'chimpanzee' rather than 'thousand' tomorrow."

Balke stood up, muttering, his frown back in place.

"No one will hear you anyway."

9 April, 1300 Hours

Indicated airspeed was 125 knots, but it seemed they were flying much faster. Standing at the open door, Bobbie watched the ground rushing beneath him. He'd had trouble remembering it was the left door, even though from his perspective—facing the tail of the C130—the door was on his right. He knew they were flying at 1,250 feet and he remembered the blackhat yelling at Harrison who'd dared to question this seemingly incredible low altitude.

"This is the Army, not sport parachuting!"

If he'd been hooked up to a heart monitor, Bobbie knew three loud beeps would've brought a nurse racing to his side yelling *he's out of control,* but he wasn't hooked up to a monitor. He was attached to an anchor line cable; secured by a snap hook and safety wire to a static line.

Watching the red light, Bobbie's thoughts flew by more quickly than the ground. Why in hell had he been selected to be first to jump? Probably because Sergeant Airborne was a tad taller than he was. Or maybe it was because the blackhat—like everybody else all along—had mistaken Bobbie's self-assuredness for bravery. Whatever the reason, there he was waiting for the green light.

They'd been in the building, all rigged up, standing quietly. The blackhat called out.

"Let's goooo! Airborne, Chalk Number one! Get on the black line!"
Then he'd screamed again, "Is that clear?"

Bobbie's heart had jumped. *Beep! Number one.*

"Clear, Sergeant Air*borne*!" twenty voices had responded.

Carp had whispered, "Don't sweat it, Bobbie, when I slap your butt you'll know I'm right behind you."

The huge door had opened and they faced the fat tail of their bird—the maw as big and dark as one of those caves at Carlsbad Caverns.

Beep! Number two.

Once in flight, they'd responded to the Jumpmaster's shouted instructions.

"Siiiiix Minutes!"

"Outboard Personnel, Stand *up*!"

"Hoooook up!"

Yelling over the noise of the engines, the jumpmaster had waved his index finger up and down.

"Cheeeck static line!"

Both hands behind his ears this time, he'd bawled again.

"Sound off with equipment check."

"OK! OK! OK!..."

Their shouts resounded twenty times through the fat body of the airplane. Each jumper checked the person in front, the last one in line turning around to be checked by the one in front. Tugging on the static lines, they insured that safety wires were in place. True to his word, Carp had made sure Bobbie's yellow static line was attached to his parachute, and slapped his bottom. Preparing for a safe handoff to the jumpmaster, Bobbie had kept a large bite of line below his grasp.

He shouted, "All OK, Jumpmaster!"

Opening the door, the jumpmaster set the blast shield and watched the ground for the drop zone and his release point. The wind, whipping cold through the aircraft, added to the noise.

Only a minute ago the jumpmaster had held up his hand; and then, bringing his index finger and thumb into close proximity—as in a pincer grasp—indicated thirty seconds. Those seconds went by too fast. Bobbie's imaginary monitor beeped for the third time.

"Staaaand by!!"

Handing off the coil, Bobbie stood with his knees bent, most of his weight on his back leg, fingertips spread evenly over the ends of his reserve parachute. Intent now on the light, Bobbie cleared his mind. Red, red, red. Green!

The slap on his buttocks was harder this time.

"Go!"

Bobbie stepped out, yelling, "One chimpanzee, Two chimpanzee, Three, chimpanzee..." It was an eternity.

The opening shock brought his head up, and he checked to assure he had a good canopy. Bobbie was looking up the prettiest light green silk skirt he'd ever seen. The ground came up quickly under his bent knees and feet, held firmly together. Hands held in front of his face, he kept his elbows bent. Touching down softer than he had from any of the towers, Bobbie made sure the five points of performance hit the ground. Triumphant fists in the air, he stood up remembering back twenty-five years.

His father—home from the office and still dressed in his suit and tie, hat firmly in place—had tossed him into the sky. Catching Bobbie in his strong arms, he'd thrown him higher and higher...

Like skiers after a day on the slopes, Bill and Jennifer joined Bobbie and Carp who were eager to talk about their experiences. It was catharsis, and they knew it. Hearing the laughter, they were joined by Annie and George. Kurt and Harrison wandered into the barracks and joined the group.

"I was scared, but when that parachute opened, I looked down and knew exactly where I was going to land."

Still flushed with excitement, Annie raised her voice.

"One of these days I'll tell you how loud I yelled. I could give Sergeant Lee some competition. I know his secret."

Smiling at her, Harrison didn't ask. He was learning that this mild-mannered girl would tell them when she was ready. Annie kept most things to herself, sharing private thoughts on rare occasions.

Harrison said, "I know you don't want to hear from me, seeing as how I'm accustomed to this form of entertainment. However, I must say I almost lost it up there today. It's different. And that's a fact. I hope my courage comes back for the next one!"

Bobbie stretched and wandered to his laptop. He'd spoken with Balke. It didn't surprise him that the Commander had urged him to keep his ears to the ground. The situation was escalating by the moment, and Bobbie wouldn't be surprised at anything that happened at this point. Like Tahoe and Balke, Bobbie was bothered by a vague uneasiness that had nothing to do with jumping. He wasn't the only one.

10 April, 0600

Bill drew a black line through the first jump listed on the menu. Jennifer had typed and printed the schedule from Sergeant Airborne's shouted instructions.

JUMP#	DRESS/EQUIMENT	EXIT
# 1	*BDU's and OD parachute helmet*	*Individual*
# 2	*Combat Equipment:*	*Mass from one door*
#3	*No Equipment*	*Mass from both doors*
#4	*Combat Equipment*	*Mass from both doors*
#5	*Combat Equipment*	*Mass from both doors, night*

Combat Equipment consists of rucksack with food and ammunition and weapons case. Second and Third jumps will be at 1000 hours and 1500 hours on Wednesday. Fourth and Fifth jumps will be at 1500 hours and 2100 hours on Friday.

Dropping the neatly outlined jump schedule, he picked up the Washington Post he'd found at the PX. Hidden on the back page were two short paragraphs. Shaking his head, Bill spoke softly.

"This could be serious," he said to Jennifer.

With very few details, the article reported a kidnapping in Taiwan seventeen days earlier. The politician was still missing.

Chapter Twelve
Keeping Watch

Whose fault is it when the tiger or the wild bull escapes its pen, or when the tortoise or the valued gem is damaged in its box?
The Analects of Confucius

Fort Benning, Georgia
Easter Sunday
15 April, 1630 Hours

The quiet day hadn't been disturbed by any of the usual sounds. No small arms fire could be heard from the rifle ranges across the road. There were no basic trainees singing cadence. The grinding clank of shifting gears from cattle cars transporting soldiers to training areas was absent.

It was so still that Bobbie found himself listening for retreat, usually broadcast at 1700 hours. He'd been at his laptop all day, typing notes on what he called the "aviation problem." He intended to brief Bill, Carp and Harrison on the situation. Whatever happened—and Bobbie could feel something coming as surely as that bugle call—he wanted the computer expert close by. At first, Harrison's braggart ways had annoyed Bobbie, but there was no denying the man knew his business.

The report was filling three double-spaced pages, and Bobbie struggled to make his deductions clear and logical. He was convinced the situation was explosive.

"Carp, come here a sec, please? I want to run this by you."

Pulling his head out of the pillow, Carp yawned.

"Sure thing, pal. What's up?"

Taking a closer look at Bobbie, Carp squinted.

"You growing back your 'stach?"

Bobbie ran a hand over his upper lip. He'd been clean-shaven since Airborne School. Distractedly, he answered Carp.

"Gonna shave it tomorrow. Listen, I've got this outlined—the airline thing. Check me as I go along. See if you have any questions. OK?"

Sauntering to the small table, Carp pulled up a chair. Bobbie had made a pot of coffee in the hotel sized automatic carafe, and Carp poured a cup.

"First, I want to get you familiar with some of these acronyms."

Carp laughed, "More?"

"Different, Carp. ALPA stands for the Airline Pilots Association. FAA, well you know what FAA stands for. How about FARS?"

Squeezing his brows together, Carp answered, "Federal Aviation Regulations?"

"Yep. And then there's an acronym for each airline's world headquarters. OK so far?"

"Sure."

Bobbie peered at the screen, glowing bluish white in the dimly lit room. Most of them had learned to sleep with Bobbie's screen as a nightlight.

"All major airlines seem to have a "fence"—that's what I'm calling it for now—between pilots and managers. The fence exists because the pilots, on one side, are concerned, above all, with safety and the daily life of flying. Management, on the other side, is sitting in an office concerned with making big money for the company."

"But, Bobbie, isn't that true in any company? Even yours?"

Scowling at the computer, Bobbie grunted.

"Yeah, I suppose. But these managers don't have a contract and there aren't any unions. They want to keep their high paying jobs and they do it by getting the most from their employees and by spending the least."

Looking at Bobbie over the top of his cup, Carp nodded.

"Sounds like good business to me."

"Sure," said Bobbie, "But the way they do it is the kicker. Management arranges to spend the least by hiring new pilots and getting rid of the older pilots. A band-new pilot can be hired for $30,000 a year, up to $50,000 the second year. At retirement age a 747 captain can be making as much as $240,000 a year."

Carp pretended to choke.

"You're shittin' me!

"No way, Jose. I've looked at it carefully and verified the figures."

Bobbie stood up and walked around the table, pouring out the last of the coffee. Pushing the screen around, he remained standing; looking down and moving the cursor to the line he wanted.

"Mangers arrange to pay out less in wages by demanding more hours from fewer—and newer—pilots. They pressure the new pilots a little bit, and when they give more hours, they push for even more. Two things happen. Care to guess?"

Carp pursed his mouth.

"My guess is that the new pilots, getting pressure from the company to fly more hours, will take more pushing than the older, more experience pilot. I mean they probably want to keep the job."

Bobbie smiled at his friend.

"Exactly! Management wants new pilots because they'll bend to flying more hours, and their salary is lower."

"So," asked Carp, "What's the second thing that happens?"

Lifting his head Bobbie spoke slowly, his voice quiet. His business career had taught him the value of drama in presenting a case to clients.

"Pilots get pressure from the FAA. The Federal regulations are quite clear about how many sequential hours a pilot can fly. The FARS describes in detail the psychological impact from flying too many hours. The rules set down are very explicit and there's a narrow box determining the number of consecutive hours a pilot can fly. No pilot wants an FAA official showing up in the cockpit, demanding to see how many hours he's logged."

Bobbie scowled and held out his hand, mimicking an official.

"I'm curious, may I see your log book?"

Carp chuckled at Bobbie's impersonation.

"I've got a question, Bobbie. Has anyone ever tried to climb the fence?"

Rubbing his chin, Bobbie shook his head.

"From what I've been able to find out from my sources, there have been some attempts. But historically, those who have tried to climb the fence usually get drawn into the moneymaking aspects of management. They succumb to the existing conditions, defer to higher management, and hide from the responsibility. The managers continue to sweep problems under the carpet, waiting until somebody trips over the pile hidden there."

Fascinated, Carp quickly asked a series of questions, firing them rapidly, not giving Bobbie time to answer.

"This is happening? Today? How about safety? Doesn't this mess affect passengers? Do the experienced pilots quit? Are they fired? What about all these so-called pilot slowdowns and pilots on strike, refusing to fly?"

None of the questions surprised Bobbie. Carp usually got the heart of a problem quickly.

"Let me start by saying that ALPA gets involved when a situation has escalated to the point when the more experienced pilots refuse to break the FARS and won't fly. The press gets involved, saying that pilots are on strike. In reality, the senior pilots are not flying because of the regulations governing their hours. You with me so far?"

"Of course, Bobbie. Go on, please. This is an incredible tale you're weaving."

"Carp, believe me when I tell you I wish it *was* a tale. It's happening, man, and I'm worried."

Seating himself across from his buddy, Bobbie adjusted the screen, referring to his notes.

"So, when some story hits the news, management probably thinks about law suits against the news agency that broadcast or printed that the pilots are on strike. And of course, the lawyers—on attack mode—are right there; a pile of snakes with their rattles going."

They both doubled up, aware that Bobbie had a law degree and knew all the best lawyer descriptions. Bobbie quickly became serious, returning to the review.

"At this point, an airline's headquarters may get involved and begin to throw out any manager they feel is not doing the job. Things begin to settle down for a while. But the fence is still there and no one has ever climbed it."

"Wow," said Carp. "This could explain some of the delays. It can't always be the weather, right?"

"Of course weather is a factor, but you're correct. Delays are not always weather-related, although that may be the reason given."

Bobbie shrugged and readjusted his body, trying to ease his tense shoulders.

"Another source told me that there've been a few pilots—he described them as 'weak characters'—that have climbed the fence. They fail at management because they have marginal ability to begin with. They have a sort of disloyal or false character and can be manipulated. They fail in the administrative arena and try to return to flying. The pilots won't take 'em back."

The two men were silent for a moment as Bobbie saved the document. Glancing at Carp, Bobbie stood up.

"Let's get a beer."

The two men left their quarters, deep in thought. Sixty-two days of Ranger School was ahead of them.

Retreat sounded, clear in the still, spring air. Bobbie glanced at his watch.

Two thousand five hundred and fifty-three miles away, a teenage impassively watched an explosion rock San Francisco International Airport. Positioned near a hangar, an aircraft suddenly blew up. It was not as spectacular as it would have been at night; nonetheless it could have been seen and heard by anyone who happened to be at the airport. The fireball glowed white in the center as streams of yellow and red flames circled the fuselage and found the wings. When the JP4 ignited, the black smoke raised high in the air. There appeared to be minor damage to the hangar. The airplane was totally destroyed. The boy walked quietly away from where he'd been watching, deep in thought.

* * *

Columbus, Georgia
1730 Hours

The fragrance of onions and garlic simmering in olive oil and tomato puree filled the air. Master Sergeant Scott Claridge lounged in front of the TV. The relaxing sounds of his wife—who he openly acknowledged as his best friend—bustling around the kitchen lowered his lids. He dozed.

Pasta on Easter was a tradition they'd begun when the first of their three children was born. Now sixteen, the boy had been joined first by a daughter and then another son.

Military life had been good for Scott. He had a supportive spouse and children who adjusted easily to the many changes. At only thirty-five years of age, he looked forward to retirement and a change of occupation in three years. Maybe he'd write a book.

"Ellie Mae, settle down."

Scott murmured at his Great Dane who was crowding him on a couch that was exactly two inches longer than his six-foot one-inch frame. At a little over two hundred-fifty pounds, the Ranger instructor and his dog threatened to exceed the weight bearing capacity of the sofa.

Enjoying the peace of his home before the next round of training, Scott was content.

Even as a boy he was content. His mother, raising two huge sons—alone for the most part—had always described him in a few short words:

"Scott is himself. All the time."

When he was seven years old, Scott's father had died in Viet Nam. The family was still not in custody of the remains.

Both boys chose military careers; Scott's brother now served with Seal Team Six.

"Dinner's ready!"

Rousing himself, Scott drifted to the dining room and lit the white candles.

Stretching his large frame in various directions, feeling the sleepiness fade away, Scott looked forward to the next morning. He'd been assigned the task of training seventy-seven civilians. It was a first for Rangers. Scott intended to see that the low profile, exceedingly talented—from what he'd learned—group would receive the best he had to offer.

"No baby-sitting or molly-coddling," he'd been told, "Treat 'em like anyone else."

Watching over trainees, forcing them to excel, was what Scott did best.

Seating themselves in their usual places, the family held hands around the table. Scott led the blessing.

"God, please bless this family, our country and give us peace. Amen."

None of the Rangers he'd trained could ever imagine their instructor in this setting.

* * *

JFK International Airport
1800 Hours

Carrying a bouquet of pink calla lilies tied with a pale pink ribbon, the bride had been radiant. Most brides are, but she was exceptionally beautiful. With a creamy, chocolate brown complexion, the tall and graceful Vienna Winder had became the wife of Doctor Jonas Campbell less than five hours ago.

Dr. Campbell was the first black Episcopalian minister to serve at Saint John the Divine, the huge stone church in downtown Manhattan. He was also the youngest.

The newlyweds boarded an airplane and left JFK bound for Israel and a two-month honeymoon, which would begin with a tour of the holy land. They were in the wrong place at the wrong time.

* * *

Quemoy, ROC
16 April, 9 AM Local Time

Sometimes things happen and it isn't until later that the path—the course of events leading to the situation—can be clearly seen. One simple incident, leading to another and then another often brings people together, entangled in each other's lives from the beginning.

At sixty-two years of age, Fang Mei had never spent much time in front of a mirror. She wore her hair—black, with only a few stray strands of gray—cropped closely to her head and arranged in wispy bangs across her forehead. This not only made for low maintenance, but also gave her face a certain gamin quality; youthful and becoming.

The family name, Fang, could be translated to mean *flower*. Her parents had given her the first name Mei, *beautiful*. Still slim and athletic, Fang Mei wore blue jeans and modern T-shirts with outrageous slogans printed across the front. This amused her family, but Fang Mei's strong personality kept them from mentioning anything. Today's T-shirt was hot pink embroidered with two white daisies positioned neatly across the bust. Elaborate script announced: *They may be little but they're all mine.* Fang Mei's youngest grandson had brought it to her from America. Only the younger generation understood the message.

Never remarrying after the death of her husband, Fang Mei lived alone on the island of Quemoy. Also known as Kinmen or Golden Gate, the island had been her home for over forty years. From her grandchildren, Fang Mei had heard about another Golden Gate, near San Francisco. She often wondered if she'd ever travel to see the entrance to the bay and the bridge that was named for her island.

Nestled close to the coast of Mainland China, the island was barricaded and built mostly underground Two hundred and fifty miles directly east across the Taiwan Straits, was the city of Kaoshung on Taiwan.

At times, Fang Mei would travel by fishing boat to Taiwan to visit her large family. Most of them lived in Taipei.

Leaning on her hoe, Fang Mei's normally smooth face was wrinkled in thought. Two weeks ago Fang Mei had seen something that disturbed her greatly.

Walking along the old board sidewalk at sunset, she'd watched as a powerful launch motored slowly toward a rotting rarely used wharf. Partially hidden by trees, Fang Mei watched as two men roughly pulled a smaller man from the cabin. The small man's arms were tied behind his back. Thanks to her grandson, Fang Mei immediately identified the silvery stuff. It was duct tape. She even knew the words in English, and smiled because she remembered them. Her smile had faded quickly when they dragged the man across the old timbers. He was blindfolded.

Moving slowly and quietly, Fang Mei stepped backwards until her feet touched the edge of the boardwalk. Ducking quickly behind one of the trees, she'd watched them half-carry the struggling man. Forcing the man ahead, they pushed and shoved him towards an old structure hidden in the scrubby trees.

For several days she did nothing. But a week ago Fang Mei had called her brother in Taipei. The Taiwan Air Force Chief of Staff had laughed at his sister, telling her she was daydreaming. When he hung up the phone, the man rubbed his chin. He suspected that it was Cheng his sister had seen. With the phone call, he'd discovered where they'd taken him, but he certainly did not want his sister involved in the political maneuvering. He'd handle it his own way.

Puttering in her small garden, Fang Mei brushed her hands on her jeans. What she had seen troubled her deeply, and her brother's attitude only added to her unease. Straightening her back, she walked determinedly towards her small house. She'd made up her mind to ask her friend to take her across the Straits to Taipei. Fang Mei intended to visit her martial arts master. He'd know what to do.

Chapter Thirteen
Comfort Level

Yield and become whole. Bend and become straight. Hollow out, and become filled. Exhaust, and become renewed. Small amounts are obtainable; large amounts are confusing.

Lao Tzu

Fort Benning, Georgia
16 April, 1230 Hours

The flight plan from Southern California had included a stop in Oklahoma City to refuel. The other stop was noted in Lisa's logbook, but it was not something she could discuss. The flight had taken a little over eight hours. Contacting the tower, Lisa was cleared to land. Two weeks of an FAA approved training program had added a CASA 212 type rating to her ticket.

The man in the right seat nodded approvingly as the airplane touched down lightly, fixed gear squeaking evenly. Ground control directed Lisa along the taxiways to the designated parking area. The high-pitched whine from two Garret 331-10 turbine engines squealed annoyingly. Lisa shut down the airplane, carefully following the checklist. She was exhausted.

"OK, Lisa, you're a good pilot. Gimme your logbook."

The newly hired co-captain signed her off. The man had been working as an FAA Operations Inspector and was quick to accept the new job. His first assignments had been to give Lisa her check ride and to remain on stand-by as part of STC staff. He was well paid.

"You know how to reach me," he called over his shoulder. His name was Dan, and he seemed to know where he was going.

Stretching her neck to release the kinks from the tension of flying, Lisa gathered her few belongings. She looked back into the roomy compartment, admiring once again the transformation of the cargo area—now outfitted with nineteen seats upholstered in deep blue. The high wing configuration of the airplane afforded passengers a clear view of the ground. A neat galley had also been added along with a lavatory.

The instrumentation had been upgraded and included a Global Positioning System. The four radios—two for communications and two for navigation—were standard and required for any aircraft operating under FAR-Part 25. Lisa had flown the last leg using a view-limiting apparatus—to simulate instrument conditions—clipped to her sunglasses. It was part of the required check ride, and Lisa found the array of instrumentation easy on the eyes. They'd even installed air conditioning. It was a beautiful airplane, and Lisa patted the door as she exited aft of the cockpit.

The upswept tail bore a red circle with STC boldly painted in the same deep blue as the passenger seats inside. Red and blue stripes followed the outline of the fuselage, flowing smoothly below the round windows and around the nose. The N numbers were in red: N35388. It looked like any other commuter aircraft, but it wasn't.

April 18, 0800 Hours

Five groups of veteran soldiers—Merrill's Marauders who'd served in World War II; RICA from the Korean War; TRRA from Viet Nam; LRRP; USARA; and the 75th Ranger Regiment Association— supplemented the training staff at Ranger School. Previous engagements in Panama, Granada, Somalia and Desert Storm, gave these advisors the expertise to provide the best possible training. Knowing this, Jennifer gritted her teeth.

Face down in the worm pit—to avoid the barbed wire strung overhead—her thoughts became audible.

"Those guys probably stayed up all night thinking of the most disgusting, personal-worst war-time experiences to come up with this crap!"

She yelled at no one in particular. They were all grunting or groaning anyway, and her voice got lost in the general sucking noises of twenty bodies crawling through the muck.

"RAP week! Perfect." she muttered, lips close together to avoid getting any more sludge in her mouth, "Only I wouldn't call it Ranger Assessment Phase, I'd call it *Revolting And Putrid.*"

Jennifer's fastidious nature was disgusted. It wasn't the physical effort that bothered her so much. It was the indignity of being covered with the slimy, stinky mud and water that enraged her. She could feel the gunk creeping down the back of her BDU pants and over the tops of her jungle boots. Extremely uncomfortable, Jennifer found herself thinking about food. She laughed at the absurdity.

The morning had started with running until they were drenched in sweat. Sawdust in the pits below each instrument of torture on the obstacle course stuck to their bodies when they fell. It was like rolling chicken in flour and egg mixture. Jennifer's stomach growled. The nasty, five-lane trench probably *was* filled with worms. She tried not to think about that possibility, or of her incredible hunger.

The days went by and members of the STC Squadron found that their perspective about what had previously been considered uncomfortable had changed completely—replaced by a more realistic viewpoint. The most persnickety would discover that an obsessive need for cleanliness was nothing compared to the gnawing, ever-present hunger. There was no time for luxuries such as bathing, food, sleep or days off. Weekends did not interrupt the training schedule.

Scott told the squadron they could expect a fifty-three percent drop out rate by the conclusion of the sixty-two days. He also told them that small unit leadership would be the focus of the course.

"Small unit tactics such as raids, ambushes and reconnaisaance will accomplish this," he growled, "There will be no formal leadership classes. *Everything* we do will instill leadership in each soldier. The principles of leadership give you the edge. Don't ever forget it."

Scott's southern drawl rolled over them like soft strands of cotton, but the content of his verbiage was ruthless. Over the weeks ahead, the Squadron would find that his stories of previous sorties with earlier classes were horrendous tales bordering on sick humor.

That first day, his account involved two Nigerian soldiers who were training with the Rangers, and was so disgusting that Jonsey's mouth fell open and Scott had to tell her to shut it before the flies got in.

The subject came up when Scott was explaining that a brilliant move on the part of a soldier could earn what he called a *major plus spot report*. If they did something bad, it'd be a *major minus spot report* on the record.

"In the old days, Rangers, we took survival classes in Florida. These two soldiers from the Nigerian Army were doing poorly. We couldn't fail 'em because they'd go back home and probably get executed. So we gave 'em a chance to redeem themselves."

Scott's lecture took place as part of the squadron stood at attention, waiting for their go at the worm pit. He was oblivious to their discomfort. George and Annie tried to ignore his neatly pressed uniform and clean face. Glancing surreptitiously at Don and Lisa as Scott turned for a moment, Annie moved her head slightly in his direction, rolling her eyes.

Nothing escaped his notice. "I saw that, Ranger!" Scott yelled, and he continued his story.

"We'd taken the objective and had stolen all the animals. They rigged up this gate and tied up a goat to the poles. Then the two soldiers were told if they slaughtered the goat they'd earn a *major plus spot report*. The instructions were very clear, I can tell you, but these two men didn't get it straight."

Pausing to peer at their sweaty, sawdust-covered faces, Scott grinned at the memory.

"One of the guys approached the goat with a hammer. He'd been told to give out a Zulu war cry as he knocked the animal over the head. He missed, and hit the goat on the nose. The goat struggled and the soldier fell, straddling the goat's horns. The other guy went at the goat with an old rusty machete, hacking away. Problem was, he hacked his friend instead. The both wound up in the hospital."

Not getting a response from the squadron, Scott turned away from them. "I guess you had to be there," he grumbled.

* * *

Jerusalem
5:30 PM Local Time

Tea on the balcony consisted of caviar on toast points, assorted sandwiches and the ever-present dish of olives. Lazing in the warm sunlight, Jonas and Vienna laid plans for their day trip to Nablus. They planned to leave early, and had hired a taxi with a driver purported to know his way around.

Watching them smile into each other's eyes, the hotel staff hovered solicitously around the newlyweds, vicariously enjoying the shimmer of romance. It would be the couple's last peaceful evening for many weeks.

* * *

Quemoy, ROC
Midnight, Local Time

Fang Mei tossed restlessly. Her small suitcase lay packed but still open on the table near her bed. In the morning she'd add her toiletries and a few small, hand-made gifts for her grandchildren. Sleep came and went as Fang Mei went over her plans.

"Don't forget the bank. Did I remember to put in the shopping list? Should I bother to call brother? Lao Shir is expecting me tomorrow."

She'd checked earlier. The man was still in the small house.

* * *

Fort Benning
2030 Hours

Dragging up the stairs to their quarters, STC Squadron were bedraggled and completely worn out. Dan the pilot was sitting on Bobbie's bed. Taking one look at Bobbie's face, he stood and quickly handed Bobbie the newspaper he'd been reading.

"Lisa said you'd probably want to see this."

Uncomfortable in his surroundings, dressed in neatly pressed jeans and white shirt, the pilot swiftly left the building.

Bobbie glanced at the small headline, circled in red.

"Airline receives Bomb Threats. Terrorism suspected."

Tired as he was, Bobbie's adrenalin kicked in. He quickly scanned the account of an anonymous telephone call received by the air carrier on Easter Sunday. There was no doubt in Bobbie's mind: that was not the act of a terrorist.

* * *

Scott's sensitivity and concern for the members of STC Squadron under his guidance followed the usual pattern. However, it was because of the Master Sergeant's intuitive nature—coupled with his experience— that he'd immediately noticed the uniqueness of the people and was quick to capitalize on their capabilities.

It was his idea to refer to them as the STC Squadron, and it was his job to find people's comfort level and jar them out of it again and again. From the first days of training, Scott realized that these professionals were quite different from those who usually came to Ranger Training. For one thing, most Rangers consisted of U. S. Army personnel ranging in rank from Sergeant E-5 through Captain—not many senior NOC'S or officers above Captain attended Ranger School. Once in training, no rank defined the students. They were all simply, "Rangers." Even though Scott had personally supervised the training of U. S. Army personnel and officers from military groups from various parts of the world, this was the first time he'd been associated with a civilian group.

Secondly, the education level of these people was far beyond anything Scott had experienced. He was quiet about his praise, but he was awed by most of them. One group in particular, caught his attention. Scott had never seen fifteen people come together so quickly, as if they were all thinking exactly the same thoughts at exactly the same time. Others had many of the same capabilities, but this particular team inspired him to push even harder during the demands of training.

The third thing that set them apart was the fact that he hadn't had to assign buddies the first day. This group had already selected their own Ranger Buddy. Scott had heard a rumor that this had happened before they'd even attended Basic. There were many unanswered questions about the group.

"Okay folks," Scott muttered to himself that night before he slept, "My orders say I'm supposed to treat you like anyone else. Let's see what you can give me tomorrow."

He didn't know that Bill, even after the most rigorous days, would continue to drill the Squadron at night in the specifics of STC. Scott would find out soon enough.

* * *

Baqa'a Refugee Camp, Amman, Jordan
19 April, 8:00 AM Local Time

At the same time Vienna and Jonas sat down to breakfast on the veranda of their hotel, Faris called his friend Dabir on his cell phone. They were only a block away from each other, but having a cell phone was a status symbol and the teenagers used them incessantly. The two boys could have walked two minutes down the dirty street to have the conversation in person, but this wouldn't have been as "cool." They'd picked up the Americanism browsing at the Internet Cafes in Amman. Carrying a rifle was also very cool.

They made plans for a hike to Nablus, ten kilometers from the compound, in the West Bank. Faris wanted to see his uncle. Uncle Fadil had money and stature. The self-appointed mayor of the small town, his influence would assure that Faris could get the car he so desperately wanted.

Unaware of her son's plans, Kamilah went about her daily chores, which—for the most part—consisted of "constantly renouncing sloth." That's what Kamilah called the futile attempt to keep her house clean.

Since the 1967 War two thirds of the population of Jordan consisted of Palestinian refugees, one of who was Kamilah. Her seventeen-year-old son was born in the compound, as she had been thirty-four years earlier. She'd named him Faris—the Horseman, the Knight—and he was the light and hope of her life. Daydreams, prompted by family discussions about returning to Israel, had faded since Faris was born. Kamilah, whose name meant *Perfect*, continued to hope that her knight would free them from the filthy camp crammed with over 63,000 souls.

Tattered and worn even when Faris had taken them from a dead soldier, the boots were held together with various bits of string and tape. The cell phone was more important than a new pair of boots. The soles were still intact and kept the sharp rocks from biting into his feet.

Walking briskly, avoiding the checkpoints, the boys made the trip to Nablus in less than three hours.

Nablus, Israel
11:00 AM Local Time

Faris and Dabir reached the top of the hill overlooking the quiet town. The taxi carrying Jonas and Viena pulled into the main street of Nablus and headed for the ruins.

Faris snorted, "Look at them. They have money for a taxi. They are going to look at their 'holy place.' That's why they come here—to look and pray. Do they leave any money here?"

Dabir returned hotly, "Never! They come and look and leave. Sometimes they poke at the ruins, like those guys up there."

Pointing to the archeological site on the mount west of Nablus, Dabir ducked quickly.

"Patrol!" he warned.

Both boys knew how to drop and hide and scramble to avoid being seen. They'd been doing it all their lives.

Quietly, with practiced stealth, Faris led the way to the large house at the end of the main street. He tapped lightly at the front door.

"Uncle, Uncle. It's Faris. Let me in."

Massively built, immaculate house robes flowing around him, Fadil opened the door. The next hour was a complete frustration for Faris. Fadil claimed to have no money for the car. Leaving the boys in the small courtyard behind the house, Fadil went about his business.

"I've got to have that car, Dabir. What can we do?"

Dabir shrugged. His name, roughly translated, meant *Secretary*. That's exactly what he was. He could follow Faris' orders, but had no thoughts of his own, other than how to find food and electricity to charge his coveted phone.

Hitching up his trousers, kicking his poor boots at the stone-covered yard, Faris thought hard. Then his face lit up.

"I know. Ransom! We'll kidnap those tourists up there," and he pointed in the general direction of the ruins.

"Uncle will know how to get money for them. Let's go!"

Dabir hesitated.

"Come on! I have to have that car. They told me if I have that car I can do great things for them."

With no real plan in mind, Faris led the way. Both boys carried their rifles. Later, no one could explain why no shots fired. They didn't know that the boys had no money for ammunition.

Faris thought fast. They'd need a distraction. Pulling Dabir along, he pointed to the pile of tires in front of the house.

"Get those! Roll them down there, into the street."

While Dabir made a pile of tires in the silent street, Faris found a can of gasoline, and rummaged quietly in a drawer in the kitchen for some matches. His uncle had shut the door to his bedroom that also served as his office. There was no sound from within.

Aside from the taxi and a few workers on the hill, the small town was very still. It was noon.

Knowing the chance he took, bringing the young couple into an area that could be dangerous, the taxi driver looked in all directions as the trio climbed the hill to the ruins. His taxi had interchangeable license plates, and he'd simply pulled over and turned them as they'd approached the Nablus area. He'd done it hundreds of times for pilgrims who wanted to see the Mountains of Good and Evil and the ruins, rich in religious history. Until today, there had never been a problem.

Out of the corner of his eye, the driver saw the black smoke behind him. Instantly on alert, he beckoned to Jonas. "We have to leave!"

Jonas turned to see two young men charging toward them, rifles pointed directly at him. It was only a moment. The boys were young, strong and armed. At a motion from Faris, Dabir struck the taxi driver over the head with the butt of his rifle.

The workers at the ruins were invisible, having stretched out on the ground for a nap.

Marching Vienna and Jonas down the rocky hillside, Faris saw that the burning tires were keeping the residents' attention. The boys roughly pushed the couple behind a row of tall evergreens, and down the steep incline to the outskirts of Nabuls. No one saw them. In less than twenty minutes, Faris and Dabir forced the couple through the back gate and into the house.

"Uncle. Uncle. I have prisoners."

The look on Fadil's face frightened Faris.

"What have you done, Nephew?" he thundered.

"Ransom money, for my car, Uncle."

Fadil's next words stunned the boy.

"People like you do not kidnap people. They kill them."

Regaining consciousness, the driver staggered down the slope to his taxi. In his haste, he flooded the engine. It took several attempts to start. He couldn't see the attackers, but he was terrified that the noise would catch their attention. Making his way slowly through the streets, taking the back way, he felt dizzy and disoriented. Twice he had to stop the car to shake his head. Blood dripped down the back of his neck, and he swiped at it with the sleeve of his shirt.

At one of the stops, he caught a glimpse of a big man, the two boys and the young couple. Putting his head down below the steering wheel, he peeped over the edge of the window panel. An abandoned shack, half a mile from the end of the road, was their destination. Shoving and pushing the couple, the three opened the sagging door and shoved them inside. The big man carried something. Was it a rope?

Returning to Jerusalem, the driver said nothing for two weeks.

* * *

Fort Benning, Georgia
20 April, 1200 Hours

That morning at PT one of the four Ranger Instructors had screamed at them. The one consolation was that the volume of his voice didn't come close to Sergeant Lee's.

"You're gonna do pushups until *my* elbows explode!"

Informing them there would only be one meal a day, the instructor said, "Today it's lunch."

They'd been reminded again; the building was no longer called a mess hall. In order to be politically correct, it was the DFAC, and they had to pay a price to eat. Stationed at the door, an instructor asked them a question. Only a good answer would allow them to get their meal.

"So, what can you tell me about your Ranger Buddy," was his usual query.

This questioning was not as unreasonable as it seemed. It was not mere prying. It was part of the training, a way to make sure that each Ranger knew as much as possible about each other. The instructors didn't know that the Squadron had already been through the filtering process at Bliss before they started their training, and knew more about each other than most family members. Therefore, the responses took the instructor by surprise.

"Lisa? Oh, she flies our airplane. Had to miss ground week at Airborne to get her rating."

"Yeah, Harlem's my Ranger Buddy. She drives us all crazy because she's so organized, but she can put out a forest fire."

After five or more such responses, the instructor found himself wanting to hear more.

"Annie? Oh, she's a singer. Performed in New York until she joined up."

"What do you want to know about him? He's a doctor. Doc Kurt. Did his residency in Philadelphia. General medicine."

Jonesy replied, deadpan, "My Ranger Buddy's an expert in anti-terrorism. And he's a part-time bodyguard for someone whose name I can't mention."

That night she explained to the group that she hadn't really lied, that Steve was her real buddy. They were too tired to comment.

22 April, 0300 Hours

For weeks Harlem had nagged Mike to sleep in his clothes.

"Just in case, Mike, please?"

He'd wave her away, "Semper Fi, babe!"

Rolling over, he'd fallen asleep in the next breath. That night it caught up with him. Rudely awakened by all four instructors who'd taken out the fireguards and set off grenade simulators, the Squadron leaped out of their bunks and into the street.

"Where's your Ranger Buddy?"

Rubbing her face, Harlem had no idea where Mike had gone, and she said so. It was the wrong thing to say. You never leave your buddy.

"Ranger, make like a Koala Bear, now! And do it upside down."

Lithe and quite capable, Harlem wrapped her arms and legs around the indicated tree, slowly turning herself head down. The only problem was, the bark was wet. She slowly began to slip and finally hit the ground. While the instructors continued to encourage the mayhem, she slithered away and began searching for Mike. She found him, low-crawling down the street, naked, weaving his body around the big rocks.

"And *who* are you?" yelled an instructor.

"I'm his Ranger Buddy," Harlem choked out, barley refraining from laughing.

"Get down there with him, sweet pants Koala bear. Hold his hand and low-crawl your hearts out!"

It was the heat of the moment, and Harlem didn't take offense. Her brothers had called her much worse.

Their humiliation didn't end there. During PT, the instructor picked Harlem out of the Squadron.

"Now if you know where your Ranger Buddy is, you call him."

Swallowing hard, Harlem called out, "Hey, Ranger Buddy."

Dressed in his socks, boots, and hat and nothing else, Mike joined her.

"Hold hands now, Ranger Buddies, and we'll take a walk with the rest of the class."

Their first period of hand-to-hand instruction followed. It was something none of them ever forgot. There was naked Mike, crawling all over Harlem during hand-to-hand.

25 April, 1900 Hours

With the sun hitting their left shoulders, they'd been on the trail all day. Four people had dropped during the march. Kurt had informed the medics trailing the line that it was heat exhaustion, compounded by the rigors of training. Approaching their objective, there were seventy-two of them.

The trail wasn't really a trail; it was an unimproved dirt road, heading northeast from Camp Rogers. Scrub pines, oak and other deciduous and coniferous trees were rich and green from the unseasonably wet winter. Small, dog-sized deer, rabbits, squirrels, armadillos, skunks, possum and rattlesnakes were in the forest, but supposedly only came out at night.

They'd had a safety briefing, which Scott had introduced by saying, "Stay away from Jake the Snake."

Twilight approached. The PI trooped the line.

"Hey! Shitbirds! Tighten it up! Pull it together. I do *not* want to see so much space between you!"

Scott turned, walking faster now in the opposite direction. He continued to shout comments as he made his way around the end of the Squadron and doubled back to the front.

"Lookin' good! Time for some marchin' music!"

Over his shoulder, Scott pointed directly at Annie. "I hear you're a famous Broadway star, Ranger. Give us some tunes."

For some reason, Annie had been marching to a rhythm already set in her head. It was suddenly easy, there in the woods, to let out her voice. If she started low enough, she wouldn't have to warm up.

Freeing her hands, she began clapping, pronouncing the beat for the others.

"Duh! *Duh!* Duh-DuhDhu*Dhu*. Accent the second beat. Make it hard!" she called out.

Clear and clean in the twilight, her voice rose above the sounds of marching boots. setting a faster pace.

"Tau-Mie, tell me! Where'd you get that name?

"Tau-Mie, tell me! Where'd you get that name?

"I heard it was unusual circumstances.

Flaming dances.

Young carriers of bullets.

"Help me pull it out!"

Annie sang the words rhythmically, in perfect cadence, pronouncing each word as cleanly as the bullets she sang about. It took incredible artistry and talent to make the words fit the beat; but Annie was a pro. It was pure sixties rock and roll, with a terrible theme.

"Taum-Mie, tell me!

"I heard it was war time. Dead Time. Dread time. All alone time. No time.

"I heard it was somewhere in the dead of night,

"Somewhere in the dread and heat,

"Somewhere all alone, in the Southeast part of our world!"

"I heard it was your father, a hero, a war man, a sad man,

"Named you for that child-carrier of bullets dead at his feet.

"I heard it was a time we can't forget, must not forget,

"Your father, my mother, your father, my father

"Our Children.

"I heard it was war time, scare time, dead time, dread time

"Life time, world time.

"Tau-Mie, tell me, where'd you get your name?"

Holding up his hand, Scott stopped the Squadron. He turned slowly, speaking in a hoarse undertone.

"Holy Mary, Mother of God."

The way he said it, they knew he wasn't swearing.

"How do you know about those things, Ranger?"

Annie's signature smile, big and bright, flashed in the setting sun.

"My mother wrote it—it's about my half-sister. Her dad died in Viet Nam."

* * *

The eighteen-mile march concluded the first week of Ranger School. It was ugly, but ninety-five percent of them made it through. It was a record. The ones who failed were too smart to feel like failures. They knew that not everyone had the same talents, could pass every test. They were still part of the STC team, on call and willing to do whatever necessary to make STC successful. The ones who made it were philosophical about the remaining days. It was a mindset.

The only comfort in Ranger School was the knowledge that they could do more than they thought they could.

Chapter Fourteen
Military Tactics

I dare not be the aggressor, but rather the defender; I dare not advance an inch, but would rather retreat a foot. This is to move without moving, to raise one's fists without showing them, to lead the enemy on but against no adversary, to wield a weapon but not clash with the enemy's. No disaster is greater than taking the enemy lightly. If I take the enemy lightly, I am on the verge of losing my treasures. Hence, when opposing troops resist each other, the one stung by grief will be the victor.
Lao Tzu

Camp Darby
26 April, 2200 Hours

Memorization was not his strong point, and James whispered relentlessly in the darkness, "FFU, ORP, RRP...FFU, ORP, RRP."

It was driving Jasen crazy and he bent closer to his buddy, "Go to sleep, James."

Animal sounds came from the woods. Clear skies and the waning moon were hidden from view. They'd set up the patrol base in a circle. Covering each flank, three M-60s were at their twelve, four and eight o'clock positions. James shifted under his poncho liner, trying to fit his head more comfortably on the backrest of his rucksack.

Lack of food, the sixty-degree temperature—it felt like thirty—and the need for sleep that wouldn't come, came to blows in James' entire being. He was tempted to ask Jasen to "spoon" with him. At times Buddies did this—cuddling bodies together for warmth.

Instead James held his tongue jammed towards the back of this throat. His whisper was almost silent; a vague undertone that blended into the sighing of the trees.

"Gimme your woobie, Jase, I'm frozen."

Pulling the poncho from his shoulders, Jasen quietly placed it over his buddy. The civil rights expert was content to crouch in the stillness. He rarely had a chance to reflect on personal thoughts. Annie's song was still running in his head. He was relieved to discover that Ranger School no longer included live fire training.

By now they were familiar with the priorities of work. Kurt had repeated it to the twelve people in his squad.

"Okay, people, here's the deal. Security is first priority. Second priority is weapons maintenance. Third is eating."

Rotation of assigned duties gave each of them a chance to achieve the necessary grades. While James had cleaned his weapon, Jasen pulled security. Then they flip-flopped. Pulling out his MRE, James had gulped the remaining food, barely taking time to chew. He'd made it last all day, eating a bite now and then when he couldn't stand the gnawing hunger another moment. Keeping watch, Jasen could hear him swallow heavily. Again, they'd traded places, but Jasen's food for the day was already gone. They'd been allotted a thirty-minute sleep cycle, but James wasn't sleeping.

"Friendly Forward Unit. Objective Rally Point. Reentry Rally Point. I've got it now."

Reviewing the scenario, hoping he'd perform well, the archeologist dozed.

Yesterday, the eighteen-mile, tactical march had brought them to Camp Darby. The day had ended badly. With their goal in sight, a line of trainees had marched along the edge of a washout. They'd been cautioned, but for some reason—probably lack of sleep—the forewarning escaped their attention. One person angled too close, and the next followed. By the time the third pair of boots hit the rim the dirt began to crumble. All twelve had bumped and rolled to the bottom of a thirty-foot gully. Hearing the shouts and rumbles of their bodies and gear, Scott shook his head.

"Hey! We're down here!"

Scott had kept walking. Ignoring their shouts, he led the rest around the washout. He'd figure out a way to extract them later.

27 April, 0400 Hours

They were back in one piece, but if Harrison thought about it too much, he'd kick himself. He should've been able to find the opening. The RI's AAR had been painful. It was pure luck, in Harrison's opinion, that they wouldn't have to repeat the phase.

He'd been able to hold it together all night, but only by concentrating on keeping Kurt from losing it. During brief periods when they could talk, Kurt would discuss the weight of the rucksacks and which one of them had the most blisters. They realized the whole thing was about getting dirty, going without sleep, working until you hit the inner core and the realization that you can't do it alone. They'd all had to get past that barrier, fighting through pressure and tension. At Harrison's suggestion they'd changed the conversation to the ocean, and the beach.

It wasn't that they hadn't been advised. During the first week, Scott had devoted an entire hour to what they'd be carrying before introducing a vast array of military skills they'd master.

"An eighteen-mile march, or staying in the field, is not that much fun. Although the mission load is dependent on the mission specifics, you can count on carrying between fifty and eighty-five pounds."

It seemed more like a month ago—rather than a week—that Scott had picked up an empty rucksack from the table in a classroom at Benning.

"You will always have your night vision device, aimpoint sight, ANPEQ-4—that's your night laser sight—personal hygiene kit, weapons cleaning kit, poncho liner, extra pair of socks and T-shirt, rations, water and ammunition."

Swinging the rucksack back and forth in front of them, Scott spoke soothingly, intimately. The swaying and his voice were hypnotic. Eyelids had drooped.

"Your rations are MRE—Meals Ready to Eat. Your poncho liner is your blanket, your woobie."

Scott grinned wickedly as he saw one pair of eyes close fully.

"Ranger! Front and center!" he'd bellowed at Carp, who had begun to drool, oblivious, in a deep sleep. "In the old days, Ranger, we used to make a sleepy-head drone like you go to the back of the room and hold up a big rock with the Ranger tab painted on it. You'd hold it until you fell asleep. The rock on your head would drop you. We'd drag your sorry ass out back and make you do pushups to wake up."

Weaving slightly, trying to make sense out of Scott's words, the tall carpenter pushed out his chest, taking deep breaths.

"So if you see some RI with scars on his head, most of 'em came from dropping rocks in the classroom, not enemy encounters."

Screaming at Carp, Scott had directed him out the door.

"The rock is gone, but the pushups remain. I want a hundred. Wake up, Ranger. Wake up!"

Glaring around the room, Scott had picked up the rucksack again.

"Who's this guy's Ranger Buddy?"

Bobbie stood.

"You can tell him the rest later. You'll be wearing your LBV—oh, and your first aid kit will be in here. You'll carry your M-4's. Some of you will carry radios and others will carry demolitions. Remember, what you carry is mission dependent. Most of the missions center around small unit tactics…"

The lecture had continued as if there had been no interruption.

Tonight's raid had been their first—and most difficult. It'd only lasted seven hours, but it'd seemed a lifetime. Spending most of the day in the planning bay, Kurt had stood at a chalkboard set up under a flat roof that barely kept the rain off. Five other squads were similarly engaged. At RI changeover, the RI had established the chain of command.

"Ranger Kurt, you get to be Queen for a Day. You've got ten minutes to get your shit together."

Harrison had blinked slowly, knowing the rest of the Squad got the joke; funnier because the RI didn't realize what he'd said.

The five-paragraph operations order had been described in detail.

"Listen to what you're told, and you'll pass. No sweat."

Listening and understanding were two different things. What with the need for sleep and huger nibbling away at their reserves, it was easy to listen; difficult to understand—and even harder to accomplish. Words like: Situation, Mission, Execution, Service and Support, Command and Signal flowed from the RI's mouth like warm honey. They struggled to comprehend the details of call signs and radio frequencies.

The RI had named two team leaders, subordinate to each squad leader. Assisted by Harrison as RTO and Annie as machine gunner, Kurt would navigate. Kurt's suggestion for a two-hour sleep rotation had brought the ever-alert Scott to his side. Tapping Kurt on the back, Scott waved a finger at him, pulling him aside where the others couldn't hear.

"If you give them boys two hours, you won't have any security."

Taking the hint, Kurt had walked back to announce they could sleep in thirty-minute rotations. The planning, under Kurt's direction had gone well. Making Kurt navigator was the only mistake.

Led by Kurt, Harrison and the others had managed to get through FFU Charlie. From the inner circle of the patrol base, at all four cardinal points, was a path through concertina and barbed wire. Half a mile long, windy and treacherous with razors and barbs, the paths led from the base to the woods. Going out from the patrol base was one thing; finding the small opening at the other end, returning in the dead of night, was another. Barbs surrounding the small opening in the line had torn at them as they'd walked into bad guy territory.

Kurt had identified the ORP, and moved ahead to scope out the enemy layer. He knew that the encampment consisted of dedicated OPFOR—opposing forces—structured the same as a regular Army platoon, but acting as the enemy. With Support laying down a heavy volume of fire, and Assault aggressively charging cross the objective, the raid had been a rousing success.

They'd moved back to the ORP, collecting gear, checking for casualties; readying everything to get back to the reentry point. That's when things had fallen apart. Trying to locate the break in the wire where they'd come out was like finding a doorway in the middle of the woods. After stumbling for thirty minutes through the trees, Kurt and Harrison thought they'd found the place.

The RI's After Action Review, shouted overly loud—in Harrison's opinion—had dropped Kurt's head.

"On the leader's recon for the FFU, Ranger Kurt's inability to land navigate placed him three hundred meters west of the FFU."

Delivered in bursts, the review had two purposes—to explain why the patrol had been compromised, and to watch the squad for reactions.

"In Ranger Kurt's quest to find the FFU he was engaged by the defending unit. Ranger Kurt and his Ranger Buddy IMT'd away from the engagement and moved back to the RRP."

Beginning to shake his head, the RI had spoken scathingly.

"While they were IMTing back, I walked behind them, in disgust— disgust, I tell you. I've been to county fairs where the clowns outperformed what you did today. Ranger Kurt, your navigation was piss-poor."

Six weeks later, Kurt would redeem himself and earn a major plus spot report.

They planned all day, went out all night—coming back at dawn to begin again. The next twelve days consisted of raids, ambushes and reconnaissance mission, one after another like inexorable waves. It was an endless blur of repetition.

* * *

Columbus, Georgia
5 May, 0600 Hours

"Scott, you're up early."

Patting the covers, his wife encouraged him to return to bed.

"Naw. I gotta do some thinkin', sweetheart. You go back to sleep."

It was Saturday, and Scott had surprised his wife at three in the morning. Leaving the Squadron in the capable hands of the other instructors was not out of line. Scott needed a few hours at home alone to review some things surrounding the group under his tutelage.

For one thing, he'd learned something that had left him dumbfounded; but had answered some of the questions that had plagued him. They obviously trusted him, and for some reason this pleased Scott immeasurably. Scott had already figured out that orders for a civilian group to be admitted to the school, would probably have come from the TRADOC—the entity overseeing the activities of Rangers at Benning. What surprised him was that TRADOC had been contacted by SOCOM, who had been contacted by JSOC. Orders to JSOC had come down from the National Command Authority. The Squadron under his training had contacts all the way to the top.

They'd told him that their instructions had included the possibility of sharing this information, should they decide to do so. They explained that Balke's friend, General Jamison, had personally selected Scott. The funny thing was, Scott had never heard of the man.

Additionally, there was the way the entire Squadron avoided the Blue Falcon. Each Ranger student knew they had to be on their game at all times. No one wanted to be a Spotlight Ranger; but the temptation was usually too strong. It was far too easy to avoid undue notice by swinging the attention to one's Ranger Buddy, letting any blame fall there, rather then on oneself. Scott had seen it over and over again. It always happened. The instructors expected it and used it to their advantage. Stress from the high risk missions, the peer reports, lack of sleep, need for food, all played a part in producing this phenomenon. The effect was called Buddy-Fucking—Blue Falcon.

Scott could observe Blue Falcon, swooping predictably over STC Squadron. The next day, it vanished. The entire group—whether they were separated into two-Buddy teams, twelve-person squads, or larger platoons—somehow avoided the very human tendency to rat on a friend to avoid criticism.

The previous morning, when the squads had returned, he'd found Bill, Jennifer, Lisa, Don and the other eleven working in pairs, performing smooth, slow movements that reminded Scott vaguely of unarmed combat. He'd never seen anything like it. They should have been sleeping, and he told them so.

"You look like a bunch of those weighted, round-bottom dolls," he'd whispered.

Bill had motioned Scott over, "Join us, if you like."

It was unprecedented, but he did. After an hour, Scott had started to move away from the group. He turned back.

"Ya'll know about Blue Falcon?"

They'd nodded. Kurt stepped forward, speaking softly.

"When I was doing my residency there were hours and hours when I didn't sleep. Then some emergency would come in. I didn't get the operation; I had to assist someone else who'd get the glory for saving a life. I learned early on to support all the players. Next time it'd be me, relying on them."

Each question they answered brought up another one.

* * *

Jerusalem
7 May, 1100 Hours Local Time

The taxi driver had never entered the hotel; only picked up and dropped off guests. It was two weeks ago that he'd been hit over the head. When he'd told his wife, she'd nagged him every day to report the event. He gave in to her demands, creeping to the front desk. Keeping his face covered, he spoke quickly, in short sentences.

The astounded clerk called to the driver who had whirled, running through the lobby and out the front entrance.

"Come back!"

Hearing the commotion, the manager came to the front desk.

"What is the matter with you? We never shout in this hotel."

After explaining, the clerk stood by and watched as his employer picked up the phone.

"Is this the American Embassy?"

* * *

Camp Darby
15 May, 1100 Hours

The truck found them at Darby Queen—reportedly the nastiest obstacle course in the civilized world. Teamwork was everything. There was no way you could complete the course without it. Carrying a large canvas pouch, the driver made his way towards the RI.

"Put it down, Private. I'll take it from here."

The RI watched the squadron straggle back from the course to stand in formation.

"Form up. Form up. We're gonna have six hours R & R before we head out to the mountains. You get to do peer reports."

Pointing to the canvas bag at his feet, the RI grinned.

"First things first, however," and the RI let out a roar, "Mail Call!"

No privacy was allowed. The instructor stood in front of each person receiving letters or packages, watching carefully to make sure no contraband—gum, cigarettes or chew—were enclosed.

Mike opened a box with his name printed on the label. He didn't recognize the return address. Lying neatly folded on top was a white T-shirt. As Mike shook it out, wondering who'd sent it, the Squadron caught a glimpse of the imprint. In beautifully embroidered black script was the message:

Semper Fi! Be Prepared. Wear something at night!

No one ever admitted sending it to him. Months later, Mike mailed it to Fang Mei to add to her collection.

* * *

Jerusalem, American Embassy
20 May, 0600 Hours Local Time

For nearly two weeks, the Ambassador had thought again and again about the so-called kidnapping at Nablus. He'd been unable to verify the report with anyone. The couple in question was honeymooning. They could be anywhere. If what the hotel manager had told him were true, the couple would have been missing for a month. Surely someone would have called to inquire. He'd taken the short trip to Nablus, and finding nothing out of place, returned to his office.

The hotel was still trying to identify the taxi driver, but no one could find him.

It was too bizarre to be true, but he couldn't stop thinking about it.

These days, the Embassy had one very simple regulation regarding visitors to Israel:

"You're on your own," tourists were told.

Nonetheless the Ambassador felt he had to do something. He remembered meeting a Navy Commander at a State dinner he'd attended. They'd spent several hours discussing music, and their careers. The highly decorated Naval Officer had hinted at some new group being formed, some special diplomatic corps…the Ambassador couldn't remember the details. Perhaps, with his connections, Balke would know what to do.

The Ambassador waited three more weeks before making the call.

* * *

Dahlonega, Georgia, Camp Frank D. Merrill
27 May, 0500 Hours

Human nature normally dictates that a group will choose the most capable person to do a specific task. This tendency often backfires, as Ranger students repeatedly pick the same people to do the same tasks. Those chosen wear themselves out and become ineffective. In the case of STC Squadron, the reverse was true. Squad leaders learned early on to pick the least capable person. The physicist from San Francisco, Don, had pointed out the fallacy.

Doing poorly as RTO, Bobbie was chosen for that position until he got the hang of it. Kurt learned land navigation perfectly. Scott had never seen a group that learned the basics so quickly.

Thirteen days ago, a Blackhawk, UH-60, helicopter had dropped them in groups of twelve. For a week, half the class had practiced lower mountaineering; rappelling, knot tying, scrambling up and down sixty-foot cliffs. Comprised of platoon-sized elements, patrols had filled the nights and days of the other half.

During the second week, Ted had arrived. He'd participated in small unit tactics, observing with the other RI's. The SEAL was impressed with the Squadron.

When the team had a moment to rest or eat, Ted and Bill would take them through various stances, speaking softly—or not speaking at all. Leaning casually against a tree, Scott observed, wondering what motivated these people.

As he watched this morning, a phrase from the Greek philosopher Thucydides, surfaced:

"Of all the manifestations of power, restraint impresses men most."

Scott was impressed.

Annie stood braced against a two hundred foot cliff. Nearing the conclusion of the upper mountaineering phase, she and George were roped together. They'd practiced stirrup climbing, boulder climbing and free climbing, but it was these last few days that they'd been completely in their element.

There was something about Tennessee Valley Divide and Mount Yonah that enthralled them. It wasn't only their surroundings. They took pleasure in the feeling of freedom and the thrill of being tied together, dependent only on each other as they climbed higher and higher.

Worried about their size match up, the RI watched them carefully. There was more than one reason for his vigilance. At times, daring Annie to belay his weight, George yelled out, "Falling!" Challenging Annie several times, when there was no real fall, the RI was more than a little annoyed with George. The other reason was more important.

The RI questioned Annie's ability to belay the weight, if George did fall. In a way, he felt sorry for George because his buddy was at least thirty pounds lighter.

Suddenly, slipping from his perch, George plummeted.

"Falling!" he cried out, this time in earnest.

Rapidly, Annie had him locked in. The engineer fell only a few feet. Annie's major plus spot report left her in a glow for several hours.

* * *

Debbie DZ, Eglin Air Force Base, Florida
30 May, 2100 Hours

They had thirty minutes from the time they touched the ground. Jumping from the C 141 Starlifter under cover of darkness, their mission instructions were clear. They were to pick up ranger buddies, form into fire teams, and make their way to the assembly point. The directions they'd been given were easy enough to follow: the northwest corner of the drop zone, at eleven o'clock.

Harassing fire plunked at them, but they knew it was all part of the scenario. No one would shoot them in the face.

* * *

Yellow River, Florida
10 June, 0200 Hours

"Here we go," Bill quietly called to his boat crew, "Ones! Enter the boat. Twos! Enter the boat. Threes! Enter the boat."

As coxswain, he'd give the paddle count. The small, F470 Zodiac held twelve. Kurt, navigating, sat in the middle of the boat along with the rucksacks. Poncho over his head, he held the map carefully on his knees. From the faint glow of the red-lens mag light, he barely made out their position. It was pouring down rain.

Bill's quiet instructions rose above the sounds of the paddles. They'd practiced until—even half-asleep—they could keep the paddles from smacking into each other.

"Even numbers, give way together! Odd! Steer in the river. All! Give way together!"

Bill was the best, and his voice lulled them.

"Dammit!"

The call was louder than it should have been, and Bill thought they'd unexpectedly hit a stump. But there was no jar. The rhythm broke as all eyes fastened on a water moccasin, wriggling at the end of one of the paddles. Poking his head out of the Poncho, Kurt identified the serpent.

"No worries, folks. Relax. Shake it off."

The paddling continued.

Eyes again on the map, Kurt called softly to Bill.

"Left bank, two hundred meters."

He was dead on.

* * *

Fort Benning, Georgia
13 June, 0400 Hours

Upon their return to Benning, Bill called his teacher in Taipei. Although Bill's Mandarin was at sixth grade level and Lao Shir's English was broken, they communicated quite well. Normally in contact through Email or phone at least once a month, Bill was eager to converse with the elderly master.

"Lao Shir, it's Bill, in America."

It was a term of respect—not the man's name—and meant *teacher*

What Bill's teacher told him prompted him to call Commander Balke.

* * *

15 June, 1200 Hours

With even less fan fare than the ceremony at McGregor, STC Squadron graduated from Ranger School. The quiet ceremony was held in the Ranger Hall of Fame. The only guests were Steve, Ted, and Scott's wife and children. Delivering a low-key congratulatory speech, Scott looked out over their faces. He knew he'd hear from some of them again. Calling Bill forward, Scott shook his hand warmly. He handed Bill a small black box.

"A gift from the RI's, Bill."

Inside the box was a Ranger's Ring—specially crafted. Set in 18-karat gold was a blue sapphire. Scott pointed out the three letters engraved on the inside of the band. He'd obviously paid attention during the Squadron's quiet nighttime discussions.

"Star, Truth, Country," he said.

Walking slowly from the building, Bill and Scott said goodbye.

"I understand you plan to retire in three years, Scott. Do you have any plans?"

Pulling a battered business card from the pocket of his BDU's, Bill handed it to Scott.

"Call anytime."

Chapter Fifteen
The First Boy

While your parents live, do not wander far.
Let your sojourning be only in specified places.
The Analects of Confucius

Soquel, California
16 June, 1800 Hours

A second explosion, even more stunning than the one on Easter Sunday, not only destroyed the aircraft—another empty 747—but also blew away half the hanger and a jetway parked nearby. As it grew dark, the brilliance lit up the entire area.

The boy shivered. Hugging his knees, he wanted nothing more than to sit on his mother's lap and plan the rest of it in her comforting arms. Her footsteps clattered on the wooden steps and she walked into his private room, unannounced. His head snapped up, guilt written clearly on his face.

"Bobby, what are you doing?"

Jumping up to throw his arms around her neck, Bobby kissed her loudly.

"Not much, Mom. Just playing around."

Alice Hendricks knew her son as well as any mother could know a teenager.

"Okay, Bobby, where were you all day, and why didn't you answer your phone? We gave you that phone so we'd be able to keep in touch."

Bobby shrugged, "A bunch of us, Mom, drove around. You know I can't talk in front of them."

Smiling indulgently at her only child, Alice felt her heart contract. He was so beautiful.

"Okay, but dinner's ready, and I'll bet you're starved. Your father had to go out of town again. He's still hoping for a flying job, but it looks like he might have to settle for something else."

Conversing quietly, arms around each other's waists, Bobby and his mother climbed up the stairs.

Midnight

"Mom, don't worry. I'll be back soon. I need some time alone. My phone is off, but I'll turn in on tomorrow, I promise. I love you. B."

Bobby read the note one more time before slipping it into an envelope. Tiptoeing across the hall to his parent's bedroom, he could make out the lump that was his mother. She was sleeping soundly.

When he reached the dining room, Bobby propped the note against one of the silver candlesticks. That's where they always left messages for one another.

Without a sound, Bobby went to the basement. Picking up his disc player and a selection of CDs, he jammed them into his backpack next to his cell phone and a ticket to New York. The flight was scheduled to leave San Francisco at 7:00 AM. He was ready.

* * *

San Francisco International Airport
0545 Hours

It was a whole lot easier than he thought it'd be; they never even looked at his disc player. They let him put it in the little basket along with his phone and keys, and handed it back to him after he passed through the metal detector. In his shirt pocket was the receipt from long-term parking. Bobby took a deep breath and sat waiting to be called to board the airplane.

0745 Hours

"We're sorry for the delay, folks, but we can begin boarding now."
Bobby smiled as he handed his boarding pass to the agent.
"Have a good flight."
Bobby knew there would be no flight.

0815 Hours

Leaving his seat belt unbuckled, Bobby waited patiently as the airplane taxied to position. He'd been listening to ground control on the headset provided by the airline. There'd be another delay before they'd be cleared for takeoff. It was all working perfectly. His chance came when the cabin crew took their seats. Removing the disk player from his backpack, Bobby stood up, crouching in the dim lighting.

With ease, he slipped past them all. They never even saw him, busy with their own thoughts and conversations. The key worked exactly right.

He was in the cockpit.

"I've got a bomb!"

* * *

Fort Bliss, STC Headquarters
17 June, 1000 Hours

The CASA landed smoothly at Biggs airfield.

All but two of the passenger seats were filled with fifteen members of STC Squadron and the two advisors. Eager to see the inside of the new airplane, Steve and Ted had hitched a ride from Benning. The rest of the group went home to be with family and friends until the first of July. The planned rotation would keep no less than twelve people at Bliss at all times.

Balke had provided a van. Parked on the apron, the driver flagged them down.

"STC? I don't know if this'll hold all of you."

Piled on top of each other, duffels squeezed around their feet, they headed for Fort Bliss. Pulling into a parking space, the driver looked over her shoulder at Bill.

"Commander Balke told me he wants to see you all. Now, Sir."

Pounding up the stairs, they trooped into the room. Balke was waiting. Anyone who knew him would recognize his expression immediately. Time could never completely wipe out habits that were formed before and during tense situations. Balke was on alert mode, deliberately calm. He greeted the returning squadron.

"Folks, let me congratulate you on fine work. Reports from your instructors gave you highest marks."

Balke rubbed his nose deliberately, moving to stand in front of twenty folding chairs.

"Please find a chair. This will be a briefing."

Chairs scraped as seventeen people, now silent, found places.

"I got a call thirty minutes ago from Captain Jack up in Berkeley. There's a hostage taker on an airplane at San Francisco International. FBI is on the scene. Nobody knows who the hostage taker is. They believe it could be a terrorist, but Jack disagrees. Nothing fits the profile. He wants our suggestions, folks."

Looking directly at Bobbie, Balke paused.

"Okay, Bobbie. What're your thoughts? You've called me twice about some inside information you think you have. Does this fit in somehow?"

Without missing a beat, Bobbie began to fire questions.

"What time did Jack call? Why did he call us? When did this happen. How long ago? How many passengers? Who exactly is on the scene? What about the press?"

Looking around the group, Bobbie continued thinking aloud.

"Harrison, I'm gonna need you, man—Carp, you too. Lisa, we'll need that plane of yours, and your co-captain. Have him get the CASA refueled. Don, I want you on media. Kurt, you'd better come too."

Bobbie grew silent, nodding at Balke, who began to answer Bobbie's questions.

"Jack called at 1030 hours—0930 his time. Turns out that the FBI commander is an old buddy of his. Jack told him we're experts. The airplane was taken as it taxied to position—uh, at 0815 Pacific Time—a little over two hours ago. Including crew, there are 325 people on board. Airport, Daly City, San Francisco, San Bruno and FBI are there. No press yet—that they're aware of."

"I'll need some equipment, Commander."

"Jack will get you anything you want, Bobbie."

Balke continued, "Lisa, they've established a base of operations at a Coast Guard Air Station positioned at the northeast end of the airport."

Balke hesitated momentarily, "One last thing, Bobbie. It's only a rumor, but Jack thinks they've got a recording of a voice."

When Bobbie climbed aboard the airplane they'd left only an hour ago, something popped into his mind. Later, when he put all the pieces together, he'd recognize the hypnologic suggestion. It was Father's Day.

San Francisco International Airport
1000 Hours

For the first hour, craning his neck to watch out the left window, he'd seen cars and trucks racing crazily towards the airplane. They'd veered off and disappeared underneath the belly of the jet. Two large, black vehicles were parked next to a low building about two thousand feet away, behind the airplane's left wing. When they'd first pulled up, Bobby counted at least fifty people piling out of the armored vehicles. All of them carried guns. They were still swarming around the airplane.

They hid behind their trucks and cars, peeking up at the cockpit. Once in a while they'd yell at him through a bullhorn—or maybe it was the pilot they wanted to talk to. Bobby had covered his ears, carefully keeping the headset cord to the disc player positioned in one hand. The men in the cockpit had only moved once.

Bobby had yelled, "Don't get up! Stay in your seats or I'll pull it out!"

The captain had started to answer.

"Shut up!" Bobby had screamed.

Bobby saw some of the men outside positioning themselves around the airplane. A few walked away to go inside or behind the building. They were probably eating and laughing. Bobby's stomach growled, and he bit his lip.

They'd taken turns peeing into a bag the captain provided, and there was bottled water to drink. But there was no food.

Since he'd told the pilot how the bomb worked, they'd left him alone.

He'd told the pilot to turn off the radios after delivering the report. At his instructions, the crew had stopped asking questions.

It was hot in the cockpit, and his hands were sweaty. Holding the disc player was very tiresome, and his right hand on the headset cord kept slipping. Every now and again, he'd wipe it quickly on his pants.

The initial burst of adrenalin had worn off long ago, and Bobby wasn't sure what to do next. The truth was, he'd never known exactly what it was that he wanted.

1540 Hours

"Ground, CASA November 35388, request taxi to Coast Guard Station, North."

Lisa's voice was expected by ground control, and directions followed instantly. Light winds from West/Southwest had made a fuel stop unnecessary, and the 994-mile trip from Biggs had taken exactly four hours and forty minutes.

The airport was a mess, and at first the tower had directed her to divert to Marin County. An alert FAA official in the tower immediately countermanded the instructions, clearing Lisa to land on a short runway normally used by the Coast Guard.

The active runway was blocked by the silent 747.

The CASA's short runway performance was as excellent as they'd been told. They could pick out Captain Jack, standing in front of the building.

"FBI's here, Bobbie, good to see you."

Escorting them inside, Jack introduced the team to the FBI operations commander who greeted the team warmly.

"Thanks coming, folks. As you can see, it's a zoo."

Motioning around the building, the commander's hand came to rest on his jacket pocket. He pulled out a rumpled white handkerchief and mopped his face.

Regional mutual aid SWAT teams from San Francisco, Daly City, San Bruno and San Mateo police, and the airport police—who had followed the mutual aid binder—were already in place by the time the FBI had arrived. Coordinated at first by SFPD, they'd set up negotiations, tactical, communication links, emergency medical, relief and refreshments. Turning over field command to the FBI was not a problem. It was standard procedure.

Six-person tactical teams, trained for rapid deployment, were ready to move. Their orders—to enter immediately, locate and neutralize the situation—were in a holding pattern. Team leaders, assistant leaders, point and scout people, high group snipers and their backups, stood ready. Each team member had changed into BDUS. Most had worn jeans and light jackets over their T-shirts when they'd arrived.

They'd put on soft body armor. Hard body vests with ceramic plating to increase the withstanding capabilities, were also available. Many wore ballistic helmets, black and imposing. Their gloves were a NOMEX product, and they'd donned bala clavas; full face hoods. Flash bang goggles were in place and all of them carried some type of fully automatic weapon—HK 53, 33 or MP 5. Some carried two. Most side arms were equipped with TAC lights or laser sighting systems.

Four people had been assigned to each of the airplane's eight entry points. The total number of personnel, including three STC, stood at one hundred and twenty.

The commander sighed, "Airport Police, SFPD, Daly City PD, and

San Bruno PD swarming all over the place. We've got crisis teams, tactical teams, high groups, negotiators...there must be a hundred or more people out there, and no one's got a clue."

Glancing at his watch, the FBI agent looked up at the small group standing shoulder to shoulder in the small office the National Guard had turned over to him.

"It's been dead silence since the first report. Any ideas?"

Bobbie was angry. For the last four hours he'd been mulling over possibilities. Now he was ninety-nine percent sure.

"Sir, can I hear the tape?"

Headset in place, Bobbie listened carefully.

Bobbie knew exactly what they'd been trying to do when he'd accepted the headset from the primary negotiator. The negotiator had been trying to talk to the hostage taker. The secondary stood back, eyes wide open at the change in procedure. She'd been prompting her senior, helping with questions, keeping him on track—all to no avail. They'd chosen words carefully, attempting to become friendly and sympathetic. There was no response.

It was doubly frustrating because they were hampered by the necessity of keeping to the policies—don't give up anything, don't exchange anything.

The intelligence officer had tried to get information for the team, but with nothing to go on, it had been an uphill battle. He didn't know if weapons or drugs were involved. Hell, he didn't even know who was up there.

In charge of all communications between the teams, the liaison didn't run messages because there weren't any.

The fifth person on the negotiating team was the press officer. Normally interacting with other Public Information Officers in other units, he had a direct link with the teams. He was not prepared to brief any media.

The situation was in total deadlock when Bobbie had asked to listen to the tape.

"I've got a bomb!"

There was a brief silence, then the pilot's voice.

"Tower, 747 heavy, unable to comply. Bomb in the cockpit."

Then silence.

Bobbie rewound the tape.

"I've got a bomb."

Once more.

"I've got a bomb."

Yanking the headset from his head, Bobbie stared intensely at the commander.

"Back 'em off, Commander."

The FBI field commander's jaw had dropped.

"I can't do that," he said to Bobbie.

"Sir, I have reason to believe your terrorist hostage taker is actually a young American. Possibly the son of someone the airline has recently fired. Can you get me a list of all pilots recently laid off or retired from this airline, and someone who knows them personally?"

The commander nodded, quickly opening the door and waving to an airline official that'd been on standby all day.

Within fifteen minutes, Bobbie had his list. It took him another ten minutes with the airline official to select three names.

Three quick phone calls took another five minutes. Carp crossed off all but one name. Alice Hendricks didn't know where her son was. The airline official—sweating now—read the name with a shaky voice, adding details from memory.

"Captain Bob Hendricks. Lives in Soquel, near Santa Cruz. Wife's Alice. Son's about seventeen—named after his dad. Bobby. Bob retired, oh, maybe six months ago."

The anger in Bobbie's dark eyes bored directly into the airline official's forehead.

"Retired, or laid off. Which is it?"

He couldn't look the man in the eyes.

"Uh—well, he was asked to retire, if that's what you mean. They decided to hire some new boys and, well…Bob was getting close to retirement anyway."

Bobbie shook his head in disgust.

"Carp, call Alice back. Tell her you're coming to visit, and that you need to see her son's computer. Harrison, I need you to go too, man, but leave Kurt here…just in case. Find out where that kid's been on the Internet. Lisa, find the closest airport to, uh—Soquel. Don, watch for any media, and keep this group working together! Carp when you hang up from Alice, get a car to…"

Lisa flagged him, "Watsonville. It's ten minutes from Soquel."

"…Watsonville airport. Lisa'll tell you where to have it sent."

Bobbie turned to the FBI field commander, speaking quietly.

"Sir, that boy in the cockpit is scared and unstable. He probably doesn't know what he's doing—other than striking back at those who stole his father's career. I'm sending my team to the boy's house. They'll find out what we need to know, and bring the boy's parents back here. In the meantime, back 'em off!"

Bobbie turned, nodding towards the door leading to the apron.

"I'm headed out there, Commander, and I want to see all the teams away."

Bobbie stopped momentarily, facing the commander.

"In the meantime, if you've got more to say, put on a headset. Let everyone hear, including the boy—if he's listening."

Grabbing a headset, the Commander followed Bobbie through the door. He pulled at Bobbie's arm. Bobbie ignored him, taking a stance in full view of the airplane.

"Commander, please comply. We need to give that boy some space, some time."

Then Bobbie stood quietly. Not moving. If the boy were watching, he'd be able to see the headset, and his lips moving. Maybe he'd turn on the radio.

"Commander?"

Eyes on Bobbie, the FBI official adjusted his microphone. He had a decision to make. Jack had vouched for this team. The BSHNT leader was a personal friend of his. They went way back. What he said say now could end in tragedy, or it could save many lives. He took a deep breath.

"Okay folks. Move away from the airplane."

He looked intently at Bobbie, "You've got an hour. Then we move back. That's all the time I can give you."

The field commander walked back into the building.

Dressed in BDU's, Bobbie stood staring at the huge airplane.

"Carp, first thing, ask Alice if her son's a skier."

They were flying over a beautiful mountain, the ocean in sight ahead of them. Tiny cars wound, bumper to bumper over a narrow, winding, four-lane highway beneath them. Carp had been dozing. He'd learned to sleep anywhere.

He yawned, "Sure thing, Harrison. What're you doin'?"

Harrison's fingers had been flying over the keyboard of his laptop since takeoff.

"If Bobbie's right, this kid made the bomb at home. I'm writing a program to find out where he got information, in case the kid was smart enough to get rid of any URLs."

Stretching, Carp gazed out the round window.

"Must be people coming back from the beach," he commented.

Harrison continued to talk in a low monotone.

"See, information is stored in these blocks, ½ K or 1 K, or 2 K, depending on the particular file system. So there's a block of say, 1,024 bytes, which can store about 1,000 characters. The blocks are scattered around the disc. There's pointers...well, anyway, when you delete files, all it does is erase the entry in the master block, and puts it on a free list. I'm writing a program that'll arrange 'em in the right order. I can do it faster than trying to find a program that's already written."

Not computer literate, Carp had no idea what he was talking about. He watched the Pacific Ocean growing closer and closer over the nose of the airplane.

Soquel, California
1615 Hours

"Something's happened to Bobby. I know it, Bob. What's going on?"

Hendricks soothed his wife who was clutching their son's note. She caressed the paper, smoothing it, reading it over and over again.

Arriving home at three this afternoon, he'd opened the door to his nearly hysterical wife. She'd waved the note in his face, screaming at him.

"Bobby's in trouble, Bob," she shouted, as if it were his fault.

The phone calls had aroused Alice even more.

"Carp. What kind of a name is that for an official? Who is he? Why does he want to see Bobby's computer? What's he done?"

By now, Alice was crying openly, her sobs wracking at her body.

"Honey, hold on, now. Everything's fine. We'll find out soon enough. If it'll make you feel any better, I can have Grace come by. She's your best friend."

As he reached for the phone, the doorbell rang.

"I don't want Grace, I want Bobby," she snapped at him.

"Mr. Hendricks, my name is Carp. This is Harrison. Lisa is our pilot."

Bob took one look at the trio, dressed in Army battle dress; with some strange patch on the shoulders, and his heart sank. Some National Guard Unit, he wondered?

"Can we come in, please, sir?"

Alice came to stand by her husband. It was a bad dream. She'd wake up soon and find that all this would be a nightmare. But she didn't wake up. And it was a nightmare—real and devastatingly frightening.

"Mr. Hendricks, we have reason to believe that your son, Bobby, is holding a bomb in the cockpit of a 747 at SFO."

Carp's words, spoken calmly, nevertheless brought Hendricks out of his silence.

"Come in, please, come in."

Walking quietly, Lisa stood on the other side of Alice, not touching her.

Carp asked, "Mr. Hendricks, is your son a skier? Has he been skiing recently?"

Bob looked at his wife.

She nodded, "Yes, he was at Squaw, I think, last weekend. What's going on?"

Hysterics held at bay, Alice was numb with the effort.

"Where's your son's computer?"

1700 Hours

"Yeah, Bobbie. I've got it. C-4, picked up at a ski resort. The kid's smart, but not too smart. He's gotta be under tremendous stress. Be careful."

Harrison listened, cell phone held in his shoulder as he looked at the screen.

"Near as I can figure, the kid molded it in his disc player, rigged maybe a two inch fuse to the blasting cap, ran it to the detonator in the jack of the headset. Probably using the batteries. Yeah. When he pulls the headset, Boom! Maybe, *maybe,* one minute delay. Oh, and Bobbie, the kid has this incredible game. Looks like he practiced blowing up airplanes. C-4 is stable, but the kid's not. Use caution."

Poking around the basement floor, Carp had discovered traces of the grayish-white substance still clinging to a foil wrapper stuffed in a wastebasket. Carp could imagine the boy, jimmying open a storage shed at the ski resort, finding the explosive in an ammo box, knowing that the ski patrol now preferred to use it for avalanche control...it was common knowledge.

Huddled in a corner, the boy's parents watched and listened, not interrupting the proceedings. By this time, Lisa was holding Alice's hand, squeezing it gently now and again.

"Try not to worry, Alice. We'll fly you to San Francisco. It's going to be fine."

Alice reached out a tentative hand, running her fingers down one of Lisa's red ponytails.

"You have beautiful hair, Lisa."

Her boy was in trouble, and talking about normal things relieved the pain.

San Francisco International Airport
1745 Hours

"The boy's parents are on their way, but I've got to move my people back into position."

213

"Give me the hour, Commander. It's only been forty-five minutes."

Bobbie breathed slowly. He knew the chance he was taking. He'd been through the training. Captain Jack had set up several scenarios for them while they were at McGregor. Bobbie didn't want that for this kid.

Bobbie weighed the boy's stability against the high risk he was taking. His experience in the courtroom or at negotiating tables told him to wait. Patience, coupled with experience usually won the case. He only needed to wait it out. He looked at the airplane, willing the boy to talk.

The man stood there. Bobby could see him; he wasn't moving at all. It was silly, but Bobby felt as if they were talking. The soldier had watched him for the past hour. All the people in their black and blue clothes and facemasks had moved away. He checked again. There wasn't anyone outside except the man. Bobby's hands were shaking and his head hurt. The man in the army suit didn't have a gun. Bobby couldn't wait any longer.

"Turn on the radio."

"He's talking!"

The RTO yelled to the FBI commander.

"He wants the soldier who's standing outside!"

Pounding through the door, Bobbie was already yelling instructions.

"Nobody come outside! Get those stairs hauled into place!"

He was back outside in less than twenty seconds, already speaking.

"Hi, Bobby. Here I am. You have the headset on?"

"Yeah."

Bobbie knew the boy was a serious contender. He might only be seventeen, but he'd made a bomb. Bobbie had to treat him as an equal. He started speaking slowly, carefully.

"First off, my name is Bobbie—spelled with "ie" at the end." Bobbie didn't move.

"I know what happened. I'm aware that your father was laid off. He's a pro, a class act. The company shouldn't have treated him and other experienced professionals the way they did."

Silence.

"Bobby, you hear me?"

"Yeah."

Not once did Bobbie sigh or breath heavily. He stood as quietly as he'd been standing before, in exactly the same place.

"Do you know my father?"

"I'm here to help you both through this, Bobby, if you'll let me."

"OK."

Behind him, Bobbie could hear quiet cheers from those monitoring the conversation.

He moved one hand slowly behind his back, signaling to Carp. The noise was silenced.

"I'm gonna start moving towards you now. I'll make sure you can see me the whole time."

"OK."

"Over on your right, I'm gonna have them move a stairway up to the door. Tell the captain to have one of the stewardesses open the door."

"OK, Bobbie."

The boy sounded very tired.

"I've made sure that no one in the airplane will bother you, Bobby. I'll be out of view for a few seconds, but I'll be here, right at the top of the stairs. We'll walk down together."

"OK."

"Bobby, I'm waving. Can you see me?"

"Yeah."

Above him, Bobbie could see the boy, waving back as he walked closer to the airplane.

"OK, Bobby, be sure you bring that disc player with you, but don't worry. Nothing will happen unless you pull out the jack."

"I know."

"Can you see the stairs moving towards you, Bobby?"

"Yeah."

"I'm walking under the airplane now, Bobby. Out of sight for a second."

"OK."

"Look out the right window, Bobby. See me?"

"Yeah."

"Stairs are here now. And I can see the door opening, Bobby. Are you ready?"

"Yeah."

"Give the captain the headset. You hold that disc player."

"OK."

"I'm walking up the stairs, Bobby."

In front of him Bobbie saw the young man, taller than he'd imagined. His light brown hair was damp. He was pale behind his tan. The boy was exhausted. His body sagged. Bobbie caught him with both arms.

Chapter Sixteen
Business Encounter

When intelligence and cleverness arise in men, like motherless children
they plot to increase individual enrichment and gross hypocrisy develops.
Lectures on the Tao Teh Ching by Man-jan Cheng

Baqa'a Refugee Camp

According to statistics, eighty percent of the world's thirty-four million refugees are women and children. If anyone had brought this to her attention, it wouldn't have meant anything to Kamilah. Her days were filled with unease and concern for her son. Whether or not she was a part of this statistic made no difference. She would have worried under any circumstances.

Every morning, for the two months Faris had been away, Kamilah would go to his corner. Shaking out his bedding, she'd pray he'd come back that day. Kamilah knew where he was. Dabir had delivered the message breathlessly.

"Faris is staying with his uncle in Nablus. He won't be back for a while."

Panting and sweaty, Dabir hadn't accepted her offer of water.

Standing at her doorway, her son's friend had stared at her for a moment before backing into the street. Kamilah had watched him running away; skinny knees pumping madly, taking him out of view—one of over twenty million refugee children, lost in clouds of dust.

Fort Bliss, STC Headquarters
17 June, 1845 Hours

The large room was empty, chairs scattered, duffel bags removed. Penny, Balke's aide, had been sent for coffee and sandwiches. In his old office, Bill sat with Commander Balke.

"Bill, I'll need some more details; all you can give me."

Arrangements had been made for the team to stay at the Inn, and all but Bill had gone to check in. They'd return any moment for another briefing over lunch.

"Commander, I only spoke to my teacher for a few minutes."

Abruptly, Balke stood, staring out the window silently. Turning suddenly he waved his hand at the phone on Bill's desk.

"I had to have another phone line. It's been ringing continuously. My aide—you met her—helps out. She's been invaluable these past few days."

Frowning in concentration, Balke returned to the subject.

"Let's go over what we know about the situation in Taiwan. Two days ago, you spoke to your teacher, right?"

Bill nodded.

"A kidnapping, you say? He told you that another student of his, an older woman living on some island near Mainland, saw the event?"

Slowly rising from his chair, Bill clasped his hands behind his back.

"Lao Shir told me that his student saw two men push a bound man into a car driven by a third man. They arrived on Quemoy late afternoon—April 16th. I put it together with something I read in the Post. I have a copy of the article somewhere."

Balke reached for a file on his desk. "This one?"

Looking at the clipping, Bill nodded.

"Yes, Commander. Lao Shir told me that the woman's brother—an officer in the Taiwan Air Force—didn't believe her story."

Balke smiled grimly, looking at the file, "Taiwan Air Force Chief of Staff..."

Balke shoved the file at Bill, pointing, "How do you pronounce this?"

Wrinkling his brow, Bill peered at the romanized spelling.

"Fang Xueng. It's pronounced, *Fung Shoong*. Fang is the family name. His sister must be Fang Mei—the one Lao Shir told me about."

Balke lifted questioning eyebrows at Bill.

"That'd be spelled Mei, pronounced like *May*," Bill told him.

While he penciled the name in the margin, Balke added, "Yeah, well his rank is equivalent to a Major General."

Bill and Balke exchanged glances. Balke's quick words echoed Bill's thoughts almost verbatim.

"I have a feeling he did believe sister May."

* * *

San Francisco International Airport
1800 Hours

Don handled the negotiations. Bobbie's decision to include the physicist in the team had been based on the fact that he was Lisa's buddy. As it turned out, Don's persuasive abilities played an important part in the youngster's release.

Pointing out that the boy's father was, after all, a twenty-five year employee of the airline, Don's suggestion to the Airport and San Francisco Police Departments and the FBI commander was acceptable. The boy was released into the custody of his parents. The decision was influenced by the fact that the airline representative would not press charges. There would be a hearing of course. The boy's actions demanded retribution. Alice and Bob Hendricks would be notified later about the time and date. They led their boy away, holding him close, patting and comforting him.

"Make sure the passengers know it was a false report. Okay, so they sat on the runway for nine hours. It doesn't take a bomb threat for that to happen!"

Kurt spoke to the airline media person, convincing her that in the best interests of all concerned, there should be no hoopla. It was just one of those things that happen.

"Give 'em a free ticket somewhere. That'll make 'em forget anything they think they saw."

"Thanks, Commander, it was good to meet you. Glad it all worked out."

Talking to the FBI commander, Jack and Carp were full of smiles and good will. They soft-pedaled everything perfectly. None of the teams involved needed to know the details. It was settled. No bad guys to shoot. The SWAT teams packed up and went home.

Gritting his teeth, Bobbie spoke in a soft undertone to the airline representative.

"All I need from you right now is a place for me and my buddy to sleep tonight and a ticket to Chicago tomorrow; the earlier the better."

* * *

Fort Bliss, STC Headquarters
1900 Hours

"We've got two other situations to deal with—one's in Israel, the other in Taiwan."

The briefing had started while they'd gulped down the sandwiches. They were used to eating fast, and reminded themselves that they could wolf down as much as they wanted.

"A week ago I got a call from the American Embassy in Jerusalem. The Ambassador and I met at an executive dinner and he remembered me. It seems that someone saw a honeymoon couple taken at Nablus, on the West Bank—nineteenth of April."

James' head snapped up, as Balke continued.

"Sometime in late March—we're not sure of the date—a high-ranking politician was forcefully taken from his office in Taipei and is possibly being held on a small island—Quemoy, I think that's how you pronounce it. We have only a few details. The information is sketchy."

Balke's expression was a mixture of concern and vague excitement. They all felt the same way. STC was in business.

* * *

San Francisco
18 June, 0700 Hours

They'd been offered two rooms, but the men had elected to share one. They'd talked most of the night, calling Balke several times. Bobbie's plan, outrageous and daring, needed approval. Finally, at three o'clock in the morning, Balke had called back. Tahoe had given the nod, although Balke did not mention this fact to Bobbie.

Carp woke to Bobbie's smooth tones, talking on the phone.

"Yes, well, sir, as I said, I heard a rumor, that's all. Yes. Yes."

Bobbie grinned at Carp.

"As I said, I represent M & L Negotiation—in Hartford, Sir. Yes. Exactly."

Turning his back to Carp, keeping his face straight, Bobbie continued.

"Yes, today if possible. I'm in San Francisco at the moment, but my plane leaves in an hour. I can meet with you at three; or would five be better? Yes, as many as possible. No problem."

Bobbie listened for a moment, moving and tightening his shoulders in frustration—but he kept his voice even, professional. He was the expert; helpful and in control of the conversation.

"As I said, Sir, I heard that your airline may be the subject of a hostile takeover, and my company is interested in handling the negotiations. Yes. Yes. That's us. Good to know, Mr. Franzen."

"Yes, sir! Very good. See you at three sharp."

Hanging up the phone, Bobbie turned to Carp.

"I didn't lie. A hostile takeover is exactly what that boy attempted."

* * *

STC Headquarters, Fort Bliss
0800 Hours

"I've been to Nablus, Commander. I know the area quite well."

Penny, Balke's aide, had brought donuts. Coffee in a huge thermos was also available to the eleven STC personnel.

"The main thing is to find that cab driver, James. Pick your team."

James didn't hesitate. As soon as he'd heard 'Nablus,' he'd been working it out.

"Okay, Jasen, this is it, Buddy. Steve, wanna go to Israel? Jonsey, I'll need you, darlin'. Harlem, Mike! I've got work for you. Find out everything you can about…"

Flipping the pages of his notebook, James found the place.

"…about Vienna and Jonas Campbell; Manhattan."

Looking around the room, Bill grinned.

"Guess that leaves the rest of us with Taiwan."

Balke shook his head solemnly.

"Slow down, Bill, they haven't asked for our help."

"They will," Bill said, and he continued looking around the group.

"Jen, we'll need some sort of cover story. Check it out. Find us something. Annie and George, ever been to Taiwan? Ted, I have a feeling you'll be needed. Any chance you can join us?"

The SEAL laughed, "I'm attached permanently to STC, Bill. I'm all yours."

* * *

San Francisco International Airport
0800 Hours

At the security gate, Bobbie and Carp, still dressed in BDUs, stepped to one side. They nodded to the uniformed guard. Bobbie opened his briefcase, taking out a small packet.

Looking over their permits and checking their identification, the guard led them around the metal detector.

With a bright expression, the airline representative met them— boarding passes waving in the air. Nodding curtly, Bobbie tried to be civil to the man who escorted them down the jetway and into the airplane. Indicating the first class seats, the man smiled ingratiatingly. He was holding out his hand. Bobbie and Carp looked at each other and grinned. One by one they clasped his smooth palm.

Carp said, "We were ordered to Chicago, you know, and then diverted here yesterday. From there I think we go to Boise."

Carp babbled on, "So, thanks for the lift. We had fun."

The representative didn't know exactly how to respond to them.

"Thank you again, gentlemen, have a good trip," and the man actually tried to salute them.

Watching him leave the airplane, bucking the crowd of boarding passengers, Bobbie and Carp were very busy with their seat belts. As soon as they knew he was out of earshot, they exploded in laughter.

"Pray he doesn't tell his bosses we're going to Chicago," Bobbie choked out.

* * *

Quemoy, ROC
11:00 PM, Local Time

Fang Mei was not sleeping well. Attempting to keep herself busy, she worked long hours in her garden. She no longer made the journey to Taipei to see her family. She had to keep watch. Somehow she felt that he was safer because she was there.

It'd been early April when they'd brought that poor man to her island. Each day Fang Mei made the short trip to the little house where they were keeping the prisoner.

On several occasions she'd been able to get close enough to peer into the window at the back. Once she saw him playing some sort of game with one of his captors, and another time she saw him staring back at her. His expression didn't change. Either he thought she was one of them, or that she was simply a curiosity-seeker.

The vigilance of the guards was constant. Fang Mei had counted seven different men who rotated duties. They'd moved their rapid motor launch, tying it to another rotting wharf—one that was closer to the house. Once a week or so, it would roar off across the straits, returning the next day. Try as she might, Fang Mei could not find out who they were. It was as if the island was fearful.

While visiting her teacher in Taipei, Lao Shir had cautioned her not to interfere. He didn't give Fang Mei any reasons for this warning. Bill could have told her. Lao Shir knew more than most people realized.

To soften the admonition, Lao Shir had added, "Don't worry. Your brother will have a change of heart."

Although it took nearly three months, Lao Shir was right.

* * *

O'Hare International Airport
1430 Hours

Bobbie and Carp strode quickly through the terminal. Except for Bobbie's briefcase, they had no luggage. They'd stored the rest of their gear on the CASA before leaving San Francisco. During the flight, Carp had looked around the cabin, smirking at Bobbie.

"Enjoy the ride, Buddy, these seats cost our friend back there over two thousand dollars. I wonder if it'll come out of his paycheck?"

Bobbie grunted, "I guess we'll never know, will we?"

The flight had included breakfast and a movie, but the two men had ignored both. They'd spent the first hour discussing Bobbie's "presentation." Both had slept soundly the rest of the flight.

Picking a cab from the row, Bobbie handed a slip of paper to the driver.

"We have a three o'clock."

The driver settled in his seat. "No problem."

Neither Bobbie nor Carp had adjusted to civilian surroundings. Their minds and bodies had accepted the challenge yesterday the same way they'd accepted the Yellow River in the middle of the night. They knew the priorities, and responded as they'd been trained.

Yesterday, they'd been in the CASA or at the airport. Carp's brief visit with the boy's parents didn't interrupt the flow of activities that were very much like the missions they'd rehearsed.

The huge building loomed over them as they stepped out of the cab. The street noises and jostle of people were overpowering. They were used to silent night raids and the sounds of gunfire, not traffic.

"Buddy, we're not in Kansas any more."

Carp's dry humor settled Bobbie's nerves.

Taking the elevator to the top floor, they arrived in what was a wonderland of plush carpeting and quiet elegance. They'd showered and shaved this morning, using the Army issue kits still in their bags. Their jungle boots and slightly rumpled uniforms were out of place in this bastion of wealth and power. It all served to harden Bobbie's resolve. They announced themselves to the receptionist at exactly three o'clock.

The expression on her face was a mixture of good manners and disbelief. Incredulity won out as she recognized the names from the appointment book open on her desk. She'd been expecting suits. Never having been this close to soldiers, she struggled for composure.

"Yes, they're waiting in the conference room. I'll show you the way."

Bobbie had to give her credit. She walked steadily ahead of them towards a huge set of paneled doors mounted with tall gold handles. But her hand was shaking as she tapped lightly. Smiling calmly, Bobbie reached around her.

"I'll take it from here, Ma'am. Please don't disturb us."

Bobbie pulled open the doors. Followed by Carp, he walked directly towards the group. Two vacant chairs awaited them, but were ignored. Constructed of deep red cherry, the massive table filled the room. Silver coffee services—one at each end—and plates of sandwiches were positioned neatly on the gleaming surface.

Used to MRE's, eaten a mouthful at a time, usually in the dark, the gap between what they'd been doing a week ago and what was in front of them was too much to assimilate. Exchanging a look, Bobbie and Carp automatically went to the priorities of work. They followed the plan, ignoring their discomfort.

"Good afternoon, gentlemen. By now you've heard the report that one of your airplanes was threatened yesterday at SFO. I'd like to fill in some of the details for you."

At the far end of the table, a man stood up.

"Who the hell are you? How did you get in here?"

"I called you from San Francisco this morning," Bobbie replied evenly, and he placed his briefcase on the glossy table.

Slowly the CEO sat down. Ten men sat with dazed expressions. Bobbie began to speak.

Using the techniques he'd mastered a lifetime ago, Bobbie took them through the entire scenario, from the first virtual bombing to the talk-down late last night. Poignantly and with total clarity, he told them exactly how the boy had made his bomb. He explained when Bobby had first decided on retribution. Choosing his words carefully—he didn't want any of them to misunderstand one facet of the story—Bobbie took them through the writing of the note to the reasons for the boy's anger.

"Gentlemen, *this* is what you caused."

Snapping open the briefcase, Bobbie reached in and threw a sheaf of papers on the table. Paper clipped together, the pages slid across the polished wood.

"My report, gentlemen."

Carp moved slowly to one of the vacant chairs, sliding his long body into the red upholstery. He reached for the coffee urn, but his gaze stayed on Bobbie. Slowly, Bobbie looked around the table.

"You've been so busy making money for yourselves, increasing your own salaries, making stockholders smile that you forgot about the people you serve. I won't apologize for calling you hypocrites, although I don't judge you. That's not my place."

Bobbie leaned both hands on the table now, pulling himself closer to the group.

"Gentlemen, there are needs that must be met. The airline industry as a whole is in trouble. I'm not telling you anything you don't already know. The passenger load has increased, volume of flights has increased, air traffic control is saturated, ATC systems need to be modernized—I don't need to mention all the problem areas. You know them better than I do."

Shaking his head slowly, Bobbie was silent for a moment. What he had realized that day in the gym—when he was still deciding whether or not to become STC—was true. Uniforms command as much respect as a blue shirt and red tie. No one said a word.

"These days, gentlemen—more than ever—you need experienced, senior pilots. To throw out the best captains in order to lower salary costs is stupidity of the highest order. To compromise safety in the airline industry could be considered criminal."

Removing his hands from the table, Bobbie stepped back.

"It's up to you to decide whether or not your airline wants to be the leader. My report includes everything I told you today."

Pausing now, Bobbie nodded at Carp who sipped the last of his coffee and stood. Bobbie closed the briefcase and Carp reached over and picked it up. Both men stood together at the end of the table close to the enormous doors.

"Fix the problems, gentlemen. Start today."

Pointing to the papers that had wedged against one of the silver trays, Bobbie spoke again.

"I'm sure the press would have a field day with what's in there."

The CEO jumped to his feet.

"That's blackmail!"

"It sure is, Mr. Franzen. It surely is. Good day, gentlemen."

Making a neat about-face, Bobbie and Carp walked to the doors.

The men seated at the table could see the black grip of the pistol jammed in the back of the waistband of Carp's pants. He'd forgotten to put it in the briefcase.

"He's got a gun!"

Carp turned back to the table, smiling easily.

"Oh, yeah. Sorry, I forgot to put it away. We've been on duty. Don't worry, it's licensed."

Striding through the reception area, boot sounds muffled by the carpeting, Bobbie whistled under his breath. Carp recognized the tag line of Annie's song. Marching to the beat, they left the building.

"*Tau*-Mie. *Tell* me, w*here*'d you *get* that *na*-me."

The presentation was over.

Chapter Seventeen
Red Tape

Those born with an understanding of the universe belong to the highest type of humanity. Those who understand it as the result of study come second. Those who study it with great difficulty come third. And the people who find it too difficult to attempt study, come last.
The Analects of Confucius

Quemoy, ROC
19 June, 0700 Hours Local Time

Head hanging nearly to his waist, fists on his forehead, Ambassador Cheng was despondent. The designation *Ambassador* was not really accurate, but it was more understandable to foreign diplomats than his official title—Assistant to the Chief of the Legislative Yuan. As a high-ranking political leader, Cheng's main function was overseeing the operation of the Executive Yuan, but being fully aware of all facets of diplomacy was also in Cheng's job description.

In addition, he was the admitted expert in understanding cross-straits relationships, which could be intricate. But Cheng liked to explain that the connection between the People's Republic of China—PRC, and the Republic of China—ROC, was no more or less complicated than understanding the history and formation of any two nations with close family ties. It only seemed multifarious to the Western world.

Frequent visits to the United States took Cheng to the Taipei Economic and Cultural Office in Washington D. C. The label was demanded by diplomatic protocol and the offices were not referred to as the Taiwanese Embassy.

Cheng's was the steady voice of reason, sorting out misunderstandings and explaining realities for major world powers. His most important task, however, was to encourage and maintain open dialogue between the parties within his own country—factions that debated continuously over complete independence versus unification with Mainland China. Cheng's workload was enormous. He'd been used to sleeping in short naps, sometimes at his desk. Now he had nothing to do but sleep, and think.

They had allowed him to rinse his shirt and underwear a few times, but they provided no change of clothing. He scrubbed his face and hands at the sink, but there was no soap. No razor was offered. His face itched continuously. Cheng tried not to think about the crawling things in his bed.

By now Cheng realized who his captors were, and why they were keeping him hidden away. They were nothing more than ruffians probably hired by the World United Formosans for Independence or the Organization for Taiwan Nation Building or some other splinter group, to keep him quiet. Cheng's efforts to encourage reunification while keeping Taiwan a separate and distinct democratic state were making too much headway to please the independence groups. They wanted his voice silenced.

Watching them come and go, he'd listened to their muffled conversations filled with street slang. It had taken Cheng less than a week to put it together.

Keeping track of time was not difficult. They'd returned his wristwatch.

The duct tape had been replaced with plastic ties—interlocking and stronger than the fabric tape—and his wrists were now fastened together in front of his body. He'd grown used to using both hands as one. The plastic slid up and down, affording better circulation.

Hearing sounds from the other room, Cheng stretched out on the cot, feigning sleep. The younger of his two guards clumped into the room, peering down at him.

"*Chir fan*," he muttered, letting Cheng know that it was time to eat.

Watery rice soup simmered on the stove. Cheng didn't mind the breakfast they provided. He often ate the same thing at home. He didn't even mind the fact that they ignored him as he ate. Silence was better than what they'd discussed last night. Cheng didn't know whether they'd been serious or simply trying to frighten him.

Purposely allowing him to overhear their conversation, they'd exchanged gruesome stories—Chinese martial arts legends mixed with American crime family assassinations.

"I watched a program about how they took care of uncooperative clients. They would tie up the victim, hang him upside down in a secluded place, shoot him in the head, drain out the blood and then cut him up into little pieces."

Their laughter had terrified Cheng, who buried his head in his hands.

"But if there was someone they really didn't like or if they had to make a special example of him, then sometimes they would take a pistol with a .22 short round and fire one into each kidney. He wouldn't die right away, but the bullets lodged in his body would cause a long, terrible, suffering death from lead poisoning."

The boy had sneered, lifting his chin in Cheng's direction. The other one had slowly pulled a small volume—well thumbed and bound in pale green cloth—from the pocket of his black leather jacket. Cheng could see a knife stuck in the boy's low-slung belt as he yanked on the book. There was no title, or printing of any kind on the cover. The boy found a passage, reading loudly, squinting now and then at Cheng.

"*Now you will hear the swallow sing. As the attacker closed, Yang inserted his two fingers into the man's windpipe. The man made a sound like a swallow singing, and expired.*"

The stories continued until midnight. Cheng had wrapped his knees in his arms, lying on his side, trying to ignore them.

* * *

STC Headquarters
20 June, 0930 Hours

"Bill, we can't proceed without some sort of appeal from Taiwan. They've got to make the first move."

Relaxing for a few moments, Bill and Commander Balke sipped their ever-present cups of coffee.

"I've checked with the ministry in Washington. They won't admit anyone's missing, despite that news clip."

Balke covered the Taiwan file with both hands, pushing up with his arms. He paced.

"It's like it never happened. Maybe you understand it?"

Over his shoulder, Bill could see Jennifer at her computer. She raised her head and smiled at him through the glass partition.

"Commander, I've got Bobbie looking into the news agency in Taipei. We should have something soon. In the meantime, you do understand that the man's important, right?"

"Sure, Bill, I know," and Balke opened the file.

The two men were silent, each pondering the delicate situation. They both knew that the red tape surrounding the Taiwan situation was nothing more than a waiting game.

Cheng had been successful in keeping the status quo. Trade agreement negotiations between Taiwan and the PRC had been going well. The United States and Russia were pleased, hopeful that all would prosper from the increased business. All the parts were neatly in place. Now, all that had changed and no one would discuss the missing piece: Cheng.

"I think I've found what we need."

Jennifer tapped on the glass, holding out a document.

"It's a business deal. Taiwan wants a piece of the action, so to speak," Jennifer grinned widely, "...on Quemoy. Like Macao and Hong Kong; you know. Gambling. They're proposing a casino and resort on the island; Las Vegas-style."

It was perfect.

* * *

Taipei, ROC
21 June, 0100 Hours Local Time

"The problem is under the table, a very secret thing. Nobody can talk about it. They are not allowed to talk about it."

Fang Mei listened patiently to her brother. She had arrived in Taipei, tired and out of sorts only four hours ago. Her trip had been a last-minute decision, motivated by what she had observed yesterday. In the small house, the prisoner had been sitting too still, head hanging down. Fang Mei had watched for several moments to make sure that he was still breathing.

"You cannot get involved, *jiejie*, give me peace."

At his use of the endearment—elder sister—Fang Mei's eyes filled. In return, she spoke softly, calling him younger brother.

"*Didi*, there may be a person who can help. Would you be willing to talk to someone else? I can arrange a go-between."

Fang Xueng lifted his head, placing his hands near but not touching his sister. He had always been like her own child, born many years after she was. She had played with him, nursed him, taken care of him and watched his rise to high position in the Air Force. He knew that she was proud of her younger brother.

"Go-between? Go-between! This is not a marriage, Fang Mei. This is...it is...nothing. There is nothing to talk about."

He wavered. And Fang Mei knew it.

"Brother, listen. Lao Shir has a senior student—an American—who knows many people in Taipei. He is Caucasian, but he has lived in Taiwan. He speaks Mandarin and Taiwanese. The student can talk to your friend in the Army...I think the family name is Nei..."

"General Nei!" Fang interrupted his sister, "Your teacher's student knows General Nei?"

"Yes, brother. And the student can make a suggestion. Lao Shir assured me he is most discreet."

General Fang Xueng breathed slowly. He would never do anything to jeopardize his family, his name or his position. There were many political hazards involved with attempting a rescue operation. His attempts at negotiation had left him exhausted. He was a military man, not a politician. Maybe there was a better way to deal with the situation on Quemoy. Perhaps there was a way to save Cheng without endangering his family or losing face.

* * *

El Paso, Texas
21 June, 0630 Hours

"Nice place, Mike."

"Can you believe it? The same apartment opened up last week."

The team sat on the floor, nibbling pastry and sipping coffee. James looked at each one. They looked like grad students—archaeology students, ready for a dig. He grinned.

"OK, folks, we get our equipment at the market in Tel Aviv, and then go to Naublus. Introductions have been sent. Dr. White has given us free run of the site."

"How about the taxi driver? Jen actually found him?" Jasen asked James.

"Sure did. She'd been there, you know, to Israel, and had a ton of information in her journal. Can you believe it? She nagged the hotel until they found him."

Jonsey began to collect paper cups, disposing of them in Mike's paper bag garbage can.

"First thing, we get back, I'm gettin' you a real wastebasket, Mike."

Mike laughed, "You can use my shower if you want, Jonsey, a quick one before the flight?"

Gathering her gear, Jonsey ignored him, turning to Steve.

"You're sure I can get that Baby Eagle in the market?"

"Oh, sure, it's an Israeli hand gun. No problem gettin' it. But make sure you have that permit with you, and pack it in your suitcase when we come home."

234

Harlem added, "If you don't find what you want in the market, try the Bedouins. I hear they have weapons…smuggling is a tradition with them, you know."

The mention of weapons brought a moment of silence. They were preparing to go into a foreign country where hostilities were so prevalent that American tourists were cautioned daily. In addition, they were to conduct a rescue operation with only the American Embassy sanctioning the mission.

"Who's got the pictures?" Steve asked as he pulled out his cell phone.

James patted his backpack.

"And the tickets? Harlem?"

She nodded, "Yeah, and all your passports; right here."

Their plan was simple.

* * *

Lake Tahoe, California
0700 Hours

"Fine, Steve. Yes, I read it. Did you get my Email with the directions?"

Tahoe stood quietly in the foyer of the three-story house nestled in a stand of sugar pines. From her vantage point she was able to see the lake, sparkling in the morning sun. She was not looking forward to the drive down the hill to Reno, and the subsequent flight to the East Coast. The fact that she'd only be gone for ten days didn't make leaving any easier.

She held the phone with one hand; the other clasped the morning paper. Folding it carefully, she laid it on the small table, glancing again at the short article.

"Airline Bomb Threat a Hoax."

The brief report included a short statement from the airline, which said that precautions were taken due to telephoned threats—but that at no time was there any danger.

"Our friend will expect you day after tomorrow. You and the Jones girl will spend the night with the group at the hotel in Tel Aviv, but rent a car and drive to Caesarea early on the twenty-third. It is north, along the sea."

Turning her head, Tahoe nodded at the man who was pointing to his watch.

"Steve, take care of everything. I will be at the Cape. You know how to reach me."

Tahoe picked up her handbag and laptop. She was ready. Holding the man's hand, Tahoe stepped into the truck. She only spoke once during the forty-minute drive. The man was used to her silence.

"Take the Mount Rose highway, would you?"

* * *

Biggs Airfield
El Paso, Texas, 0830 Hours

Six team members took their places in the CASA. The flight to Tel Aviv was scheduled to leave Los Angeles at two this afternoon.

"Harlem, did you check everything?"

Crossing her eyes at James, Harlem immediately regretted it. The contact lenses she'd taken to wearing only a week ago, still bothered her.

"Damn! I'm gonna do it, Mike. LASIK surgery. Soon as we get back."

Lisa's voice came back to them.

"Buckle up folks."

Harlem leaned towards James, softening her expression.

"Sorry about that. Yes, I've got the book here."

James reached for a small red-covered spiral notebook. As the CASA taxied to the end of the runway, James flipped the pages, reviewing the tightly written schedule.

"Relax, man, it'll be fine," Jasen reassured him.

James clenched his jaw and leaned back as the airplane lifted.

* * *

Nablus, West Bank, Israel
1730 Hours Local Time

Resting his hands on either side of the jamb, Fadil stuck his head through the doorway of his office.

"Faris, it's time for them to eat."

The gentle reminder irritated Faris. He'd fed them every day at the same time. Why should he forget today? They were fine. Maybe a little dirty, but that wouldn't hurt them. Making his way slowly to the kitchen, Faris scooped out cups of the steaming mixture from the double-stacked pan on the stove.

"They eat too good," he muttered under his breath, and he slammed the lid with more force than necessary.

Carrying the pail, he stalked out of his uncle's house. Hearing the boy's departure, Fadil sighed deeply. Bewildered by the teenager, Fadil didn't know where to turn. He'd taken on the responsibility of his dead brother's child, but the boy's behavior and harsh responses were predictably defiant.

Fadil knew that fanatical groups crawled through the refugee camps. It was probably someone from the Palestinian Islamic Jihad or the Islamic Resistance Movement who had approached his nephew— promising God-knows-what in return for jobs they demanded. The HAMAS and the PIJ regularly recruited young people for their heinous activities.

Fadil had heard a news report about one such youngster—inspired by HAMAS literature—who'd rammed his car into a group of Israeli soldiers hitchhiking along a highway. In a way, the kidnapping had served a purpose. It kept Faris near him; under his supervision for a time. Maybe his influence would help. But so far, Faris had resisted him at every turn.

Still determined to get the money for a car, Faris nagged him daily. No amount of reasoning on Fadil's part penetrated the boy's hard head.

Taking angry steps towards the isolated shack, Faris pulled the cell phone out of his jacket. There was no beep, no signal. He'd forgotten to charge it. It didn't matter; the only one he called was Dabir and Dabir hadn't answered his phone for over a month.

Faris' treasured Mauser was slung over his shoulder. His uncle had tried taking both the phone and the rifle from him, but Faris had resisted so strongly that Fadil had given up.

If only he could get some ammunition. With a magazine in the weapon, he could steal money from somewhere—enough to buy a car. There was no way Faris could know that those who had promised great honor had forgotten all about him. The angry, lonely boy marched resolutely towards the hide-away.

"Dear, what can I do for you?"

Jonas whispered to his bride. Her beautiful face was streaked and mottled. Matted hair resisted his gentle fingers as he attempted to smooth it. She shivered and pulled away.

"How can you look at me?" she shouted.

They'd tried yelling; banging on the door until their hands and arms were bruised and swollen. The deep cut on Jonas' left hand was draining now, and the infection seemed to be clearing up. Fadil had sent a small coffee pot, and they'd boiled water to cleanse the wound.

At the back of the shed they'd managed to scoop out a depression in the hard ground. It had taken them several days because their feet and hands were bound with rough rope. Once completed, they kept the small pit covered with a piece of the firewood that was thrown to them once a week.

The one time Fadil had come, he'd peered into the squalid surroundings and returned with a stack of newspapers and some coffee. He'd also included a supply of matches with a warning.

"If you attempt to burn the building, I will shoot you."

The fact that he'd spoke English surprised them, and Jonas tried to find out why they were being held. Fadil had ignored them, slamming and locking the door.

The coffee had run out over a month ago. They regulated the use of the newsprint carefully, but the stack was growing smaller and smaller. Crawling was a way of life. Standing upright was exercise, as was jumping and shouting. None of their efforts were ever acknowledged. Only

Faris—silent and sullen—came each afternoon, with a pail of food and a plastic jug of water.

* * *

STC Headquarters
1500 Hours

Striding towards the phone, Balke's head was aching slightly. This was caused by nothing more than lack of sleep and very little food. With a medium rare steak and a full night's sleep he'd be fine. Commander Balke, like most in the military, thrived on situations surrounded by intrigue and action. He stepped more lightly these days. The teams had surpassed his expectations.

They'd only been back from Benning for five days and they'd already taken care of that touchy situation in San Francisco. Now another team was on its way to Israel. Situated comfortably in the offices, they were hard at work.

They continued to train with Bill, Steve and Ted every day. Twice Balke had walked to the gym, watching them quietly. They had an edge about them; a certain way that they moved—a way of carrying themselves. Each person exuded confidence. Relaxed and calm they moved quietly.

When together, they teased and laughed, but underneath the light-hearted banter was a knowledge that came from a higher type of understanding. Nothing seemed too difficult. They had an uncanny ability to stretch time. It continually amazed Balke. They always had time—time for each other, time for him, and time to accomplish each detail.

Watching them move through the training, Balke was reminded of some intricate ballet. Speaking in low voices, consulting with one another, it was always the same. They were a unit, completely at ease with one another, tough and competent. Balke had never worked with a more consistent group.

Yesterday, early in the morning, he'd watched them. Steve had been standing to one side of the gym, arms crossed, legs spread apart. Balke walked closer. All on-duty personnel were practicing. The group had returned from San Francisco—Bobbie and Carp had arrived late the night before.

"Tell me exactly what you're practicing for."

Balke's blunt question didn't take Steve by surprise.

"It's a motion study, Commander. In a way it's a sensitivity drill."

The fact that they were holding knives, the handles wound with parachute cord, seemed a contradiction to Balke; and he said so.

Steve explained, "We're doing lock flow drills; dead drills, mobile drills, live drills…see? There's direct attack, and that's angular…"

Steve pointed first to Annie and George, then Jasen and James.

"Those knives…?"

Steve smiled, "Made 'em myself, Commander. They're aluminum practice knives. But we go through the same drills with sticks or with hands only."

Balke watched silently for a moment, listening to the constant murmur of quiet voices.

"They're talking. What are they saying?"

"Commander, I can only guess, but I'll bet Harrison and Kurt are talking about surfing. Probably Mike and Harlem are plotting some rearrangement of our offices. And Annie and George are, I'm sure, discussing the opera. With Bill, it's cars."

At Balke's look of surprise, Steve explained.

"We don't talk about what we're doing, Commander. We're not thinking about the practice. It's gotta be second nature, understand? If we're robbed of our audio and visual senses concerning the activity itself, we begin to train our subconscious."

The clanging of a knife hitting the floor caught Balke's attention. Steve seemed to know before it happened and was already walking towards a couple.

"Lisa, don't overextend. Keep to the twelve motions."

He returned to Balke's side.

"Bill's probably the best at this; he's had tons of practice. And he understands the more subtle aspects of yielding. He plans every move. He thinks way ahead of the opponent. Watch how quick he is."

They never stopped training, or thinking. Because of their ideas, readily shared with him, Balke had found ways to work through what seemed to be impossible tasks.

Balke made his way through the office, scanning each position. Bobbie was seated in front of his open laptop, staring at the screen. Carp sat next to him, dozing in the chair he'd wheeled close to Bobbie. Don's desk was empty; he'd accompanied Lisa to Los Angeles. With their heads together, Jennifer and Bill were working out the details of their cover—should Taiwan contact them. George and Annie were off on some errand; getting information Bill needed. Also at his computer, Harrison quietly called out details to Kurt, who sketched neat circles around his scribbled notes on helicopter agencies in Taiwan.

"I still think our best bet is that Seagull Squadron," Kurt mentioned softly.

Pushing back his chair, Bill wandered over to the two.

"I agree. They fly the Sikorsky…how did you find out about them anyway, Harrison?"

"News, my man, the news," and he shoved a single page he'd printed.

"Well, well, well…they failed at that rescue operation. Hope they can come through for us, if we use them."

Their voices soothed Balke. They were busy. They were the best. The throbbing in his temples retreated. He reached his desk and picked up the phone.

"Commander Balke."

Tahoe's calm voice took care of the last remnants of the headache.

"Did the team get off?"

"They'll arrive in Tel Aviv at 2:15 PM local time tomorrow."

"Commander, I will be seeing our friend in Washington. Please make sure you contact the Ambassador as soon as he gets to his office tomorrow morning."

Balke knew he wouldn't get a full night's sleep, but he'd ask Penny to take him for the steak anyway. He wished Taiwan would call.

Chapter Eighteen
The Other Boy

*If we begin too late to enforce order, when the will of the child has already
been overindulged, the whims and passions, grown stronger with the
years, offer resistance and give cause for remorse. There is nothing more
difficult to carry through than breaking a child's will.*

The Book of Changes

Tel Aviv, Israel
22 June, 1800 Hours

Directly opposite Independence Park, the twenty-story hotel
soared above Nurdau Boulevard—the Mediterranean visible from
every room. On the ninth floor Jonsey floated in a hot bath. It had
been Steve's suggestion. Constant turbulence during the flight had
unsettled Jonesy's inner ear, which told her—even four hours after
landing—she was still jiggling around in the 747. The rough air had
reminded her of an old-fashioned glass washboard. The choppy
waves and troughs had made the airplane bounce like an ungainly
dolphin the entire flight.

"Soak in a tub for an hour or so, that'll help," Steve had suggested.

While the rest of the group settled in, Jonsey floated. She found herself daydreaming about the hours ahead. She'd been looking forward to this trip more eagerly than circumstances warranted.

"Stay focused," Jonsey reminded herself firmly.

They were here to do a job, quickly, silently, and then leave. The comfort of the warm water lulled her. Her thoughts wandered. An entire day, alone with Steve...Harlem's voice, startled Jonesy out of her reverie.

"Get dressed if you want to hear what the taxi driver has to say!"

* * *

Taipei, ROC
Midnight, Local Time

He couldn't put it off any longer. Caught between two factions, Fang Xueng had to make a decision. The Chief of Staff had reported his sister's observations, and for endless weeks there had been ongoing debate.

Shouted opinions, complete with desk pounding, had exhausted Fang. Those who felt the release of Cheng should be undertaken by military force were in direct opposition to other, more conservative members who counseled caution for fear of retribution. The more cautious members had a valid argument. Their families could be in danger from the radicals if they employed the militia to free the Ambassador.

Having assumed the responsibility of mediator, Fang was caught in the middle. Fang Mei's suggestion, although it had seemed ludicrous, returned to mind again and again.

It was late, but this was the first time he'd given her plea serious consideration. Lao Shir was respected and well known throughout Taipei. Before Fang changed his mind, he dialed the number of his sister's teacher.

Fang Xueng sighed in relief following the conversation with the aged philosopher.

* * *

"I took them to the ruins. They were on the hill. I was behind. I saw smoke. Two boys were running. One boy hit me with his gun."

Pushing aside the blue and white plaid turban, the taxi driver pointed to a pink scar at the base of his neck. James glanced at the business card he held in his hand

"Doud? That's your name?" The driver nodded. "Doud, did he fire his weapon, his gun?"

"No. He hit me. I fell down. I opened my eyes. My face was in the dirt. I was dizzy. I got up. They were gone."

The man couldn't have been over five feet four inches tall. Although a turban covered most of his head, they could see he had very little hair. Tucked neatly into washed out blue jeans, his flannel, zip-up jacket was faded and worn. He wore a beeper clipped to a black leather belt that was strapped high on his waist. Nearly toothless, Doud's mouth was surrounded by deep creases. His features were centered in the middle of his face, giving him a puckish look.

"What did you do?" James asked.

Speaking quickly with a heavy accent, Doud gestured expansively.

"I walked to my taxi. Tires were burning in the street. The blood was coming down."

Shaking his head at the memory, the driver stopped for a moment.

"Did you see them again?"

"Yes. I was afraid. I had to stop driving. The blood. I was dizzy. I saw the big man with the boys, and my tourists. They told me…" Doud fumbled for the right word, "…newlyweds. They are from New York."

James leaned closer, smiling encouragement.

"Yes, we know. They came here on their honeymoon."

The strains of a Mozart string quartet drifted through the lobby of the hotel. The waiter brought them soft drinks and small bowls filled with olives and nuts. Reaching for the olives, Doud glanced around the elegant room and quickly drew back. He clenched his palms together, forcing his fingers between his knees. He hunched his back, looking at the floor. He was obviously nervous, but eager to be helpful.

"Honeymoon, yes. The big man dragged them. I put my head down, like this. But then I looked a little. He had brown rope, like hair. The boys were happy. The big man was very angry—I saw him. The boys tied them—hands and feet. The big man, I know him, pushed them. They fell down. The big man shut the door. The place, the old building, is far from the street. I can take you."

Speaking quietly, James asked, "Doud, you know this man?"

"Yes. I know him. He is important. Not here. In Nablus, he is important."

Opening his daypack, James drew out the pictures of Vienna and Jonas.

"Are these the people you took to Nablus?"

"Yes. Yes. Black people. Like you, sir."

"And the big man in Nablus, what's his name?"

"I do not know that. But I know his house."

* * *

Caesarea, Israel
23 June, 0900 Hours

Keeping his hands firmly on the wheel, Steve was having difficulty concentrating on his driving. Flashes of morning sun came through the tall eucalyptus trees along the edge of the road and bounced off Jonsey's hair. The black lengths of it hung loose to her waist. She'd debated for some time this morning, but Harlem had encouraged her.

"It's your best thing, Jonsey," she'd said, "Wear it down. You're not going to be climbing mountains or crawling through mud today, are you?"

Although nearly fifteen years separated them, Steve and Jonsey had been drawn to each other from the first. The mutual attraction was something they'd never had a chance to discuss—until today.

Glancing at Jonsey, Steve spoke softly, "Someone told me once that there is a moment in time—one single moment—when you know you've waited your whole life for just that moment. And everything you've done has led you to that moment; a perfect second in time."

Jonsey whipped her head towards him, the song she'd been humming fading in her throat.

"Steve, are you talking about now, this day?"

"Naw. I'm talking about the first time I saw you."

She looked directly at him; saw his blue eyes, crinkled from the sun at the corners.

"*Yo también*," she answered quietly in Spanish, "Me too."

Headed north along the coast, they approached the old Roman port city of Caesarea. For thousands of years, it had been a favorite summer place for the wealthy. The small city was an oasis. It seemed miles away from the turmoil that threatened the country on all sides. Halfway between Tel Aviv and Haifa, Caesarea boasted Israel's only golf course. Concerts at the ancient amphitheater brought locals as well as tourists to the city. Jennifer had told Jonsey about the beautiful stone structure.

"I danced there, Jonesy, in the amphitheater, with some kids who'd come to practice. It was sunset. They taught me a few steps. I'll never forget it. I'll bet that anyone who's been there dreams of going back."

Jonsey could imagine Jennifer, blonde hair curving down her back, dancing to Israeli folk songs in the sun. Jonsey stuck her arm out the open window. There was something mystical in the air, some special fragrance that floated over her open hand. It took only a moment to recognize the familiarity.

"This reminds me of California, where I'm from, Steve."

Steve didn't comment. He'd heard it before.

"Can you make out those directions?" he asked.

"No problem. Left here. Next will be a right. Yes. OK. Now left, straight for a while. It should be at the end of this street."

They headed directly towards the sea.

"There. That's it."

Overwhelmed by what was in front of her, Jonesy experienced the same unreality that had affected Bobbie and Carp in Chicago. Ten days ago she'd been hoarding bites of food, sipping tepid water from her canteen, slapping at mosquitoes. It was impossible to adjust in so short a time. Steve grinned at her. He knew what she was going through.

Two stories with a flat roof, a pink stone villa sprawled between wide open landscaping. Grassy areas, palm trees and vast white walkways surrounded the structure on three sides. From her vantage point, Jonsey guessed that the house had close to six thousand square feet of living space.

Jonsey and Steve approached the entry past an ornamental pool. Huge picture windows reflected their images—scruffy archaeologists in khaki shorts, carrying backpacks.

Steve found the key, hidden precisely between two flowering pots.

"Steve, this belongs to a surgeon, right?"

He nodded.

"I'm in the wrong science."

All three sides of the huge living room were glass, framed in oak. Their footsteps echoed off rosy tiles; each one a different size. A six-foot wide staircase led to the bedrooms; five of them, each with a private bath. Steve dumped his backpack on a king-sized bed in the center suite, and motioned for Jonsey to do the same.

Slowly spreading the contents on the immaculate bedspread, Jonsey picked up one of the new handguns. On their way out of Tel Aviv this morning, they'd stopped at the market and she'd bought two; one as a gift for Annie. Jonsey drew a deep breath, taking in the surroundings.

"And this doctor will be here tonight, and…"

Turning towards her, Steve laughed, "Let's take a walk."

Later, lying together on the bed, Steve took her smaller hand in his.

"Life is so fragile, Jonsey," and he carefully bent two of her fingers between his powerful thumb and forefinger.

"The lessons you've learned, the ones I've learned are only the beginning. We all need to remember the basics; that softness can overcome hardness."

Dropping her hand, he caressed her bare hip.

"Tomorrow, keep that in mind. We'll do what we have to do, but this country it completely unstable. Our mission is to save two people without turning it into a major event. We go in, we get out."

Steve rolled over on his back, throwing his arm over his head.

"We've been all over it. You know what we have to do." But Jonsey could tell that Steve had something on his mind.

"What's up?" she asked.

"It's just a feeling. Nothing important. Go slow tomorrow, Jonesy."

Steve relied on his intuition. It had saved him many times.

"I will, Steve. You know it, Buddy."

At her unruffled look, Steve relaxed. They'd be fine. No sweat. It was simple.

* * *

Nablus, Israel
0900 Hours

Doud eased back on the gas pedal and squinted towards a large house on the corner.

"There is his house. The big man."

James nodded. They'd speak with him later.

Turning left at the next street, Doud wound the taxi slowly through the quiet neighborhood until the street ended. Beyond a long narrow field lay an expansive olive grove. Reducing the speed even more, Doud turned left and pointed a finger towards the middle of the orchard.

They could make out a ramshackle barn about half a mile away, but only because they'd been shown where to look. The weathered structure was hidden between grayish trees, nearly invisible.

"They are in there," Doud pronounced solemnly.

There was no one in sight, but James wanted to keep up the cover of archeology students, taking in the sights.

"Don't stop, Doud. Take us to the ruins."

Nestled in a valley between Gerizim and Mount Ebal, Nablus dozed in the morning light. Less than one hundred and fifty thousand people lived in the area. Some grew wheat and olives, or raised sheep and goats.

A few made soap from olive oil, and an even fewer number dyed wool to be woven into colorful shepherds coats for the tourists.

After the War of 1967, Israeli forces had occupied Nablus for nearly thirty years. But in 1995 they vacated the city—part of the agreement establishing Palestinian self-rule in the West Bank.

The ruins at Nablus date back to 2000 B.C. The town was linked to Jerusalem by a well-traveled highway. At first glance, the city appeared to be sleepy and peaceful. But like the entire region, tranquility could be replaced by violence—often erupting suddenly without warning.

At the archeological site on the top of the mount, James leaned against a low stone barrier. He'd put his water bottle next to him. Harlem snapped a picture, enjoying the incongruity of a modern plastic container sitting atop ancient remnants.

James found that his recollections of the place were quite precise. He gazed out over the hillside they'd just climbed. Dressed in his favorite old white turtleneck and tan field shorts, James was in his element.

"Today we'll be looking at the ruins. We're here at the invitation of Dr. Smith. We're observers. Remember."

James was repeating what they already knew, but the in-field briefing was essential.

"See that grove of tall juniper running behind the building with the round white top?"

James narrowed his eyes, scanning the entire area carefully. They all did the same.

"That's where we'll head. It'll have to be on foot, but it's not eighteen miles; more like a mile and a half I'd say, from the shack."

His eyes came back to them. To observers, the conversation would appear to be a lecture on the antiquity around them.

"We have no idea what kind of shape those folks are in, but if they've been tied up all this time I'm guessing they're gonna need help."

Pretending to be good students, Jasen, Harlem and Mike nodded, jotting imaginary field notes.

"Then, down through this area, follow the path. The red flowers—they're Adonis, by the way—are still blooming. Later than usual, but they'll mark the way even in the early light."

Looking around, James made sure they could identify the steps.

"The wall there, where the flowers grow, will provide some cover. Follow it to the trees. Proceed down the hill to the cars. Piece of cake."

For some reason Harlem shivered, looking at the Adonis. Below them, Faris peered up at the group through his uncle's field glasses.

* * *

Baqa'a Refugee Camp
2200 Hours

"Kamilah, Faris has done something and I am sorry to say, I have not corrected the situation."

Fadil's sister-in-law lowered her head, "Tell me, brother."

The two had argued for over an hour about moving Kamilah to his home on a permanent basis. Even though they would be outside Israel, in the West Bank they could at least be together. Kamilah had steadfastly refused his offer. She knew her knight would somehow take them to their true home in Israel; nothing else would suit her.

"I will not live in Nablus—that hateful place. I would rather stay in the compound forever."

The fact that Fadil earned a substantial living from his olive orchards and other activities did not impress her. She knew that Fadil would hold his self-appointed position only so long as the locals supported him. Kamilah also knew that her husband's brother had tenuous connections with the PLO. Both Fadil and his brother's wife had stronger connections with the Israeli government, but bad blood between Fadil and his relatives in Haifa kept him from speaking out on behalf of his family. As a woman, Kamilah could do nothing.

Each month Fadil would borrow a car to make a short business trip, bringing lengths of colorful wool to drop at the hovel of the weavers in Baqa'a. The visit to his brother's widow tonight was a last minute decision. He hadn't planned to see her.

Kamilah sobbed quietly as Fadil told her about the couple in the shed.

"Today a man came to my house. He said he would take them away tomorrow morning. He assured me that my name would not be mentioned. He only wants to take them home."

Fadil's mouth trembled, and he swiped his mustache with two fingers. The big man was sweating profusely, even in the cool night air. He wore Western clothing; a gray suit and conservative tie. They were confining and too warm.

"I agreed to meet them very early. It's the best time. But I am concerned about who may be watching. I didn't want to worry you, Kamilah, and I am relieved that someone has come to take them. I feel I can trust the man and his friends. They are American archaeologists. The man explained that it was a taxi driver—the one who brought the couple here—who saw me. The man swears that the taxi driver will not mention this again."

Fadil groped for the glass of tea his sister had prepared. It was cold, but he drank it anyway.

"It is your son I am thinking about. Faris will not listen to me. In the evenings I read aloud to him from the great books. He laughs. I take him on short trips in an attempt to interest him in the history of our land. He goes to sleep."

Fadil ripped off his jacket, loosening his tie.

"I must keep him from the influence here, the people who cause the trouble. But I don't know what else to try with my nephew."

Touching her eyes with the long sleeve of her jacket, Kamilah stood and turned to one side. He could see her profile, proud and beautiful. Fadil's expressive eyes begged his sister-in-law.

"Please understand my position. I've tried to be a good man. To get involved in the politics of this nation is beyond my capabilities. I am not a scholar or a learned man. I do not want to get caught up in what would amount to beating my head against a wall. There are too many forces at work here. My only concern is for you and Faris."

Kamilah's back was stiff. It was as if she didn't hear him.

"Do you believe me?"

She turned to face him.

"You have had every opportunity to improve certain situations. You say you are not educated, but I know better. People have always listened to you, Fadil. But you never once followed through with your ideals. You got caught up in the making of money instead of the making of peace."

The sorrow in Fadil's eyes was deep. She knew he had simply given up long ago. Kamilah turned away from his pleading gaze.

"We have talked long enough, Fadil. Send him back to me. He is my son."

Kamilah moved to the doorway looking at the filthy street. Picking up his jacket, Fadil walked out into the darkness.

* * *

Caesarea, Israel
24 June, 0300 Hours

Two cars pulled out at the same time. The doctor's white Mercedes led the way. His medical pouch was on the seat next to him. He would wait for them in a secluded corner of the hotel parking lot in Tel Aviv.

"Do not worry. I shall remain until I see your car, Steve. There will be no problem."

The doctor's assurances didn't ease Steve's trepidation. The plan was to walk the couple from the barn to the ruins dressed in field clothing as part of the archaeology team. He and Jonsey would join the others on the hill at Nablus. There should be no question about groups of students, arriving at different times to gather samples and take pictures before returning to Jerusalem. It was a common occurrence.

The rental car was old, and Doud—when he'd shown Steve how to switch the license plates—had told him the car would cause no undue attention. Steve anticipated problems. It was a way of life for him.

Jonsey would have preferred to drive, but Steve pointed out that the less attention they drew, the better. She agreed. The Baby Eagle was stuck in the back of her belt, hidden under her field jacket. The trowels they'd purchased yesterday were in her pockets, along with small brushes and a larger whiskbroom. Both she and Steve carried backpacks with canvas sample bags, short-handled rock picks, bottled water and notebooks. Cameras dangled around their necks.

They drove without speaking. Following the signs to Jerusalem, they turned inland, watching the headlights of the Mercedes continue ahead to Tel Aviv.

"You're clear on the directions, Steve?"

"Yes."

Any magic from the day before was gone. They had a job to do.

* * *

Nablus, Israel
0500 Hours

"Come in, please," Fadil whispered, checking the street carefully. There should be no patrol at this hour, but one never knew. He saw only the rental car with a woman and another man sitting in the back seat. It was an hour before sunrise.

James and Jasen entered a dimly lit room. It was well furnished and quite comfortable. Fadil was apparently a lover of books, and many familiar titles caught Jasen's eye as he looked at shelves overflowing with volumes in various languages. He wiggled his expressive eyebrows at James. James kept his voice low.

"Sir, we need to get to the shack. In your opinion, will we meet with any resistance?"

Fadil shook his head. "I do not think so. Patrols are sporadic, but no one is out this morning. We will go now."

The three men didn't see Faris—on tiptoe—peering over the top of the wall.

The smell hit Harlem like a slap in the face. She tried not to show her discomfort. The couple was asleep, flat on the hard ground, the woman's knees bent into the man's backside. Their hands were bound behind them; legs tied at the ankles.

Carefully placing the backpack next to them, Harlem drew a knife from her pocket. They both jerked and groaned at her touch.

"It's OK. I'm here to cut you loose," she murmured.

Apparently they'd been able to move around enough to keep

circulation going. Their color was good. They were covered with bruises, but there was no swelling or streaks and no indication of serious injury. Their hands were filthy, fingernails torn and uneven, filled with weeks of dirt.

Harlem could tell that they'd probably fed one another, dipping their fingers into whatever food they'd been given, while the other knelt from behind. Harlem wondered if they would be rational. How had they survived?

"Who are you?" Jonas moaned.

"My name is Harlem. I'll have you out of here as soon as you can walk. And if you can't walk, we can carry you. First, I need to wash your faces, and change your clothing. While I'm doing this, I'll explain everything."

They were like babies. They smiled at her gentle touch, cooperative and silent. Harlem felt sudden rage. How could anyone do this to another human being? As if reading her thoughts, Vienna spoke weakly.

"Don't be angry, Harlem. That's where I'm from, you know— Harlem."

Harlem swallowed hard, looking at Fadil.

He stood at the door, silent and miserable, mortification written clearly on his face. He could not look at any of them. He knew he was an animal in their eyes—a person he'd hate if the circumstances were reversed.

Harlem called to him quietly, "Fadil, get the others, please." Her gentle voice sent waves of embarrassment over him. She'd said "please."

"Oh God, help me," he thought.

Motioning to Mike, James and Jasen, Fadil stood to one side as they entered the hovel. Without a word, they helped Jonas and Vienna to their feet, giving them time to get their balance.

"Can you walk a little?"

"We're fine. We've been jumping and rolling," Jonas smiled ruefully, "We've tried."

Holding Vienna under the arms, Harlem and Mike walked her around the small barn. In a short time, she could maneuver on her own. Jonas watched, smiling encouragement. He leaned heavily on James and Jasen.

"Are we ready?" James asked. Getting nods, he spoke only once more, "Let's do it."

None of them saw Faris, toes dug into the sand, pointing a rifle at them.

Faris had awakened to voices. He hadn't understood their conversation. Foreign guests often came to his uncle's house, but the hour was unusual. He had dressed silently, grabbing his rifle and moving quietly outside. From the enclosed yard he could see the car headed towards the olive grove.

Abrupt, fiery anger had burned through him. They were the ones he'd seen on the hill yesterday. They weren't scientists. They were going to free the hostages!

Visions of his car seemed to run out the ends of his fingers. He'd slung the rifle over his shoulder, balling up his fists—holding on to the dream.

Racing along the street, not caring if anyone heard his boots, Faris had followed the slow-moving vehicle.

He'd crawled the last few hundred yards towards the barn and waited.

Fadil advised that they keep to the cover of the trees, which grew to the base of the hill. He led the way, his flowing robe blending with the gray-green foliage. Moving into the open, there was no conversation. Strewn with white rubble, the grassy mount rose in front of them. They paused, allowing Jonas and Vienna to rest for a moment. The sky was beginning to lighten. Dull orange streaks began to color the horizon above the hills behind them. They had about twenty minutes until daylight.

To the left, they could make out a car—headlights off—approaching the base of the hill at its center point; the usual parking place for visitors to the ruins.

James nodded to the group, speaking quietly, "Jonsey and Steve."

Fadil led the ascent. The big man was surprisingly agile. Both Mike and James had attempted to dissuade him from making the climb, but Fadil had insisted.

Slipping a trowel from his pocket, Jasen held it in one hand. He and Jasen supported Jonas. On either side of Vienna, Harlem and Mike began trudging up the hill. When they were halfway up, they saw Jonsey and Steve slowly move towards them.

Crumbling walls of an ancient temple, its dome beginning the catch the early light, rose to their left. They began snapping pictures, and removed tools from their packs.

The group turned into the rocky path, dotted with the Adonis flowers gleaming against the low, limestone wall. They approached a slight curve to the left. Beyond the bend were the junipers. So far they had seen no one.

Vienna was gasping. They stopped again.

Fadil held up his hand in warning. "Patrol."

More trowels and brushes appeared. Vienna was given a camera. Jonas sipped from a bottle of water Jasen handed him.

Greeting the others, Steve called loudly. "How's it going? You're up here early."

Jonsey yawned, pushing at the small of her back, feeling the comfortable weight of the handgun. Steve shook his head at her; a silent warning. Five turbaned men marched towards them. They were armed, but laughing pleasantly as they greeted Fadil.

Suddenly, their ears were assaulted by shrieking. At a dead run, a boy rushed in their direction. He was holding an old 8 mm Mauser in front of his torso. The first rays of the sun glinted off the blue-black barrel.

Only Fadil could make sense of the boy's angry shouts.

"NO! No you cannot have them. They are mine! I need them for my car!"

Fadil did not notice that a magazine had been inserted into the rifle. But Jonsey did.

She shouted a warning. Fadil turned towards her. "He doesn't have any ammunition for that old gun." And he stepped in front of Faris, blocking his way.

With no hesitation, Jonsey drew her pistol, moved to position and leveled it at the foolish boy. "Put down your weapon, son." She looked at Fadil, asking him to translate.

"He doesn't have any bullets," Fadil tried to explain.

"Tell him I am firing warning shots," Jonsey yelled.

She fired two rounds into the ground at Faris' feet. Small chips from the stones flew into the air. In the next moment, Faris pulled the trigger.

Horrified, Jonsey saw a white plume of smoke curling in the still morning air—making a perfect clockwise swirl around the boy's head.

The weapon exploded in his hands, sending wood and metal deep into his chest.

Faris lay in the path, his blood mingling with the Adonis. He died, wondering how he could get his hands on some NATO ammunition that wouldn't backfire on him.

There was long silence, profound and heavy. Then Jonas fell to his knees next to Faris, bowing his head. He was weeping. Vienna moved towards him, placing her hands on his shaking shoulders. Her face was wet, shocked. She shook her head unbelievingly.

For a full five minutes, Fadil didn't move.

Faris was dead. How did he fail? What could he do?

The patrol backed away. They were shocked at what had transpired, and wondered if they should arrest the Americans. They discussed it quietly.

Fadil heard them. Shaking himself, the big man walked towards James. His face was tragic.

James started to speak, "There must have been an obstruction in the barrel, some wet sand..." but Fadil interrupted him.

"Go down the hill, please. Get into your cars and drive away. Do not look back here. I will explain what has happened in my own way. Do not get involved. These men know me. They have trusted me in the past; they will listen to what I have to say. Go now."

James turned, pulling his team together, but was stopped momentarily by Fadil's words.

"What happened to me is happening everywhere. I can no longer look the other way."

Chapter Nineteen
Taiwan Connection

In the archery contest no special emphasis is laid upon piercing the target, for the strength of the contestants varies. It is style that is important; such was the way of the ancients.

The Analects of Confucius

STC Headquarters
23 June, 2430 Hours

Annie replaced the receiver and turned in her captain's chair. Lifting her hair, she fanned the back of her neck. She'd opened a window, but there was no breeze.

"Where's Bill?"

It was after midnight, and the room was filled with the same quiet tension that had filled the offices more than six months ago—when the STC interviews began.

"He went for a drive," Jennifer responded.

Annie got up and moved closer to the window.

"That was Taipei again, Jen. There's his car."

Both women watched Bill pull into a parking space below them.

"What about Commander Balke?" Annie asked.

"On his way."

Everyone had stayed; except Bobbie and Carp. Sending them for a long weekend had been Balke's suggestion. They'd earned it.

George was working with Harrison and Kurt. They were on-line, getting as much information as they could about Quemoy. The phones had been busy all evening.

Lisa had finally reached her friend in Reno, and had talked him into seeing Bill and Jennifer tomorrow evening. Now she was on the phone again with Dan, making sure the CASA was fueled for the trip to Nevada. Don stood behind her, rubbing her neck.

Taiwan had called twice.

James had checked in before leaving Tel Aviv, but that had been four hours ago. The Israeli Embassy had called every hour since seven o'clock. Ted dozed in his chair. He was the only one not pretending to keep busy. In reality, most of what they'd been doing the last hours was pretense. They were waiting to hear from Israel.

Balke slowly replaced the receiver. His face was grim. He checked the time. It was a little after eight o'clock in the morning in Israel. He stood up, motioning to the others through the glass. They stood jammed together in his small office.

"I'm calling the Embassy in Jerusalem. You might as well hear this now."

Balke sat down heavily, reaching again for the phone. He counted the ringing—seven twofold bursts before his call was answered.

"Ambassador. The couple is safe."

Balke related the story, exactly as James had told it.

* * *

Reno, Nevada
23 June, 2000 Hours

At night, with the winds from the north, a straight-in approach to Reno-Tahoe International can be breathtakingly beautiful. Rattlesnake Mountain, rearing up out of the desert to the right, was a large dark area in contrast to the dazzling display of casinos along Virginia Street to the left. The airplane was silent. Thoughts of the tragedy that had unfolded in Israel filled everyone's mind.

Lisa spoke to the controller, wondering if he could sense the relief in her voice. It was good to be home. She had missed the high desert more than she thought she would.

"It's interesting you came to Reno. Nevada has strong ties to Taiwan. It's our Sister State."

Bill and Jennifer sat in Frank's kitchen, rather than meeting in his office downtown. He'd invited them for pizza and beer at his home high atop a ridge overlooking the city. The man had style. In another era, he might have been called dapper. Blonde, blue eyed and charming, Frank knew the casino business inside and out. Several years ago, Lisa had met the consultant at a cocktail party. She'd explained to Bill that they'd only dated a couple of times. All Frank could talk about was tourism and gambling.

When Lisa called—it must have been a year since he'd seen her—he remembered she was a redhead, and all she had talked about was water tables in the desert.

Upon hearing the proposal, Frank was happy to take the meeting; even though it was short notice.

With their heads together, Jennifer and Frank discussed business particulars.

Jennifer asked, "Is our proposal realistic?"

"Absolutely. That region is filled with a large number of high-stakes gambling customers."

Bill and Frank sat on one side of the table, the lights of the city glimmering through the large window. Jennifer faced them. The pizza was gone.

"You say you have a group that's interested in looking at ways and means to capture that area?"

Jennifer nodded.

"And you need an expert?" Frank leaned back, sipping his beer.

In his experience, people who came to him fell into two categories—individual speculators that wanted to invest very little, and those that had big backers. From what he'd heard, they had the backing. But there was something different about Lisa's friends. He couldn't put his finger on it.

He'd seen a similar proposal put together some time ago for the Taiwanese. No reason to suspect they hadn't resurrected the idea.

"Taiwan hasn't been too big on tourism, but obviously they've looked at it as an opportunity for economic development. Much of the world is finding out that tourism is a way to do it. It's a huge economic engine that's clean; and it's all imported—dollars that come into the country. There might be some local money, but what it really allows is a huge influx of money from outside the region. Is it realistic? Certainly."

Leaning over the empty pizza boxes, Frank let his eyes rest on the contract Jennifer had in front of her. She hadn't offered it to him. In all propriety, he had to wait for her to hand him a copy.

He had to admit that Jennifer's credentials were good, but he wondered what she'd been doing the past six months. He didn't want to ask. His two guests were smart, knowledgeable, and asked all the right questions, but he couldn't quite pigeonhole them.

Jennifer placed a pocket recorder on the table, asking permission to tape the conversation. Frank didn't mind.

He'd seen and heard enough. He was ready to give them the information they needed. Frank was a real showman. He spoke for over an hour.

"Gamblers in that area could go to Macao. The problem is that's one of the areas where good play doesn't like to go because it's dirty to the point that it affects the customer."

Jennifer asked, "Good play?"

"Yeah, a fair game, a fair deal. Macao is one of the few places in the world that doesn't get the best players. Good players don't like to go there. Australia, now, that's where some of the biggest and best casinos are. It's a spectacular place—the Gold Coast of Australia. They entertain and lay play to the biggest in the world. It's not uncommon, in an evening, for them to have ten million dollar exchanges with a player or two that come out of the part of the Asian world you're looking at."

Warming to the subject, Frank gave them details on regulation and control. He explained skimming and surveillance and how count is administered.

"You need an operator, or an operating entity, that has the background and is qualified to do development in that part of the world—an entity that knows its stuff and is legitimate."

Jennifer cocked an eyebrow at Frank. "You understand we're looking for a consultant who can explain these needs?"

"Absolutely. Taiwan's indicated they want to build a casino. The easy part is finding an architect and deciding how to lay out the casino floor, how to put in the lighting, how many tables are needed, and how many slot machines. Once that's set, then you've got to come up with the things that are the controls. How do we handle the drop? Who has keys to slot machines? Controls are a huge part of the casino business—if you want to know where your money is going. It's a cash business."

Shoving back his chair, Frank sipped the last of his beer.

"Look, in some Nevada casinos on a given night they can move a hundred million dollars in drop on the games."

He wiped the corners of his mouth with a linen napkin and stood up, pacing around the kitchen.

"Effective implementing of procedures and controls is what people come to Nevada to look for. Our regulatory system—thorough the Nevada Gaming Control Board—oversees what everybody's procedures are, and then approves or disapproves them. Let me give you an example."

Moving closer to Bill, Frank leaned across the table.

"You can't commingle money coming in with money going out. You do inventory control. That's why you can't cash out your chips at the table. The dealer doesn't keep cash in a stack to hand out. No. We know how much comes in at the table. At the cage we know how much goes out. Then we do a balance of the two to know what our win was for a period. It's those controls that Nevada is known for. If anybody wants to put in a casino, anywhere in the world, this is where you come."

The details Frank was giving them were exactly what Jennifer needed to finalize the proposal she'd already drafted.

"In England you've got Labbook, and in Europe you'd go to maybe

Casinos Austria. Right here you've got the University of Nevada-Reno, with its School of Gaming Management. They're hired to do most of the international feasibility studies. Let me check into it for you."

Bill and Jennifer looked at each other. Frank understood the look. They were under a time constraint.

"I know, you've got that meeting in a couple of days. Look, let me call up there in the morning."

Frank started to hedge a little, "I know they did a study on Tinian. Tinian's claim to fame is that it's where the Enola Gay took off. It was the closest airfield. It's got a long military runway—it's a United States protectorate, and the beaches are beautiful..."

Frank quit. He knew that they could see right through him. For some reason any equivocation on his part would undermine his position. He had to speak honestly.

"You say the Ministry of Tourism originated the idea, but it never went anywhere?"

Again, Jennifer nodded.

"Now you've arranged other backers. Okay. Let me see if I can get the white paper. Maybe we can dust it off..."

Bill asked, "White paper?"

Jennifer answered, "Feasibility study."

Until now, Bill had listened without getting involved in the discussion. Mostly he'd been sizing up the consultant. He knew some of Frank's background; that he'd gone into private consulting, and was well respected. More importantly, Bill measured the man's sincerity, enthusiasm and method. He liked what he saw. Frank reminded him of a primeval archer—stuck in modern times—flinging words instead of arrows, with exactly the right amount of flair. Taiwan would love him.

Bill made up his mind. "Frank, we've got a deal that could be a hell of a project for you."

Grinning broadly, Frank jabbed a finger at the contract. Even upside down, it was easy to read the large fee they offered.

"I'm in. Why not? I'll go."

* * *

Bill should have been tipped off.

Maybe it was the excitement of going to Taipei, coupled with his pleasure at being able to show Jennifer his favorite city. Whatever the reason, Bill didn't place any importance on how the plan unfolded with little effort—almost on its own. In retrospect, he probably should have been more alert to the possibility of a breakdown here and there. It wasn't until it was all over, that Bill realized his mistake.

Outwardly, the plan looked great. The team had worked out the intricacies. Of course, Jennifer's business acumen pulled it all together. George was an engineer, a builder. His input would be a valuable part of the meetings. Ted would be Annie's accompanist for the entertainment they'd planned for the bigwigs in Taipei. He'd also be Bill's backup. Lisa's contribution—finding Frank—fit in perfectly. It had all come together too easily.

* * *

Chiang Kai Shek Airport, ROC
25 June, 2200 Hours

Before landing, the cabin lights were dimmed. Descending quietly and smoothly, all eyes watched the city of Taipei flow underneath them. The 747 touched down after a fourteen-hour flight, accompanied by appreciative applause from the passengers. The enjoyable moment faded—clouded by an inauspicious beginning. They almost lost Frank.

"You think I'm stupid?" he barked, banging his shoulder bag on the floor. He faced Bill, annoyance written clearly on his face.

"You think I don't know there's a little caveat to all this?"

Bill stood quietly next to the cart piled high with various pieces of luggage. His soothing tones did little to appease Frank.

"I know it's not exactly what we told you it was going to be, Frank. But go along with it. You'll get paid quite well. And there *is* a deal here. You can put it together."

Frank picked up his bag, stalking off. He walked a few paces, and then turned. During the flight he'd overheard some of the talk. What had he gotten himself into? Still angry, he moved closer to Bill. Their faces were only a few inches apart.

"You're screwing with a business opportunity here for me, damn it! Don't mess this up." Frank was used to knowing all aspects of any deal.

Bill responded calmly, "No problem, Frank. I can explain more later. For now you've simply got to trust me."

Frank sulked, walking to the taxi with the rest of the group; biding his time.

* * *

Taipei, ROC
26 June, 1200 Hours

That morning, the chairman of the chemical company had given the team a tour of his company. They'd wound up for lunch at a hot springs north of Taipei, inland from the beach community of Tanshuei. The hot springs had been in the chairman's family for years. It was his hobby. Now the man looked forward to operating a casino on Quemoy. He was one of the major backers.

Frank began to relax. Whatever he'd overheard was put in abeyance. He started to enjoy himself, and—as Bill had predicted—the Taiwan businessmen were impressed with Frank's knowledge and charisma. Well-dressed and easy-going, Frank fit in perfectly.

Returning to the hotel, Ted and Annie spent an hour rehearsing, while George and Bill joined Jennifer and Frank in the lounge. They had a brief meeting with two representatives from the airline—the other major backer. All was going according to plan.

Lai Lai Sheriton Hotel
1900 Hours

Representatives from the Ministry of Tourism were relaxed and attentive. Vice presidents from the airline, five of them, were enjoying the high-spirited conversation. Director Woo had brought his wife. Their two sons were in school in the United States. Emma was from Germany and spoke Mandarin, German and English fluently. She and Annie hit it off immediately.

The entertainment director had arranged for a piano to be brought into the large, private dining room.

During dessert, Ted stood, clinking his glass.

"We have arranged a small token of appreciation for all of you this evening," and he sat down at the keyboard.

Annie—lovely in a shimmering pink evening dress—charmed them with both popular and classical songs. She closed with the aria from Don Giovanni—*Vedrai Carino.* The familiar music, its classical beauty filled with pure human emotions, brought everyone to their feet. The stage was set for business.

* * *

2200 Hours

"They will take us to Quemoy to look at the proposed site on Sunday. Tomorrow and Saturday we will tour Taipei—the Museums, I suppose, and other points of interest."

Bill listened intently, holding the receiver in one hand, doodling with the other.

"Yes, I think you are correct, Sir. That was wise. She is safer in Taipei. We don't expect any trouble, but that was a good decision."

Taking shape under Bill's pencil was a helicopter.

"About the Seagull Squadron, you've arranged the pickup for Sunday, late afternoon?"

Bill hunched his shoulders. He probably shouldn't have asked the question. He and Fang had already discussed the arrangements.

"Yes, Sir. Thank you."

Hanging up the phone, Bill turned towards Jennifer, "It's OK. Fortunately the man is used to double-checking details and was not uncomfortable with the reminder. He's as concerned as we are, Jen, and he brought his sister here. He's arranged to have someone else show us the place. I need to be at the airport at four."

Jennifer brushed her hair, yawning, ready to call it a day. Bill crumpled the sketch, tossing into a wastebasket.

"You'll have to come back to Taipei without me, Jen."

"Yes, I know."

"Fang told me the political situation is really touchy. Everyone is afraid of retribution—putting their families in jeopardy."

She nodded.

Bill chuckled, "We always knew we'd be in a position to provide deniability for the U.S. military. Who'd have believed we'd be doing the same thing for the Taiwan militia?"

Bill moved to a table, opening a bottle of water. He tipped it to his mouth, swallowing the contents in one long swig.

"Should be pretty straight-forward, Jen. Fang says they only have two guards on the man. At this point, no one expects a rescue."

Bill stretched out on the huge bed, staring at a black-framed watercolor of a Chinese drummer. She held an ancient two-headed drum at her waist. One hand was cocked above her head; the other held a stylized mallet drifting with red ribbons. Her skirt was red.

"The hotel manager told me the painter is from Mainland China. It's a unique kind of painting. He drips the color onto wet paper. The hotel puts his paintings in the rooms and takes a commission. They're for sale, Jen. Like it?"

Staying at the Lai Lai was Bill's decision. The hotel was upscale enough to give the appearance of well-moneyed business people, comfortable with the good life.

Looking around the suite, Bill wondered what they'd think if they knew he'd been slugging it out in the wilds of Georgia, covered in mud, nearly dead on his feet only a few short weeks ago. He also wondered what they would think if they knew the real reason he was here. Bill turned out the light, putting a stop to his thoughts. It wouldn't matter anyway. So long as Taiwan got the business, they'd be happy.

29 June, 0900 Hours

Jennifer loved Taipei. The sounds, the colors, the people filled her heart. She reminded herself of the potential danger and the importance of keeping to the plan.

"Someday, we'll come back and do it right," she whispered to Bill.

He didn't smile; only put his hand on the small of her back as they climbed the long flight of steps to the famous museum. But he pressed with his fingers, letting her know he felt the same way. They followed their guides up the endless gray cement stairways, edged with white railings—ornate and intricately carved. Tall palms waved in the breeze. The sky was dappled with clouds, providing some relief from the burning sun.

Earlier they had crossed a lovely bridge spanning huge pools where hundreds of yellow and orange koi massed, looking for food. At one end of the bridge a couple sat, dressed in white. It turned out to be a photo shoot; a faux wedding. But it added to the romance of the place. Huge lavender hibiscus—big as dinner plates—hung from tree-sized bushes above their heads.

Taking them to the beach community of Tansuei, Director Woo showed off his sleek, powerful motor yacht. While the others inspected the vessel, Bill and Jennifer walked along the beach near the marina.

Two silvery metal towers with three-inch supports dug deep into the hard sand, caught Jennifer's eye. Kicking off her shoes, she quickly climbed to the top of one, waiting for Bill to join her. They sat close together atop the twenty-foot structure, looking out over the Straights.

"They army put up these lookouts," Bill told her, turning his body to look behind them. "And they put in those bunkers. See, in the low cliffs behind us?"

Bill grinned, "Can't be too careful, you know."

This was the first time Bill had talked about Taiwan. He'd left all the explanations to their hosts. It had been over three years since he'd been here, three years since his first meeting with Tahoe.

"What you know is invaluable to STC," she'd said.

Bill knew that his practice of certain disciplines was only part of what Tahoe had meant. He was aware of his natural consideration and good manners; his appreciation and sensitivity towards the small gestures of hospitality; knowing the pride people take in their culture. It was a natural ability—something he knew intuitively and passed on to others by his example.

Jennifer had grown to appreciate the courtesies demonstrated by Bill. Following his lead, her presentations during the business meetings had gone smoothly.

"I love watching the way you relate to the people here, Bill."

He gently patted her hand.

"You know, in the west, we get sloppy. We don't always appreciate refinement or carefulness. I'm sure you've noticed, Jen, how respectful the people are—the way they treat everything, not only each other, but objects."

Bill gestured again at the unused bunkers.

"Mainland practices missile launches. Taiwan sounds air raids. The next morning, everyone bows to each other. Like family squabbles."

It was an enchanting two days.

1 July, 0700 Hours

The Bureau of Tourism had developed national scenic areas on the northeast coast, the east coast, and the Pescadore Islands. They put in parking lots, pavilions, beach amenities, trails and marinas. The private sector was encouraged to build hotels, restaurants and other recreational facilities.

The facilities on Quemoy were not up to international standards—according to the local government—and the Bureau was eager to open the area to more than local tourism. Thus, a proposal by an independent group to build a vacation paradise that would bring out-of-country money was, as Frank put it, "a plum, ready to fall."

Meetings were concluded, proposals reviewed, all that remained was a trip to Quemoy to look over the site.

Annie and George, Jennifer and Bill boarded the director's yacht that would take them across the straits from Tanshuei to the island. Already on board were Frank, Director Woo, one representative from the Board of Tourism, and Woo's wife. The original plan had not included Annie, but the Director and his wife had insisted. The trip would take four hours. A lunch had been packed.

Quemoy, ROC
1300 Hours

Just off the Fujian province of China, Quemoy somehow managed to support over eighty thousand people. Over the years, the communist mainland had subjected the island to periodic bombardment. Twenty-five years had passed since the United States had deployed it's 7th Fleet, an action which effectively avoided an escalation of hostilities. Travel to Quemoy had been restricted until five or six years ago.

The geologic base of the island was hard stone. The Army had laboriously constructed a maze of tunnels, weaving and connecting underground strongholds.

Only one area could be called downtown—the city of Chin Men—and it was in the center of the island. Cultivated land and low trees, dotted the entire landscape.

Roughly the shape of a doggie bone, Quemoy had been a fortress island. Now all that remained were the tunnels, empty except for black market transactions. Even the fishing industry had died out. It was a desolate spot, with a built in work force.

George shook his head at the perfection of the whole scenario. It was an engineer's dream. Eager to see it all, Frank asked that they motor around the perimeter of the island.

They tied up at a wharf jutting out from the end of an unimproved runway used by small aircraft. The dormant island was less than twenty miles long.

Bill had hired a local fishing boat, supposedly for the rest of the day. The aging vessel was barely seaworthy. It didn't matter. Bill never intended to use it to return to Taiwan. At the last minute, he asked Annie to stay on the island with him. Later he would regret it. Standing on the pier, Annie waved at Jennifer and George who, along with Frank, were back on board the director's launch.

About now, Jennifer would be explaining why Bill and Annie stayed; that Bill had visited Quemoy in the past and wanted to walk around the island. The hired boat would bring them back later.

Annie turned to Bill, "Let's go."

The two walked past the airstrip where, in an hour, the helicopter would meet them. Moving more quickly, they took the boardwalk along the shore, south towards the outskirts of Chin Men. They walked a full mile before they saw a young man headed in their direction.

"*Nei hau*," he greeted Bill.

"*Nei hau*," Bill responded.

The youth pointed towards a small hut off the walkway. Turning quickly, he ran into the woods. Bill and Annie stood still looking out at the straits. A fog bank was beginning to shadow the bright sunlight. It was very still. To their left, small waves slapped against a rotting wharf. A blue and white in-board motor launch was tied snugly to a lopsided post. A crumbling cement walkway led from the pier up to the boardwalk. Well-tramped sand grass defined a path leading off the boards, a quarter of mile inland to the hut.

Bill led the way. Annie followed him across the sand. They reached the hut. They knew the drill. Go in. Get out with the Ambassador quickly and quietly. Annie patted the pocket of her dungarees, letting Bill know she had the roll of tape. They went in barehanded.

"*Bu yao shuo hwa!*" Bill spoke in a harsh whisper. "Be quiet. Do not speak!"

Two guards rose instantly, one pulled a knife. Annie reached behind her, pulling Jonsey's gift from the waistband of her pants. She took a

271

stance, but Bill simply walked to the young man and quickly disarmed and subdued him.

Annie had both men bound at the wrists and ankles in two minutes. A single strip of duct tape went across each man's mouth.

Cheng was sitting on the cot. He held out his arms, tears running down his face. It took them thirty minutes to get back to the small airport. The Seagull Squadron's Sikorsky hovered overhead. In five minutes they were on board, rising towards the sky, headed for Kaoshung.

Fog was beginning to swirl around them. The pilot kept the helicopter low, explaining that they needed to stay under the overcast.

Bang! Something went into one of the turbine engines. It was thumping and spooling down when another blast went through the second engine, knocking out the blades on the turbine, stripping it instantly. The shared rotor system sent the helicopter into autorotation. They were two miles over the straights. Below them was a blue and white flash of the motor launch. Two men were firing high-powered rifles.

The short glide path of the helicopter, still headed out to sea, sent them closer to the water. A hail of bullets hit the tail boom, completely shredding the tail rotor and the drive shaft. Unable to react, unable to auto rotate successfully, the crew watched helplessly as the sea came up to meet them.

The impact broke the helicopter into a million pieces.

Chapter Twenty
A Better Way

Through repetition of danger we grow accustomed to it. Water sets the example for right conduct under such circumstances. It flows on and on, and merely fills up all the places through which it flows. If one is sincere when confronted with difficulties, the heart can penetrate the meaning of the situation. Once we have gained inner mastery of a problem, it will come about naturally that the action we take will succeed. In danger all that counts is carrying out all that has to be done and going forward, in order not to perish through tarrying in the danger.
The Book of Changes

STC Headquarters
30 June, 0230 Hours

Balke glanced at his watch, reminding himself that the caller was sixteen hours ahead. The voice on the other end was choked with emotion.

"Commander, Annie stayed with Bill. The rest of us left on the director's launch and got back to Tanshuei 30 minutes ago. The helicopter never showed up. Their ETA was 1500 hours."

"So it's the three of them?" Balke's voice was calm.

"Yes, Sir, Annie, Bill and the Ambassador, and the two pilots."

"Any other details?"

"We've got Ted on it now, Sir. He's down south at the Seagull Squadron base—place called Chiaya County. They're waiting on the weather. Fog's heavy across the Straits. Right down to the floor."

"Keep me informed."

Balke hung up the phone, looking through the glass windows of the office. All eyes were on him as he rose from the desk, and stood in the doorway.

"That was George. It's not good news."

Taiwan Straits
2 July, 0700 Local Time

Annie was singing. She cradled Cheng's head in her lap, rubbing gentle fingers over his forehead. For the past seventeen hours, he'd been drifting in and out of consciousness. She'd given him a sip of water. Now he was asleep again, breathing evenly.

Somehow, Bill had managed to salvage seven quart-sized plastic bottles of water that were intact. They had bobbed up, floating in the wreckage.

Annie had checked Cheng carefully once they'd gotten him into the raft. It was incredible that neither he nor Bill has sustained anything more than bruises.

Cheng's ordeal on Quemoy had taken its toll. His skin was hot and dry. He tried to lick his lips. Annie gave him another sip. Raising her face to Bill, Annie stopped her song.

"Bill, there are fishing boats out there, right?"

"I don't know, Annie. They tell me there's not much fishing going on right now."

"Should I call out? I can make myself heard, you know…in case anyone's out there."

Her grin was rueful. Sergeant Stanley Lee seemed light years behind her.

"He told me, Bill. Sergeant Lee, remember? He told me his secret."

Bill smiled at her, "Are you going to tell me?"

Annie grinned back, weakly. Her face was torn in several places. One deep cut over her left eyebrow should have been stitched. She touched the area now and then, wincing. It had stopped bleeding, and she'd assured Bill it would be fine.

"Well, it's simple, really. He told me, 'Be a kid. Yell like a kid.'"

Bill sat back in the orange dingy, waiting. His tongue felt swollen, and his vision was beginning to blur. He knew the warning signs. They'd get a whole lost worse. For some reason, Annie's symptoms were less. Her skin hadn't chapped—yet.

"At first, I couldn't figure it out, but then I remembered a young cousin of mine. Third cousin. He came to visit and we played a game. He's only ten or so, and when he lost the game, he screeched like a wounded squirrel. My mom's hair went up like she'd been electrocuted."

Annie's eyes, still lubricated, filled with tears. Bill wanted to tell her not to waste the moisture.

"Do you think she's worried? My mom, I mean? Does she know where we are?"

"Yes, Annie. I'm sure George has notified Balke by now. He'll call your mother."

Bill turned away, blinking into the heavy mist. At least the fog gave them the appearance of some wetness. He had no idea where they were. Ted would know how to find them.

"Bill, want me to call out?"

He nodded at the girl. Bill's hair stood on end.

* * *

Chiayi County, ROC
1300 Hours Local Time

Bulletin issued at1200 HKT 02/Jul
HEAVY FOG WARNING AREAS:
KWANGTUNG, TAIWAN STRAIT…

The marine forecast included more details about wind direction and speed, which was of no use to Tang. It was dead calm, keeping the fog on the deck. The commander of the Seagull Squadron sat with Ted, waiting in the ready room.

"Call me Tang," he'd told the SEAL, "I no longer carry Army rank."

Tang had held out his hand, gripping Ted's—harder and longer than was his usual custom. He was sure his crew had gone down and had immediately sensed that the American knew what he was feeling. There was an unspoken connection between the two men.

Over the past hours Tang got to know the SEAL fairly well, and spoke openly with Ted while they swapped rescue stories.

"Our group saved many lives following the 1999 earthquake. That was our biggest and most successful operation."

Tang's personal philosophy placed human lives as top priority. He was determined to rescue the Americans. He wouldn't fail this time.

Even now, nearly ten years later, he shuddered in shame when he remembered the event.

Fumbling through a shallow drawer in the table, Tang drew out a copy of the China Post—one of the English language newspapers published in Taiwan—and threw it on top of the weather bulletin.

Lesson Learned the Hard Way shouted the byline.

Tang told Ted the story. Ted braced his legs on the back of one chair, leaning back in the other. He listened politely, even though he'd already heard it from Bill.

In El Paso, STC had researched the Seagull group carefully, basing their decision to use them on the fact that they were no longer part of the military.

Last summer—after a breakdown in communications—political leaders had directed the military to release the Seagull group from Air Force jurisdiction. Seagull Squadron had been a private enterprise for nearly a year.

"Four workers trapped in the floodwaters, waited for help that never arrived."

Tang sighed deeply.

"Our group received the call at 5:55 that evening. We were only five minutes away."

Tang lit a cigarette and inhaled deeply.

"We followed procedure. The sergeant called headquarters in Taipei."

Tang pointed north with the two fingers holding his cigarette.

"Taipei called Police Airborne Squadron in Taichung."

Tang pointed south with the same two fingers. The smoke curled around his head. He waved it away from Ted.

"Their aircraft never left the ground. They said they were not notified until 6:57, and by the time the helicopter was ready, it was 7:10. The men had perished eight minutes earlier. It was on television."

Tang ground out his cigarette. He was determined such a tragedy would never happen again.

He told Ted fiercely, "If you hear a cry you should run to help, since a life is of the utmost value."

Running meant sending his S-76C helicopters off at top speed. The Sikorsky could lift off at between thirty and forty miles per hour in three seconds. After transitional lift, it could accelerate to cruise speeds of between eighty and ninety miles per hour, and achieve 140 MPH when necessary. The speed was academic. Until the weather cleared, they were grounded.

* * *

Taiwan Straits
1800 Hours Local Time

Bill fiddled with his watch. It was still running, which meant that the tiny GPS was probably still operative. He engaged the mechanism and kept it on for one minute. Bill lay back again. Waiting and thinking.

He'd missed too many clues, made too many mistakes. He should have known there would be more than two guards on Cheng. He shouldn't have kept Annie with him. Maybe they shouldn't have used the Seagull Squadron. They'd failed in a second flood rescue operation last year. Could he have planned a better way?

3 July, 0100 Hours Local Time

The empty bottle floated and rocked in the bottom of the raft, mocking them.

"He's coming around."

Annie's voice came through the dark. Cheng moaned deeply.

"My throat hurts, Bill."

"Don't talk, Annie. How's he doing?"

"*Shui.*" "Water, please," Cheng whispered.

"*Waw men, me-yo shui,*" Bill had to tell him, "We don't have any."

Annie splashed Cheng's forehead, scooping up a handful from the bottom of the raft. She bent over the man, smiling at him. He slept again.

"Bill, they're dead, aren't they?"

"Who, Annie?"

"The helicopter pilots?"

"Yes. Don't talk. We'll be fine."

Bill switched on the micro-GPS for another minute. He grabbed the annoying bottle and pitched it into the sea.

* * *

Chiayi County, ROC

"There it is again. I've got 'em!"

Ted's voice was triumphant.

"Tang!" Ted shouted, "How's the weather?"

Tang was proud of his English vernacular, but regret tinged his voice.

"Socked in. Sorry, Ted."

Scattered over the long green table behind Ted were cups of coffee, crumbs from the boxed lunches they'd eaten and various charts and weather reports.

The radar screen in front of the SEAL glowed on his tired face. He put one hand on his head and rubbed furiously, reaching behind him for his coffee cup. Other than the two men, the room was empty.

Lights outside the building glowed in the mist, still swirling heavily. Through the fog, Ted could see two helicopters waiting on the pad.

Lying on the floor in one corner was a twenty-five-horse power outboard engine. Ted had corked the intake. A plastic ten-gallon container of gasoline sat next to the engine. His wet suit was piled on top. Black fins lay in front of the stack, along with a facemask. They'd made sure the medic was equipped and standing by.

Ted stared at the last transmission, fixed on the screen. He poked a finger at the monitor. He knew exactly where they were.

* * *

STC Headquarters
2 July, 0900 Hours

"It's one in the morning in Taiwan. Tomorrow."

Balke's voice was jubilant and he pushed his upper body through the doorway.

"That was Ted. He's received a signal at regular intervals, so that means they're alive. Bill's transmitting."

Shouts went up from those in the large office. No one had left.

They were all there, Lisa and Don, Steve and Jonsey, Harlem and Mike, Kurt and Harrison, Carp and Bobbie—waiting for news.

Balke withdrew and closed the door. He had to call Tahoe.

"They're on radar, Ma'am. Soon as the weather breaks, Ted will be on his way."

* * *

Lake Tahoe, California
0800 Hours

Tahoe hung up slowly. Her normally calm expression had crumbled at Balke's message. Tahoe's husband gathered her into his arms. She let him.

"I'm not good at this waiting game," she whispered, "Could we have planned this better? Is this a failure, or simply a way to get through a difficult situation?"

"We've already proven STC is a better way, dear. It's only that you've been under stress, but, as usual, you've handled it well."

Tahoe moved away. She regained control quickly.

He spoke again, "Bill can handle it. I have faith in him."

Her husband watched the grin—the one she reserved for him—light up her face. Her deliberate speech softened.

"You told me they'd be fine, and you're always right."

He was the one who knew her strengths, and her weaknesses. He was the one who had stood with her, encouraged her to continue the incredible task she'd begun so many years ago. He knew exactly how strong she was. He smiled quietly.

"You know me," said Tahoe.

"Yes I do," the man replied, "And they'll all be fine. Annie too."

* * *

Taiwan Straits
4 July, 0300 Hours Local Time

They'd been in the water almost three days—sixty hours, maybe more. Bill couldn't quite put it together. He wondered how they'd lasted this long. Annie no longer sang. She didn't speak. Her care for Cheng now consisted of clasping him in her arms. They curled in the bottom of the raft, asleep or unconscious. Bill couldn't tell. He brushed his fingers over his lips again.

0500 Hours

Bill woke suddenly. He couldn't focus his eyes. Everything was blurry. He thought he saw blue sky. Annie moved restlessly and he reached out a hand to quiet her. She stared up at him, blinking hard. Neither of them could speak. Undeniably, they heard it. A helicopter was overhead. They stared vacantly, lying on their backs, holding to the sides of the raft. It rocked from the waves created by the blades, pounding above and to one side of them.

Suddenly, Ted was in the water. His grin greeted them as he lifted one leg over the side.

"Well, this isn't a Mark V, but it'll get you to Taiwan. Hang on folks. Engine's comin' down."

They were vaguely aware of a splash, and of a rope ladder being lowered. Ted threw bottles of water into the raft.

"Start sipping," he shouted. "Drink way slow!"

Ted hung there on the side, opening bottles, handing them to Bill and Annie.

"Slow, slow," he cautioned them.

Another splash and a second black-suited body swam to the other side of the raft, balancing it carefully.

"Annie, Annie!" Ted's voice was insistent.

She almost wanted him to go away and leave her alone

"Annie! Listen up, soldier! You've got to get up that ladder, Annie. Just like rock climbing. Do it! George is up there waiting, Annie. Annie!"

Trying to focus on Ted's face, Bill tried to make sense of his words. Why was he yelling at Annie? He sipped the water slowly.

Ted opened another bottle and poured it over Bill's face, letting it run into his eyes. Bill blinked, his vision slowly clearing.

"Hang on again. Gas's comin' down!"

Another splash. Ted slipped into the water, swimming for the engine and the gas can. While Ted mounted the engine and lashed the gasoline container to the side, the medic swiftly assessed their condition, concentrating his efforts on the Ambassador.

He started an IV bolus with difficulty. Cheng's system was completely dehydrated and the medic quickly reached into his pouch for a small scalpel. He cut into the back of Cheng's upper arm rapidly inserting the tube directly into the shrunken vein. Despite the rocking of the raft, the medic efficiently completed the job and firmly taped Cheng's arm using butterfly bandages to close the small incision. Bill watched, dazed and heavy-headed. He finally realized the fact that the small dingy could only carry three of them.

"I'll go, Ted," he croaked out.

"Annie's goin'! She's the better climber, and she's lighter—maybe a little less whipping around with her on the end of the rope. Shut up, man. Don't talk. Sip slow. Help her up."

The sounds were incredible. The noise from the blades slashed at them, making it impossible to hear clearly. Ted's shouted instructions hurt their ears. The ladder swung precariously back and forth. Ted grabbed it.

Bill helped Annie. Ted was right. Miraculously, Annie's skin had not chapped. Her eyes were clearer than his, and the continuous sipping was clearing her head.

She tipped her bottle at Ted, whispering, "Way slow."

Kneeling low, Bill moved Cheng's body into one end of the raft, pushing the Ambassador's knees into his chest. Each move was with the greatest effort Bill could remember making. The medic helped, making sure the IV was running wide open. He began to shout instructions at Bill.

Annie stood suddenly, and Bill grasped her calves with both hands. She wobbled and slipped, sitting down with a splash. With a grim, determined look, she ripped off her tennis shoes. She sipped more water. Wiggling her bare toes Annie reached backwards with both hands, stabilizing her body, bending her knees.

"Relax, relax," Bill whispered.

The medic waited. Annie stood up again and Bill grabbed her ankles. He slowly slipped his hands up her calves and then to her thighs. She struggled to get her balance. Everything was happening too fast. Bill looked up at the tall girl and they exchanged glances.

With that look, they were back on the Yellow River. Bill was coxswain. Annie was shaking the water moccasin off her paddle.

Neither of them said a word, but at that shared flashback, they instantly began to rely on the intensive training. They went to work.

Ted eased the end of the ladder closer to Annie. She managed to get her grip on either side of the swinging rope.

The medic yelled again, telling Bill when to slow the drip, how to count the drops and how to change the bag. This time Bill understood what he needed to do.

At the same time, Ted shouted at Annie, "Get your butt up! George's on the winch. Go, Go, Go!" And she did.

Taipei, ROC
5 July, 1000 Hours Local Time

Annie and Cheng were in the same room. They had both insisted. Under the circumstances the hospital staff made an exception. They even kept the curtain pushed aside most of the time. Flowers and fruit baskets overflowed every shelf. They would be released later today.

"How are you? Tell me the truth," George whispered.

"I'm good. Honest."

"When you flopped into that helicopter I breathed for the first time in days."

Annie smiled and wriggled herself more comfortably into his shoulder.

He'd climbed into the bed with her. No one minded. The cut on her eyebrow was already scabbed over. The doctor stood over her, examining it carefully.

"You will have a good scar."

Like the other physicians, he spoke some English.

"You are in very good shape. What kind of exercises do you do?"

Annie laughed, her blue eyes twinkling.

"Oh, I do a little running, and climbing."

From his bed, Cheng chimed in, "Do you swim?"

Bill and Jennifer walked into the room to the sound of laughter. The Ambassador was almost fully recovered. He would be indebted to these people for the rest of his life. Most of the gifts in the room were from him. He'd even arranged for his daughter to bring Annie a stuffed white bear. It sat propped now on George's chest. Cheng had named it Farr.

"You're from far, far away, and you came to save my life."

"Farr," he'd told Annie, "I like the sound."

"Bill, tell us about your boat ride," Annie asked.

At that point, Ted walked in. Bill greeted the SEAL, asking him to tell the story.

"Sure," Ted said, "I like a good story. You want the truth, or want me to spice it up a bit?"

No one answered him.

"Well, after George pulled Annie up…"

"I climbed up."

"Okay, after Annie climbed up, the medic climbed up and the helicopter flew off. Bill held on to Cheng and his bottle. I started the engine. Took one pull. I checked my compass and we motored to the beach. Bill changed the IV bag like a pro. We landed by the towers. By that time George had checked Annie into the hospital, and he and Jen met us on the beach with the ambulance. Timing was perfect."

"So, what did you do with the dingy?" Annie asked.

"Gave it back to the Seagull group. It is theirs, you know."

"No, no, I mean how did they get it back?"

"Oh, I'd told Tang where we planned to beach. He was there waiting too. Nice guy."

Ted was all business. He'd done it before.

* * *

STC Headquarters
11 July, 1200 Hours

It was hot and sticky in El Paso. Balke paced around the large room. He gripped three scrawled telephone messages in his fingers. Fifteen on-duty STC personnel were lounging either at the desks or leaning against the wide windowsills. Balke had asked them to come in for a short briefing.

"First things first."

Balke held up one of the yellow phone slips and waved it towards Bill.

"Bill, you got a call from your Ranger buddy. You remember, Scott?"

Bill grinned. He'd had a feeling about the man.

"Says he's taking an early out. Wants to come aboard."

Bill said, "Fine with me. When can he start?"

"I'll get the ball rolling." Balke said and handed Bill the message.

He waved the next one at Lisa.

"This is from Frank. He put the deal together with Taiwan. Construction will begin on Quemoy sometime in September. He wants you to visit him in Taipei."

Lisa glanced at Don.

"Penny!" Lisa yelled loudly for Balke's aid, "Could you call Frank and tell him I'm busy?"

Balke waited a moment. His face became serious.

"Folks, we got another call."

Moans greeted him, but Balke's face creased in a huge smile.

"Pack your bathing suits. You've been invited to Lake Tahoe."

Epilogue

Lake Tahoe, California
9 July

General Jamison called to commend Tahoe on the completion of three difficult missions. Tahoe's response to her brother's congratulatory call was short: "Thank you Jamie, for all your help."

George held Annie's hand tightly and asked Tahoe's permission to marry her daughter.

Jennifer showed Tahoe the ring Bill had given her. Tahoe explained it was the same one her husband had given her, delivered with exactly the same words: "I have something that belongs to you."

Bill and Tahoe's husband stood alone on the beach going through a series of slow, graceful movements taught to both of them—fifteen years previously—by Lao Shir.

At the small post office in Incline Village, Mike mailed his T-shirt to Fang Mei.

In El Paso, Balke's phone rang.